DEVON C. FORD
PHOENIX

www.aethonbooks.com

PHOENIX

©2020 DEVON C. FORD

PREFACE

All spelling and grammar in this book is UK English except for proper nouns and those American terms which just don't anglicize.

PROLOGUE

They promised something new. They promised democracy. They promised peace, fair treatment of all, freedom.

They promised an end to the dictatorship the people had known their entire lives.

They lied.

As Eve stood in the empty street of The Citadel, a place she'd sworn she wouldn't go back to, she looked up at the drones flying above with their cameras pointed down. Rolling her head on her stiff neck and trying to ignore the sharp throbbing in her side, she started walking, keeping the sword in her left hand sheathed and her right hand empty, with the fingers splayed out demonstrating her intent to be peaceful.

"Halt," a commanding voice snapped from her left, muffled and distorted by the helmet. More noises sounded to her right, but she didn't turn to them. Didn't let them know she knew they were there just yet.

"I have orders to bring you in for questioning," the voice said again.

"Orders from who?" she asked, her voice conversational and not at all intimidated, which caused more nervous shuffling of boots in the shadows.

The shadows. The place where she was born and had lived for most of her life. People were afraid of the dark, but not she. She was the thing in the dark that they should fear.

"Orders from who?" she said again.

"Orders from the city commander," the soldier told her, attempting to end the conversation. "Put the weapon down and place your hands on your head."

Eve hesitated for a second, just long enough to prompt another barked order from the man.

"I'll keep hold of it," she answered, "and I'll go see him myself. He can ask me whatever questions he wants to."

She took a step forwards, but the soldier stood tall to block her path, aiming a short-barrelled rifle directly at her chest. She stopped, cocking her head and peering at the gun curiously as if she'd never seen one before.

"I thought I was wanted for questioning?" she asked. The soldier said nothing.

"If they wanted to question *you* and, let's say for example I cut your throat, they'd be angry that you couldn't speak, don't you think?"

The soldier fidgeted, clearly swimming in water far beyond his depth.

"This is what they call de-escalation," Eve explained condescendingly, which made it worse for the soldier, given her young age. "You're threatening lethal force, when it's clear you've been sent to bring me to someone else unharmed. You need to de-escalate and find another way, which means non-lethal force or negotiation."

The soldier lowered the gun and glanced down at his

belt to grab for the handle of the taser holstered there. That was all the hesitation Eve needed.

Spinning the sheathed sword in her left hand to twirl it upwards, she caught him with a distracting blow under the chin. It wasn't designed to injure or incapacitate him, only to break the flow of his movements and allow his nervous fear to incite confusion.

Dropping low, she spun, extending her right leg as she moved to simultaneously avoid the wild blow aimed at the back of her head and to hook the ankle of that person emerging from the shadows in the mistaken belief that they had any kind of advantage over her.

A yelp of shock rang out as that person realised they'd both missed their chance and were caught. Eve stood, shoving with her shoulder and toppling her attacker forwards to block the approach of the man still fumbling to draw his taser. She turned her attention to the last one lurking, to see a young person, judging from their size and build, holding their own taser uncertainly.

She saw it probably even before they knew they were going to do it.

The slight tensing of the shoulders. The subtle shift in posture indicating the flow of electrical signals from the brain all the way to the muscles responsible for pulling the trigger.

She spun away, putting herself behind the man she had tipped off balance just as the bang of the weapon discharging split the silence of the night.

She stepped back, not wanting to have the voltage transferred to her own body as the man let out an enraged gargling sound and went rigid. She spun the sword in her hands, still not drawing it, to hold it like a staff and punch the hilt hard into the back of the first soldier, causing him to impact with the one suffering the debilitating dose of electricity.

Leaving the two men convulsing at the end of the wires connecting them to their comrade, Eve slipped away into the darker shadows away from the clumsy attempt to detain her.

And froze.

The unmistakable sound of a stun baton activating behind her brought back memories she had wanted to forget. The clacking sound of the draw was replaced by the static fizzing sound the weapon made.

This was a threat she took seriously, unlike a terrified uniform pointing a gun at her.

"I can't let you do this, Eve," a voice she recognised said. Ranging his distance from her by the sound of his voice, she knew he was close enough to reach out and zap her before she could attack him, which left her only one option.

Run.

She didn't waste time answering him. Didn't engage in any grandiose speech about being right or wrong. She just ran as fast as her battered body could carry her.

CHAPTER ONE

THE NEW WAY

Eve stayed on the south coast after playing her part in the downfall of the regime holding all of them prisoner for generations. She spent so long in the sunshine that her pale skin grew tanned and the hard edge to her personality seemed to soften.

She learned how to grow food, how to live in a world where things weren't brought to her, and she learned how to sleep deeply now that the threat of death wasn't a constant fear.

Adam and Dren left after a summer and a winter spent enjoying the peace, and none of them had ventured back to The Citadel which, according to the reports and gossip that came with the travellers to their home, wasn't the happy place they had all believed it to be after the fall of The Party.

Mid-way through her second summer above ground, news was brought to her personally with a request for her skills to be employed once again by the young woman she called a friend.

The vehicle approached slowly and given that Eve lived

at the end of a dead-end track overlooking the sea, it could only be for her as she saw no passing traffic driving by her to head east or west. She lived in an area a few miles from what had once been the safe end of the Frontier – safe for the enemy at least – and the chances of some remnant of the old regime still existing weren't insignificant, even after that long.

The Nocturnals, their genetic makeup keeping them below ground but allowing for expansion in safety, lived only a few miles to the west of her home and only visited her on foot when the sun was down.

She rested the tool she was using against a fence post running wire around her vegetable patch to keep out the rabbits and walked towards the visitors, reaching behind her back for where the two knives were sheathed. Even though they lived in peace, some habits were hard to forget.

The vehicle stopped, its whining engine cycling down to leave the area silent except for the distant rush of the water and birdsong in the air, and Eve looked at the side panel where the emblem of The Party had been painted over to leave the outline of it beneath, suggesting the insignia was as easy to erase as their memories were.

The door opened, allowing an attractive young woman to step out. Rebecca Howard beamed a smile at Eve, stepping close to embrace her warmly.

"It's good to see you," she said, still clinging on. Eve hugged her back before disengaging and looking at her. Her uniform was utilitarian but it fit her well, and the new badge adorning the left side of her chest showed what Eve thought was an officer's rank.

Rebecca followed the line of her gaze and made a noise of embarrassment which Eve suspected covered her pride.

"They made me an Inspector," she admitted. "I work in counter-intelligence now."

Eve said nothing, keeping her questions safely in her head, as spending all that time alone had taught her patience.

"It's good to see you too," she told the young woman who had switched her allegiance and risked her life on the side of the people. "Come inside, have a drink. You must be thirsty after such a long drive."

Rebecca smiled, turning to wave her entourage back and indicate that they should stay with the transport. Eve saw it, counted the three armed soldiers acting as her friend's escort, but again said nothing. Leading the way inside, she poured them both water and invited her guest to sit at the table in the middle of her small, open-plan home.

"What brings you here?' Eve asked, sensing somehow that this was not a social visit. Rebecca drank, fidgeting in her seat as though she either didn't want to say what she was thinking or else she didn't know how best to raise the subject.

"We've been having... trouble," she said ominously. Eve sat and looked at her intensely, seeing in greater detail how she appeared tired and strung out.

"What kind?" Rebecca waved her had in a small flutter as if trying to diminish the gravity of those problems.

"Oh, the usual. Some complaints over food. Problems with people not wanting to work..."

Eve resisted the urge to demand the truth, figuring in this case it would be better for it to come naturally instead of being forced out. Her early life spent with the Resistance, with Cohen, and her subsequent captivity under the control of Nathaniel had made her distrustful of too many things. She knew she was damaged, cynical, but she tried to stop that from forcing away one of the few friends she had.

Rebecca stalled, seeming unsure what to say next.

"And?" Eve gently prompted.

"And... and you know how people wanted to move out of The Citadel? Back into the country? Well, they've had... erm, *issues*, and we need help."

"*My* help?" Eve asked, wanting to be sure of what she was hearing.

"Yes."

Eve stared at her, searching her face for the truth she felt was hiding behind the words her friend wasn't saying.

"Why? You have soldiers for that kind of thing."

"*They* have soldiers too, and ones who were trained better than we were. There are... there are still some of them out there, you know, *Party* soldiers. Ones who liked how it was before."

Eve glanced at the two nails above the door to her home, seeing the familiar black stick which hid the part of her body made from sharpened steel, and imagined the weight of it in her hand once again. She closed her eyes, both enjoying the memories of feeling alive and hating them for the lives she had taken when violence was a necessary part of life.

"They?" she asked. "You have a new enemy already?"

"Yes and no," Rebecca said ambiguously.

"So why me?" Eve asked. "Why not Mark or any of his soldiers?"

"We've tried that way," Rebecca said. "It didn't go well for us." Eve stood, pacing the floor with a rising anxiety she hadn't expected to encounter, before she fired off more questions.

"I need to know where, how many, what weapons they have, what security they have..."

Rebecca held up both hands to stem the flow of demands.

"We have all of that," she promised.

"But why *me*? Why not ask the Nua for help, or the Dearmad or the Nocturnals?"

"Because we want to keep this among ourselves. We need someone to go in quietly and deal with their leaders without it turning into a war."

"You want me to assassinate someone, you mean. Just say it out loud so *you* know what you're asking me to do," Eve snapped back, unhappy that her friend had only come to see her bearing a request for murder.

"We – *I* – want you to *help* us. Taking a few lives to save hundreds? Surely you can see why this is the way it has to be, for everyone's sake."

"The greater good," Eve scoffed, having heard that line used to forgive any number of hostile actions when it suited some of the people far more than others.

She tried to be strong, to tell Rebecca she should turn around and go back to the Citadel to find someone else to do their dirty work. She wished her peace could endure as Adam's had. She wished her part in all of this was over, but she knew deep down that she would answer the call, would fight for the greater good, and that she could no more say no to her friend than she could change her very nature.

"Please," Rebecca begged. "I asked the Prime Minister for an opportunity to save lives. Doing what you do best means there won't have to be a large-scale assault. You'll save lives, Eve. Please help us."

CHAPTER TWO

BACK TO BLACK

Eve tidied up the few things in her humble home that wouldn't last, taking all of the fresh food to a compost pile outside, after packing up some to take with her.

She reluctantly removed the simple garments she wore, opening a tall cupboard beside her bed to pull out the fitted, black armour she had been given when Nathaniel had believed her to be his saviour and not his end.

She stared at it, smelled it, allowing in all of the associated feelings brought back to her by memories of when she had last worn it. Even though she'd cleaned it thoroughly, the material still held the faint aroma of blood – that metallic twang in the roof of her mouth that was never quite a smell nor a taste – and she closed her eyes as her brain flashed images at her.

Darkness. Rain. The reflection of harsh, white light on steel as she swung her blade. Blood.

So much blood.

There had been a time not so long ago in her short life when the very thought of unsheathing her sword and taking on the faceless enemy was her entire purpose for living, but after she had fulfilled her part in the plan conceived so long before she was born, she found that her appetite for conflict was spent.

Her bloodlust had been expended with so much violence in such a short space of time that she felt like she'd lived two lifetimes of violence in less than twenty years.

Bundling the armour into a ball, she stuffed it at the bottom of the pack she held, adding her other clothes to it before stepping into the black costume made by the resistance or their sub-contractors-stroke-master living underground a little way down the coast.

She automatically reached for the handful of throwing knives to sheathe them in the secure pouches on her thighs, but her hand stopped mid-reach. It was muscle memory, she knew. It was her physical body remembering the sequence of actions brought on by sheer repetition and not a conscious choice to carry blades out of necessity.

She rolled up the leather pouch of the flying daggers, adding her two other knives to the pack before she threw a large, dark shawl of knitted wool over her head to make the outfit both warmer and less conspicuous.

Pausing at the door to reach up for the sword, she let her fingers dance in the air for a second, allowing herself just one last chance to refuse the plea for assistance and not leave the life of peace she told herself she enjoyed.

As soon as her fingertips touched the cold wood of the sheath, she felt it.

It was like electricity running through her, threatening to wake up the parts of her lying dormant which she'd convinced herself were gone – erased by experiences she didn't want to repeat – but they were still very much there. Taking the sword in a firm grip, she spun it once, twirling it to tuck it vertically under her arm and walked out. She shut the door without a backwards glance and walked to the open rear doors of the transport where Rebecca sat with two uniformed soldiers.

"Thank you," she said, evidently relieved that Eve was joining her so willingly.

"I do this, then I come home," the girl answered firmly. "And it's only so more people don't have to die. I'm not… I'm not an assassin for hire."

"I never said you were," Rebecca answered with a look of hurt and concern distorting her features. "I'm just trying to find a way to resolve this so that as many people as possible can go back to their lives."

Eve sat back as the electric motors whined and moved the wheels along the bumpy track to return her to the place where she was born.

———

They stopped once to switch drivers and allow everyone to stretch their limbs and their backs, but the pace they set back to The Citadel was rushed. Arriving after dark, something that would've been risky in the recent past, they were waved through an entrance gate guarded by just as many soldiers as had previously manned the position; the only difference was the absence of helmets so the people could see that they were just the same as them and not an anonymous, faceless army of robots devoid of all empathy.

Eve knew that many of the Party soldiers had willingly changed sides, showing their allegiance to whoever was in charge, as if the politics behind their orders made no difference to them. She saw that as weakness, believing that these men and women not caring about anything and merely going with the flow were just like something floating on the surface of a river.

"You trust them?" Eve asked. Rebecca followed her gaze, seeing the young woman's eyes fall on a squad of uniformed men and women who bore all the hallmarks of a Party death squad in the costumes of peacekeepers.

"I have no choice *but* to," Rebecca answered. "It is what it is, and what we had was a city in turmoil that needed stability. Safety. We needed them, and we still do. They're on our side now."

Eve said nothing. She'd never lived as they had – on either side of the fences – and in her world of subterranean living and perpetual darkness, the sides were more black and white than the grey they lived in above ground.

That grey, the uniform colour of the buildings in the capital, was obscured by darkness now, but she could almost feel the oppression the structures brought with their imposing height and drab, depressing appearance.

"We'll rest tonight," Rebecca said as she fixed her uniform and buttoned it up to her neck. "Work tomorrow. Will you join me for supper and a swim?"

A swim. Eve had spent the summer taking regular trips down the cliff paths to deserted beaches and braved the frigid waters on many occasions, but she had never really perfected the art of swimming without making it look as though she were drowning, just more slowly than she used to. She smiled, her white teeth almost glowing in the emergency lighting in the back of the transport.

"That would be lovely," she answered, genuinely conjuring some very fond memories of the food she was given during her odd time in captivity.

The transport stopped and the doors opened, revealing a gaggle of uniformed men and women who all looked young to Eve's eyes, despite the fact that she was probably the youngest one there, and she caught more than one furtive glance at the straight, black stick she carried.

"Secure the transport, dismissed until oh-six-hundred," Rebecca ordered the four soldiers who had been her drivers and escort to the south coast.

"Look at you, giving orders," Eve muttered to her as the two young women walked in step towards the looming capital building. Rebecca shrugged, having evidently taken to being Inspector Howard easily, her manner confident but relaxed.

"People like orders," she said. "With too much time to think about what they *want* to do they tend to choose the wrong thing."

Eve frowned but kept pace, not wanting to alert her friend to the alarm her words had caused.

"You mean they choose what's best for just them and not for everyone?" she asked after they had climbed the steps.

"I mean people are – *can be* – inherently selfish and self-interested, without any regard for the needs of others. We're not all the same," she went on, sounding more than Eve was comfortable with like the Party broadcasts from before., "but we are all equal, and we should act accordingly."

"And those people I'm here for don't?" Eve asked, worrying that she was stepping on sensitive ground while others could still hear them.

"Eve," Rebecca said, "the people you're here for are actively *anti* the needs of others. They're dangerous, and they want things back the way they were before. We can't allow that."

Eve smiled her agreement but said nothing. She wished it were daylight so she could see if anything had changed since the leadership had been overthrown and the public squares painted red with executions. Following Rebecca inside the building and being waved through a metal detector that shrieked at her hidden steel, Eve stepped into the elevator when invited and watched Rebecca hit the button for the thirty-third floor and scan her retina when instructed to.

"Executive accommodation," she explained with a smile of pride. Eve didn't know where Rebecca had lived before, other than ten floors below ground, babysitting her like she was an infant who didn't understand the world, but she guessed that Rebecca was proud of her elevation in status and comfort.

"You don't mind staying with me, do you?" she asked Eve as they stepped off the elevator and onto plush carpet. "I have three bedrooms but nobody else living with me."

"So why do you have three bedrooms?" Eve blurted out, acutely aware that she'd been away from other people for a long time and her social filtering of thoughts wasn't fully reengaged.

Rebecca shrugged. "It's one of the better places, and there aren't as many overstuffed uniforms taking them up any longer."

Eve managed to ignore the obvious logical conclusion that she was about to spend the night in the former residence of an executed person, but the additional rooms indicated that whoever it was who had lived there also had a family at one time.

Rebecca scanned her eye again, opening the door to an opulent, open-plan apartment with floor to ceiling glass walls showing nothing but darkness and some dull light from street level a long way off.

"Bedrooms to your left, bathroom in the middle. Feel free to grab any of the spare ones as your own," Rebecca said, walking to the kitchen area and opening a refrigerator to pull out two bottles of water. She tossed one at Eve, not calling out any warning, as if she were testing the younger woman or just being playful. Eve detected the sound that the bottle made leaving Rebecca's skin and the tiny whistle it made as it spun through the air, and she reached out her right hand to allow the bottle into her grip.

"Thanks," she said, saying nothing more about the throw and opening the nearest door to find a small closet instead of a bedroom.

"Next one," Rebecca called from the living space. "Spare clothes in the closet which should fit you. If they don't, I need to spend more time in the gym!"

Eve opened the next door and found a double bed neatly made with crisp, clean sheets and tested it out by sitting on the end. Her slender frame sank a little before the firmness of the mattress established itself.

Eve dropped her pack, pulling out her possessions and placing them in empty drawers, before pulling open the wardrobe to find a one-piece swimming costume and dark green sports gear. She stared at it for a second before stripping off her clothes and putting on the gear left purposely for her as if she were going along with someone else's plan.

Returning to the living area with her bottle of water, she found Rebecca had stripped off her uniform and wore the same as Eve did but held two rolled-up towels.

"Ready for a swim before we eat?"

Eve nodded, keeping her face from betraying the fact she was starting to feel manipulated again.

CHAPTER THREE

HOW THE OTHER HALF LIVES

Eve woke, eyes opening but body staying completely still until her brain recovered all the vital pieces of information to place precisely where she was. She had never suffered with sleeplessness, not even after the first men she had killed, but the last one she'd dispatched still haunted her.

It was as though everything she had been through in such a short space of time, made worse after the years of waiting, had hit her all at once and caused her to grow a new level of awareness regarding the world and the people in it.

It was either a conscience, she thought, or she was being visited by ghosts. Not the ghosts of those she had killed but of the ones who had almost killed her.

She threw back the covers, standing tall and stretching before running through a short routine that moved every part of her body through its full range of movement. She decided to forego her usual exercise regime, having pushed herself hard the previous night to stay afloat in the swimming pool that formed part of the gym facilities for the upper levels of the new leadership. She felt the ache of muscles not used to working in that way, but the ache was a satisfying one and not entirely unpleasant as she'd feared.

A knock at the door made her head snap towards it, suspicious of the timing and feeling as though she were back in a glass cell being monitored twenty-four-seven.

"Hello?" she said, raising her voice slightly. The door opened and Rebecca walked in, her hair wet and curly like she'd just stepped out of another shower. Unlike Eve, she looked totally fresh, despite staying up late and waking long enough before her to shower.

"Orange juice," she said, resting a tray down on the empty side. "And some pastries. I remember how much you liked those."

Eve returned Rebecca's smile but her suspicion about her friend's motives gathered momentum every time they spoke and mentioning the way they had first met didn't exactly make her feel comfortable.

"Thanks," Eve said, walking over to pick up the glass and regard it before taking a sip and realising just how much she'd missed the taste.

Instead of leaving, Rebecca took a seat on the armchair in the corner of her room and crossed her legs, careful to arrange the towel robe she wore so only her smooth, bare legs were visible.

"I have to wear uniform, obviously, but I've laid out some clothes in the spare room you might like to try on." Eve gave her a questioning look before she could stop herself, earning a small laugh from Rebecca that sounded much more patronising than she probably intended it to.

"You're a big deal around here!" she laughed. "Can't have you walking around in that old thing." She pointed at the pile of black cloth in one corner where she'd abandoned her old fighting outfit.

Eve looked then at herself, seeing the shorts and vest she'd worn to sleep in courtesy of her hostess.

"What should I do with these?" she asked.

"Oh, just drop them," Rebecca said. "The maid will pick them up."

Eve hid her response from showing on her face and nodded. "I'll shower then," she said, almost phrasing it as a question.

"There's a fresh razor in there," Rebecca answered, "and a robe. Let me work a little magic on you before you get dressed?"

Eve smiled her reluctant agreement, not entirely sure what she was agreeing to, and walked to the en suite to turn on the shower. Fifteen minutes later and feeling fresher than she had in months, she stepped out and wrapped herself in the plush robe before walking back into the room and finding Rebecca there wearing a different robe over visible matching underwear.

"Take a seat," she ordered, unzipping a small case and bringing out small items as if she was about to conduct a small-scale interrogation."

Eve sat as she was painted and plucked painfully, before Rebecca left the room and returned to produce dark trousers and a jacket, fitted tightly around the waist, and offered Eve a choice of white or navy blouse to go underneath.

"I'd go with the blue," she told Eve. "The white might wash you out a little too much."

Eve agreed, not knowing what that meant but bowing to the obviously superior knowledge of the woman.

———

Fifteen minutes later, after a ride down in the elevator and breezing through security checkpoints, with the same four escorts as the previous day falling in step with them without any orders, she followed Rebecca through the glass doors which were the scene of her killing multiple guards during their desperate fight to take over the Citadel control room.

The area looked different now. Gone was the drab grey concrete and in place of it was fresh white paint that literally covered up the blood and bullet holes, reflecting the recent change in leadership. She wasn't fooled by it, but she said nothing.

Rebecca activated the retina scan on the elevator once more and they rode up to the command level, leaving their escort behind on the ground floor.

"Listen," Rebecca told her. "A lot has changed since you left. We no longer operate a military like the Party did; instead we've reformed to become a civil enforcement structure. We're police officers if you like. You know what that means?"

Eve had ideas, given her very polarised history lessons, but shook her head to be given the answer instead. She recalled with startling clarity the old footage Nathaniel had shown her of police quelling riots. Of water and gas being used against the masses with scarves tied around their faces as they threw glass bottles with fiery rags stuffed in their necks.

She wasn't sure if she was one of the rioters, a freedom fighter called a terrorist, or whether she was one of the anonymous uniforms dishing out pain and punishment.

"Well, we still enforce the laws, only our leaders are voted in democratically." Rebecca saw her flicker of confusion and dumbed it down for her. "That means the people are allowed to choose who is their leader, and the leader chooses people to help them. They're called the ruling council."

"I thought the Resistance council took over?" Eve asked.

"Oh, they did," Rebecca said, "and Helen's still in charge but she put herself forwards for election after the dust settled. She won convincingly."

Eve nodded again to show her understanding, not asking what had happened to anyone else who raised their hand for a shot at leadership. Being so isolated and only receiving occasional news was a good thing for her and learning of the subtle shifts in how power was wielded in the big city made little difference to her.

Council. Chairman. Prime Minister. It felt irrelevant.

The elevator chimed softly and the doors slid aside to allow them out into a long, white-walled corridor that Eve recognised, even if it had been redecorated. Another security checkpoint barred their way and although it was obvious that Rebecca was recognised, she was still asked to check in with a bio-scan.

"Thank you, Inspector Howard," the uniformed man said when the panel under her hand went green. He looked to Eve, who looked at Rebecca. The woman gestured for her to place her own hand on the scanner.

She watched as the screen ran a line down, then up the shape of her hand before it, too, turned green.

"I'm sorry, Miss," the officer said uncertainly.

"What is it, Constable?" Rebecca asked politely but with an edge to her tone that indicated she was unhappy at the delay.

"It's just that… Miss, this record doesn't have a rank or position and no obvious level of security clearance."

"And the fact that she's cleared to enter here tells you nothing?" Rebecca enquired a little coldly. The officer hesitated before standing straighter and inviting them to pass.

"Jobsworth," she muttered to Eve as they walked down the corridor. "Probably only doing his job properly because he thought it was a test."

"Do people always act like that around you?" Eve asked, curious about the huge changes in the way Rebecca carried herself from the last time they had seen one another. Back then she had been a corporal working as an administrative assistant to the late chairman, only he used her to gain Eve's trust and bestowed on her a higher level of authority.

"I'll explain later," Rebecca said as they approached a set of double doors. She turned to Eve and spoke in a low voice. "Now, just listen and take it in. Like I said, a lot's changed since you were here last."

CHAPTER FOUR

THE BRIEFING

They walked in, heads turning to them as they moved towards two empty seats near the front of the large elliptical table where a screen was showing the still image of their new regime.

Voices spoke in hushed whispers, all of which Eve could make out and she felt uncomfortable at being the subject of so much attention. They sat, and Rebecca poured two glasses of water from a pitcher on the table, passing one to Eve. Just as she reached for the offered drink, everyone in the room leapt to their feet and forced her to follow suit.

"Take a seat, everyone," a woman's voice commanded. Eve saw her then, striding to the head of the room to take a seat opposite Eve, who realised she had evidently been awarded a position of great importance to sit there.

Helen sat, waiting for the noise of the ten or so other people in the room to subside before she spoke and addressed the large ring of uniforms and suits.

"Secure the room," she said, waiting again as the double doors were shut and locked. "Ladies and gentlemen, I'm not here to waste anyone's time. We have a direct threat sitting on our western borders and the purpose of this briefing is for options to be presented and I shall take advice on which is the best one to resolve this problem before it breeds. Chief Inspector Garrett? If you'd be so kind?"

The man she looked at cleared his throat and stood, buttoning the black uniform tunic as he stood and took up position at the head of the table in front of the screen. He was a man of average height and build, perhaps twice Eve's age if she had to guess, but prematurely greying so that his hair was in contrast to his tanned skin. Eve almost gasped when it dawned on her that he was not, in fact, tanned but was of a slightly different skin tone. Other than the Nocturnals or the Dearmad and their cousins the Nua, Eve had never seen anyone who didn't have skin naturally white.

"Thank you, Madam Prime Minister," the man said. "As you know, we have encountered a group of renegades in the west occupying what was one of the smaller agricultural enclaves. This group is former Party, and their military capabilities are on a par with our own."

He looked up at some gesture from somewhere among a few people behind Eve which she detected through minor changes in the air. She guessed someone had raised a hand.

"Please, hold comments and questions until invited," Garrett said. "As I was saying, our intelligence supports the theory that they are well trained, well equipped and concerningly well armed. There is no possibility of starving them out and encouraging a peaceful surrender as they are behind walls, with food and fresh water in abundance, so our only option remains an intervention by force. Inspector Black, DRT?"

"Thank you, Chief Inspector," the man he'd invited to speak said as he stood. Eve turned in her chair to look at him, seeing a man in the tactical uniform of a soldier, without the armour and protection and certainly without the weapons she guessed he usually carried. He walked to the front, offering a glance and a nod of deference to the woman they called Prime Minister but who Eve still thought of as a factory worker chosen to be the redundancy leader of a tiny resistance. She spared a momentary thought for the unprecedented rise in power of Helen, the former leader of the Resistance who now went by her new title as if their new reality demanded it.

From her limited experience of how the Party had worked before this new government, of how people like Rebecca were promoted above their abilities because they could be useful, she found herself suspicious of the woman who acted as though she hadn't come from the same place as all of the downtrodden masses.

"For those of you who don't know me," Black announced in a strong voice as he looked directly at Eve, "I'm the tactical leader of the Direct Response Team." He picked up a wireless device and clicked a button on it to make the logo on the screen wall disappear and be replaced by a high-altitude drone image.

"This is the facility in question. Situated within miles of open land, it has only two approach roads, one leading east to west and another running to the north west where the nearest facility lies currently vacated."

He clicked the device again and a schematic map appeared overlaid showing the walls and buildings of the facility as well as the roads he'd detailed.

"Our intelligence shows that this secondary facility has been cleared of all supplies, tools, equipment and most of the raw materials used for building, which indicates that they are planning to consolidate and fortify."

Another click brought the facility up in closer detail, again with the overlaid schematics.

"My best option is a direct assault of the northern gate as they wouldn't expect an assault from that direction. It's also a possibility that they will fortify or even barricade that gate in the near future, if they haven't already. I propose a dawn attack commencing with forty-millimetre gas rounds, a reinforced vehicle to break the gates, and ten troop transports to deploy at key points and capture certain buildings."

"What buildings are these, Inspector?" Helen asked, ignoring the request to save all questions until the end.

"Command, communications, armouries," Black said as he indicated three different spots on the projected map, "along with identified high-level target residences to disable their leadership and cripple any opportunity they have to organise a response." Helen nodded, turning to the rest of the room and inviting questions from others.

"How did we get the footage?" a voice asked.

"Mobile drone deployment. The facility is too far away for even prototypes to reach from here," Black answered.

"What are the anticipated casualties?" a man in a suit at the back called out to be heard.

"I estimate sixty to eighty percent of the enemy, and at the most would consider fifteen percent of ours for this plan to be enacted."

"What's the intelligence source?" a woman asked the speaker.

"Classified," Rebecca answered for him.

"Inspector Howard, Counter-Intelligence," the chief inspector introduced her, inviting her to present her own plan. Rebecca stood, reaching under the table before she did so to lightly squeeze Eve's thigh.

"Good morning," Rebecca said, sounding far less confident and quieter than the man who had reluctantly yielded the stage to her. "Based on the same intelligence package, we're offering a solution that minimises the potential for loss of life on both sides." She allowed herself a pointed glance at Black, who was standing with his arms folded and visibly grinding his teeth, evidenced by the motion of the muscles in his cheeks.

"I'm proposing we send in a maximum of three operatives with technical support, entering the facility covertly, and making a surgical strike on the leadership. When they are extracted, we arrive in force and offer them terms for surrender. It's our opinion, backed up by extensive psychological research, that when an unseen enemy can strike at the heart of a force, their morale is eroded catastrophically and the chances of a peaceful conclusion are high."

"And the finer details of this plan, Inspector?" Helen asked her.

"I'm sure you all know who our guest is today, and if you don't know her, then you'll have heard of her actions during the change of leadership. She is willing to return to service and conduct this mission."

Eve tried her hardest not to flush her cheeks pink as she felt every single pair of eyes in the room turn to her. She kept her body and her features still as she stared blankly at Rebecca.

"How can you be certain that, even if the initial phase of your plan works," Black asked her, "the others will simply give up? Are we to surmise that there is a counter-intelligence operative at work within the group telling them... ghost stories?"

Rebecca ignored his question. "Blocking the western

gate affords them no option to escape if their defences are overrun," she pointed out. "Your plan forces them to fight and die or surrender to an attacking force and likely die."

Helen cleared her throat and turned to thank the other people in the room, dismissing them. She waited until only she and her entourage were left with the three senior officers and Eve.

"Inspector Black," she said. "Please don't think me rude, but I rather suspect that you are a hammer."

"Prime Minister?" Black asked, confused.

"To a hammer, everything looks like a nail," Garrett intoned. "What I believe the Prime Minist—"

"Thank you, Chief Inspector," Helen said, clearly unimpressed at being translated.

"And Inspector Howard, as a counter-intelligence officer, I suspect that you might see every incident from a similarly unique perspective. You see shadows and spies where Inspector Black sees nails."

She slapped shut her folder and stood, her entourage doing the same in preparation of following her out.

"Find a way to combine your plans and give me one concrete option. Both of your ideas hold merit, but I see more sense in finding some middle ground. Don't you?" she turned to leave but stopped, her eyes locking onto Eve's.

For a moment the young woman thought she might say something, might thank her for coming to their aid, but she just smiled courteously and left the room.

After the doors had shut behind them, the senior officer gave his own orders.

"You heard the Prime Minister," he said. "I'd suggest combining the plans as they are and presenting an updated briefing within the hour." He walked out then, leaving Rebecca and the stern man staring at one another.

"Should I go?" Eve asked, feeling the obvious tension between the two.

"No, you can stay," Black said. "If you can't do what she says you can, then I'll need to know."

Rebecca scoffed. "Fine," she snapped, "you can have your dawn raid, but Eve goes in first. If she can end it bloodlessly, your team saves any casualties, or at the very least those casualties will be greatly reduced by removing their leadership. Deal?"

Black looked from Rebecca to Eve and back again before answering.

"Fine," he pointed a finger at Eve, "she goes in at nightfall and we'll go in at dawn but mark my words, we *will* be coming in, whether you like it or not."

With that, he left also, attempting to slam the door that slowed and resisted him to close with a soft click. Rebecca let out a strained breath and sat heavily, grunting in anger or exasperation.

"Rebecca?" Eve said as she sat, seeing her friend's head rise from where she rested it on the conference table. "I think there are some things you aren't telling me."

She didn't answer at first, merely rose and walked to the terminal where she logged in her credentials and accessed a file, her movements on the screen mirrored on the main wall display.

The file opened after a brief time spent watching the loading icon and a further password clearance was requested. Rebecca typed a long string of characters carefully, one at a time, until a picture of a man appeared. He looked hard, determined, and was wearing the uniform of the Party.

"Meet Captain Horrocks. Former infantry commander. Spent a year on the Frontier voluntarily and came back with honours. He wrote a report that got him noticed by the Chairman and was elevated to Special Operations with a high security clearance to re-write the manual on Frontier operations."

Eve looked at him, seeing him as the kind of man she had been raised to see as an evil enemy.

"He was away from the Citadel when the regime was overthrown, but soldiers loyal to him smuggled his family out months ago. We've had... we've had a lot of people leave the Citadel to start over, and you didn't hear that from me, so don't say anything. But my intelligence supports the fact that this man is planning a counteroffensive against us here to take back power. He took over the agricultural complex and militarised it with the troops loyal to him."

"So he's locked himself up with all the supplies he needs while... what? He waits? Trains more people?"

"I don't know what he's waiting for," Rebecca answered, "but I don't know anyone who wants things to go back to how they were before."

"That guy does," Eve said, jutting her chin towards the door, indicating the last man to leave the room.

"Black? Like the Prime Minister said, he's a hammer and just wants to hit nails. If all you did was plan raids and you were presented with a problem, then you'd plan a raid, right?"

"That's not my skillset, is it?"

"No," Rebecca answered. "Which is why you're here."

CHAPTER FIVE

THE CITADEL

Eve was exhausted after an hour of being presented with details and repeating them back until she knew the internal layout of the facility as well as the people living there. Horrocks and all of his evil deeds had been listed ad nauseum until she got the point and wanted to see no more of them – she got it, he was a bad guy and was planning on doing bad things.

"I need to present to the Prime Minister," Rebecca said, logging off the terminal. "Do you want to come?"

"I'd rather take a walk," Eve answered. "Am I allowed to do that?"

"Of course," Rebecca answered with an amused laugh. "It's a free country, didn't you get the memo?"

Eve didn't know what a memo was, but she was surprised that they'd let her wander around freely after everything she'd experienced so far. She looked down at her clothes and back at Rebecca.

"I should change first, though," she said. Rebecca looked at her watch and fidgeted as she thought.

"Do you know how to get back to my place?" she asked. Eve nodded, having memorised the turns and levels on their journey to the command level. Rebecca produced her tablet and tapped at it before telling Eve that she was authorised to access the right doors and elevators.

"Just be back there in two hours, okay? Don't wander too far, we might need to move out as early as tomorrow morning."

Eve left the room with her, turning right when Rebecca went left and walking out through the security checkpoint without being challenged. She went down in the elevator, feeling awkward as she tried not to blink when the elevator scanned her retina, and felt the chill air hit her at ground level where she strode out into the bright sunlight reflecting off the concrete and white paint.

She walked, enjoying just being outside as she had done every day since she had earned her freedom, and reached the entrance where she tested out her new access levels to ride the elevator to Rebecca's floor.

Walking in, she smelled that the place had been cleaned recently, and when she walked into the room she had been given, a woman yelped in fright and held a hand to her chest as she breathed heavily.

"I'm sorry," Eve said reflexively.

"Frightened the life out me," the woman exclaimed, still wide-eyed and panting. Eve saw then that she wore gloves and an apron and was making the bed.

"You're the cleaner?"

"Janet," the woman said. "I'm sorry, I won't be long, I didn't know the Inspector had a guest until I saw the spare room had been used."

"That's okay, I'm Eve."

"Oh, I know who *you* are," Janet said with a smile. "We *all* know who *you* are." Eve was taken aback by her words, feeling somehow as though she'd done something wrong and didn't know what it was.

"Don't worry, dear," Janet told her on seeing the look on her face. "You're a hero here and we won't ever forget what you did for us."

Now Eve was truly shocked and confused, not realising her face had been plastered all over the propaganda screens repurposed from the Party's spewing vitriol films. Janet explained how they saw footage of her fighting, of her actions during the rebellion, and how everyone was so grateful for what she'd done.

Eve was embarrassed, not sure how to take the gushing compliments, and just mumbled something about doing what needed to be done. Janet shrugged as though it didn't matter to her if Eve took the credit or not, because it was hers and no amount of humility could change the facts.

"Do you mind if I just get changed?" she asked, waiting as the cleaner apologised and bustled from the room, although bustling in that way seemed at odds with her being such a small, thin woman.

Eve sat on the bed, unable to shake the visual similarities between the woman and Cohen. Both were small, seemed more elderly than they were, and both had greying hair that was a mark of achievement in the old world, because that meant they'd survived long enough to have seen a lot.

She missed Cohen. She felt responsible for her death in so many ways but there was never anything she could have done differently to save her. When she dug deeper into that logical train of thought, she knew in her heart that Cohen would have refused to cooperate on any level had it not been for her, but that just proved to Eve that the woman cared more for her survival than she did for her own.

Standing up and pulling off the clothes as if they

burned her, Eve paused while she considered the black suit or the gym gear, which were her only options. She walked from the room in her underwear into the adjoining one, searching the wardrobes until she found more of Rebecca's clothes which she knew would fit well enough.

She laid out dark jeans, a pair of lightweight boots that looked more like they belonged to a uniform than any kind of casual wear and added a black top with a hood she could pull up to disguise her features if necessary.

Tying her hair back roughly, she made to leave but stopped, going back into her room and picking up a sheathed knife from her bag which she tucked into the small of her back to sit vertically and be hidden from all but the most determined of onlookers.

Feeling more complete, telling herself that carrying a blade and not needing it was better than the other way around, she rode the elevator down again and stepped out into the street where she picked a direction at random and began walking.

It didn't take her long to spot the two people following her as she stopped to look at things, often craning her neck up high to see the tops of tall buildings, because they were both in uniform and both seemed to be loitering alone for no apparent reason.

People in uniform had somewhere to be. They had something to do, otherwise they wouldn't be in uniform and they'd be relaxing somewhere.

Deciding to test her suspicions fully, she turned three consecutive lefts at junctions until she came out where she'd started. Anyone still following her after that was a fool and had made it very obvious what they were doing.

She walked slowly, turned right and doubled her pace to wait and glance behind her in time to see the same two men round the corner together, their eyes frantically searching the street. One had his finger to his ear and looked up, giving away the method they were using to track her.

Eve grew angry then. Angry that the Citadel wasn't freed from these people and that the streets were only marginally safer than they had been under Party rule. She made another illogical turn into a narrow alley before looking up and listening for the tell-tale whine of a drone flying overhead.

She heard it, but before she saw it, a head peered around the corner and ducked back again. Eve heard muttering just beyond her ability to understand the words, making a decision to turn the tables on these people.

She looked around, checking both walls of the narrow alley, and gauged the moves required with the instinct of a woman accustomed to performing real-world gymnastics. She took two fast steps before jumping at the nearest wall, compressing her right leg ready to spring away and turn in the air to grab onto a metal pipe running along the opposite wall.

She pulled herself up, tucking her feet as close to the pipe as they could go, and leaned back to be able to see the entrance just in time for the two uniformed men to enter the alleyway tactically.

Both had weapons drawn, and both she recognised as Rebecca's escorts.

They walked underneath her, one talking and asking the other where the hell she had gone. Eve wasted no time and dropped lightly to the ground right behind them.

Both men spun on hearing the noise of her landing, and as a result brought their weapons to bear on where she had been, only she wasn't there any longer. Having rolled to the side fluidly, she rose up, grabbing the gun hand of the closest man and digging the nail of her thumb into his wrist so he couldn't release his grip or pull the trigger. She turned him, blocking the swing of the other's weapon, and leaned back to arch her right foot up under the arms of the man she was holding to kick the gun free from the other's grasp.

Standing up again, she yanked down hard the hand she was holding, tipping the man forwards as she swept her right leg to take away his connection with the ground, before establishing a new one with his face.

Tossing aside the gun she had removed from him, she lined up a kick at the one still standing until he held up both hands in front of him.

"Wait, don't—"

The kick connected, boot sole to chest plate of the uniform, and took him backwards off his feet. He impacted with the back wall of the alley hard and made a noise like a hollow drum hitting wet earth, then dropped to his knees and gasped for breath.

"Wait," the other one said, making Eve reach behind her back for the blade, "we're your protection detail."

She froze. Her fingertips moved away from the worn hilt of her knife and she stood straight as if lowering her threat level.

The man she had winded gasped in a breath and spoke in a pained croak. "We work for... Inspector... Howard."

"Why didn't she tell me then?" Eve demanded. The whine from above grew louder and she looked up to see the small drone hovering above building level. As if to ask whoever was watching her through that, she held her arms out and shrugged.

It was clear that neither man knew the answer, or they

weren't willing to tell her. She guessed it was more likely the former. Still, she made no apology, believing that they'd done a bad enough job getting beaten up by the person they were supposedly there to protect.

"Here," the first man said, holding out a small tablet device with one hand, while dabbing at his bleeding lower lip with the fingertips of his other. Eve took it, taking a further two steps back to keep a gap between them as she read, and saw a message on the screen.

Howard, Rebecca, apparently ordered them to escort her at a discreet distance and only intervene if required. She tossed the device back and scoffed at them.

"Did I look like I needed help to you?"

"You started acting funny and we thought something had spooked you."

"Yeah, *you* did by following me," she shot back. Both men had recovered enough to stand but neither looked as though they were having a good day.

"Look, I can handle myself, okay?" she said, feeling a tiny bit guilty now.

"Tell me about it," the one with the bleeding lip said sarcastically.

"Okay, so I'm going to walk around a little more and then I'm going back to Rebecca's place. Is that okay with you?"

The two men exchanged looks.

"Just send her a message and tell her what happened, or if you prefer, just tell her I saw you following me and asked you to stop."

Eve walked off, intending to see some more of the Citadel but feeling like her justified paranoia had spoiled the moment.

———

"Something urgent, Inspector Howard?" the Prime Minister asked pointedly after her comm had chimed twice inside of a minute.

"Excuse me, one moment," Rebecca answered, checking the incoming comms to see if either was urgent. Her face darkened as she read, first the message from the two officers she had sent to keep an eye on Eve and the second being drone footage of Eve beating the shit out of them.

"Sorry, Prime Minister," she said. "Please go on."

"As I was saying," Helen said. "I approve this revised plan but either way I need to see results. We can't allow this kind of... *infection* to fester. What we've built here is still tenuous and needs the next generation to grow up knowing that this is their new normal. We *cannot* allow this kind of sedition, this *rebellion* to go unchecked. Am I understood?"

Both Rebecca and Black chorused that they understood her.

"Need I remind you that we still have another, err, *asset*, with the individual skills you say you require for this mission? Should this fail, I would suggest exploring that avenue instead."

She dismissed them with a wave of her hand. Black smiled and went to brief his team, but Rebecca frowned as a memory came to her, unwanted and unwelcome, of the sight of Eve clashing with a form of 'other asset' just referred to.

Her heart went cold at the thought. Avoiding such deadly violence as she'd seen was high on her personal agenda, feeling as though their people had seen enough of it to last two lifetimes, and she vowed not to unleash that cold, emotionless and calculating death on normal people.

"Of course, Prime Minister," she said respectfully, swearing to herself that she would refuse that order if it came to it.

CHAPTER SIX

TECH SUPPORT

The door to her luxurious apartment banged open, making Eve look shocked at the expression on Rebecca's face. She was evidently furious, and it didn't take a genius to figure out why.

"In my defence," Eve started, "I didn't know they w—"

"Save it," Rebecca snapped. "Luckily, this has been contained for now, but do you have any idea how hard I fought to be allowed to bring you in? Do you have *any* idea of the consequences of this going another way?"

"I'm sorry," Eve answered, "they were following me." She was cowed by Rebecca's anger and starting to realise there was more going on than she was being told. She couldn't explain why she felt fear inside the Citadel because she didn't truly understand it herself. In the months between the ceasefire and now, she'd imagined the city would feel somehow safer, lighter and more comfortable.

She was shocked to experience the same cold feeling of impending doom and reflected that perhaps her response was borne of her fear rather than a realistic threat.

"It doesn't matter," Rebecca told her. "Like I said, I've contained it. Anyway, come on. You'll need your armour."

"Where are we goi—"

"Just come on, otherwise Black and his goon squad will just roll up and put explosives on everything."

Eve followed, leaving the apartment with her borrowed boots unlaced and enduring an awkwardly silent ride down in the elevator. They went back to the headquarters complex, only this time instead of going up, they went down.

Dark memories flooded Eve's mind and she began to feel her chest rising and falling faster until Rebecca spoke.

"I'm not taking you back there," she said quietly. "We're only going down a few floors."

Eve relaxed, worrying that she would find herself locked back in an underground cage, which would be so much worse now that she'd lived in the sunlight for months.

"And besides," Rebecca said as the elevator stopped and the doors slid open, "you might see some old friends."

Her eyes roamed the busy room, open plan and packed with desks, work benches and people carrying things.

"Counter-intelligence," Rebecca said, leading the way through the busy, loud area towards a side door that led onto a corridor with far more order and less confusion. Eve shook her head as if trying to rid herself of the memory the chaos brought to her mind.

"We encompass some research stuff here, and that high-altitude drone you heard about in the briefing earlier is because of this man."

Eve stopped, seeing a hunched young man fidgeting with a soldering iron and wearing a perpetually pinched look of troubled concentration. He did a double-take when he realised others had entered his big lab and then he smiled.

"I thought you'd retired," Mouse said, putting down the circuit board he'd been working on and stepping around the desk. "After all the stuff you went through, I mean – it must've been traumatic," he finished with a shrug which meant nothing to Eve.

"Wow, thanks. Thank you for that, really."

"You know he doesn't mean any offence," Rebecca said, obviously having learned how the awkward man always managed to say the wrong thing in social settings and always seemed to fidget like a small rodent.

"I know, but... way to filter the thoughts there, Mouse." She offered him her hand to shake and saw him hesitate as if the offered paw might infect him somehow. He glanced nervously at Eve and back at her hand before smiling a little too widely for the situation.

"It's good to see you," he said, sounding as though he were mimicking something he'd heard someone else say.

"Don't mind him," a male voice said from behind her. "He didn't get out much before and now he's worse, isn't that right, Mouse?" Jonah said, raising his voice to the fidgeting genius who just waved him away dismissively and went back to soldering.

"Good to see you, psycho," he told Eve, demonstrating a total opposite in people skills to Mouse. He moved in for a hug in spite of her horrified expression and didn't let go until he was interrupted by his sister.

"Put her down, dickhead," Jenna said. "She hasn't come all the way back here and all the way downstairs so you could maul her."

"Where's Fly?" Eve asked, seeing awkward looks suddenly descend on their faces.

"He's, err, he's not here anymore," Jonah said.

"Now everyone's caught up, perhaps you could run through what we planned?" Rebecca asked, looking at mouse and trying to hide her impatience and stress.

"You've seen the compound and target brief?" Mouse asked, dropping what he was tinkering with and walking around the bench.

"Yes," Eve answered, glancing at the twins to see their expressions darken. She pushed that aside as Mouse spoke to her again.

"And you've brought your armour?"

Eve hefted the bag and poured out the black suit for Mouse to spread it out and start messing with it. Jonah spoke, guessing that Mouse was distracted and wouldn't be offering any further commentary.

"Just a couple of upgrades for you," he explained. "Covert communications an—"

"So we can all talk," Mouse interrupted, proving that he wasn't lost in his own world as he pulled a small wire free from a tangle of others and plugged it into a hidden port in her suit.

Eve tried not to say that she knew what communications meant, closing her mouth as she noticed the impatient tapping of Rebecca's foot beside her.

"Are you all coming too?" Eve asked the others.

"Not into the compound with you," Rebecca said firmly. "They'll be with me in the support vehicle."

Eve nodded, not unhappy about it because she would only have responsibility for herself and that was how she liked it. On the same note, she was worrying more about the things they weren't telling her about the operation.

"Jenna?" Rebecca said. "You have the schematics?"

Jenna nodded, walking to a terminal and tapping at it to bring up the same top-down display Eve had seen in the big briefing room far upstairs. Rebecca explained what she was seeing as she pointed to the screen and spoke.

"Western approach road. This is your infiltration point because the barricades there mean it shouldn't be guarded."

"IR scans from multiple night reconnaissance fly-overs showed no regular attendance of anyone there," Jonah cut in.

"How do I get over the wall?" Eve asked. Rebecca glanced at Mouse, who ignored her, or else he didn't get that she was silently inviting him to chip in.

"Remember that thing you fought? Remember how it found you?" Jenna asked. Eve's memories flashed vividly and gave her the same physical reaction she'd experienced in the elevator heading underground.

"A drone."

"Short-range Personnel Utility Drone," Mouse said, grinning. "I've adapted the schematics from their prototype and made some changes. It's got a range of almost three miles now, but for this it'll be a one-way trip."

Eve kept her features blank as she mulled over being three miles and a high wall away from any support.

"So, you ride the drone in here—"

"Spud," Mouse said, still grinning.

"So, you ride the drone in," Rebecca went on, ignoring the interruption and the intentionally stupid acronym, "infil over the wall and head to…"

Jenna tapped the keyboard for the next screen, zooming in the schematic to a small complex of buildings towards the centre of the facility.

"Here. Our intel shows this is the residence of Horrocks and his family. The surrounding buildings also hou—"

"Wait, his *family*?' Eve asked.

"I told you they were smuggled out of the Citadel a while ago," Rebecca told her.

"I know, but…" Eve sighed, reminding herself of the casualty numbers projected in the earlier briefing, and told herself that this was how you made an omelette: by only breaking a *couple* of eggs. "How far from the infil?"

"Three miles," Jenna said.

"Three-point-one," her brother cut in, adding the small additional distance because it actually mattered.

"Guards? Patrols?" Eve asked.

"Random from what the footage we've captured shows. Some roving patrols on foot and what looks like a concentration of others closer to the main gate," Rebecca answered.

"Sounds like a quick reaction force to me," Eve said, knowing that her key to success and survival lay in not raising the alarm. "So, assuming I infiltrate undetected, make it through three-point-one miles of the facility without being seen, break into this guy's house and deal with him, what then?"

"Withdraw back to your infil point and wait. The main gate will be hit at dawn by Black and his DRF, the fight will be brief because, in theory, they won't be given any orders… that and the fact that Horrocks controls the facility's automated defence codes personally." Rebecca sat back after she spoke, as if the plan was as simple as she'd made it out to be. Eve tried not to let her face show that she understood a little better now why this one man had to be dealt with.

"When they launch their attack, I'll be able to get a second spud in," Mouse finished.

"How do you know for certain nobody else can activate the automated defence codes?" Eve asked.

"We have an operative inside," Rebecca answered,

"and he confirms the defence grid is shut down because the people living there could activate it by accident, so Horrocks shut it down unless it was needed."

"Who is the operative?" Eve asked. She caught the expectant expressions on the faces of the twins but was unable to read Mouse's features. She guessed it didn't matter to him, and if it didn't matter, then it wasn't something he ever gave any thought to.

"Don't worry about that," Rebecca said with finality. "Just worry about getting it done."

"Which leads us on to the fun part," Jonah said. "Wanna see some new toys?"

CHAPTER SEVEN

WEST

Feeling both conspicuous and claustrophobic in her armour, Eve sat in the back of the modified transport with the same people she'd been speaking to underground.

It fit her just as well as before, only it felt ever so slightly *off* somehow, which she attributed to the small additional weight of the radio equipment. Mouse had assured her it was digitised and encrypted, and only someone with the access he granted them would be able to overhear.

Behind them drove another transport, this one filled with a team of armed, uniformed soldiers of the new regime, wearing helmets which still showed their faces behind a small, clear screen shielding their eyes that allowed for different light filters to be applied. While that second vehicle was packed shoulder to shoulder with armed men and women, their own was filled with screens and terminals which would allow the array of drones locked to the tops of both transports to be operated.

The journey was long and bumpy, though not as arduous or lengthy as the journey from the south had been, but the rising stress of what was expected of Eve made her edgy.

Would they keep doing this? Would they keep dragging her back into the space between light and dark to do the things others couldn't? Did they see her skills as a tool sitting on a rack, only to be brought down when a certain type of job needed doing?

She told herself that after this was done, she'd make it clear that she wasn't going to do it again. That she wasn't some assassin they could dust off and set loose, like she enjoyed her work.

"We're here," the driver – one of Rebecca's detail who hadn't been injured by Eve for doing his job – called to them over his shoulder through the open hatch. The transport slowed, jostling them in the back, and stopped.

Mouse unstrapped and jumped into the chair in front of a bank of three screens to start tapping away and bringing up the displays. Beside his keypad was a trackball controller and a joystick on each side. Jonah sat down behind him at a similar setup, only with less desperate excitement, as Jenna stood and reached for Eve to pull her hood up over her hair and hand her a pair of clear, plastic glasses with a robust frame.

Eve put them on, having spent impatient minutes sitting still for the young woman to heat and bend the frames until they sat perfectly on her face and weren't dislodged by sudden movement.

"You good?' she asked Eve, who nodded back.

"Radio check, radio check," Jonah muttered into the headset.

"She's three feet away from you, you dick," Jenna chided her twin brother, opening the rear doors and inviting Eve to step out. She did, picking up her sword from beside the seat and hopping down into the low light.

The soldiers from the support vehicle were spreading out all around them, facing outwards for any hidden threat to the valuable assets.

The sun had gone down to leave a glowing strip of grey over the horizon behind them as Jenna led her away and looked her in the eye as she spoke.

"Try now," she said. Eve opened her mouth to respond but Jonah spoke to her instead.

"Loud and clear," he said, his words sounding softly inside her hood. Jenna took out three small, black cylinders and tucked them securely into the elasticated pouches on her left leg.

"Crunches?" Eve asked. Jenna nodded.

"Smaller and more refined, thanks to Mouse not needing to sleep. Just pull the ring out and toss it. It's got a two second delay." Eve thanked her but her words were drowned out by a rhythmic, echoing thrum.

"Spud up," Jonah's voice announced over their communication channel before Rebecca took control.

"Conduct flight checks and set it down. Mouse? Get the high-altitude recon drone up."

Mouse didn't respond, but a second set of muffled blades fired up and rose into the air from the roof of the second transport. The engines on this one, much smaller than the transport drone and with a nearly flat profile, were far quieter and Eve's highly attuned hearing picked up that they spun at a lower speed than the others.

She watched, seeing the black shape move against the dark backdrop of the late evening sky as it hovered and articulated moving parts, before rocketing skyward and disappearing from sight and sound.

"Standby…" Mouse said. "H.A.R.D. telemetry online."

"Hard-on… line," Jonah echoed, responsible for the other drone but unable to avoid the mockery of acronyms.

"Ugh, *child*," Jenna muttered.

"Thirty seconds to altitude," Mouse reported. Thirty seconds later, after Eve had taken the opportunity to centre herself and stretch her muscles, Mouse again updated them.

"Drone at altitude. Four thousand feet and holding steady."

"Any wind problems?" Rebecca asked.

"None," Mouse reported after a second spent checking the readouts. "All within tolerable limits."

"Okay," Rebecca instructed. "Do a full fly-over and I'll compare to previous images, then scope the infil sector. Jenna? Time to get her loaded up."

Eve allowed herself to be led to the resting drone controlled by Jonah, experiencing another uncomfortable feeling when she made out the shape of the thing. She'd seen something very similar before, and that hadn't exactly turned out to be a good day for them.

Jenna showed her how she should turn to rest her fore-arms and feet against the framework, then he strapped a wide belt over her waist to keep her attached.

"Just close your eyes if it helps," Jenna said softly as she took the sword from Eve's grip and tucked it inside the restraining belt before giving her a reassuring slap on the shoulder.

"She's good," she reported as she stepped back, mouthing silently at Eve as the rotors picked up speed and she felt the ground below her begin to fall away.

"You're good," her lips said reassuringly when her voice stayed silent.

———

Eve did not enjoy the short journey. Not at all.

The glasses kept the cold wind generated by her unprotected flight from drying her eyeballs out, but it seemed the armour wasn't built to be as windproof as it was slash proof. By the time the drone began to slow and drop lower to the ground she could barely feel her fingers and her teeth chattered incessantly.

In her ears she could hear the back and forth between the others as Rebecca coordinated the two drone controllers and assessed the images sent to her. The wind took some of that away from Eve, and her blind feeling of vertigo robbed her of more as she closed her eyes and waited for the experience to be over.

The air around her felt different as the drone carrying her sank lower to the ground, giving her the impression of a large structure blocking out the wind, and guessing it was the perimeter wall of the facility.

"Okay, you're inside," Rebecca said in her ear pointlessly as the drone hovered still.

"It hasn't landed," Eve whispered back.

"It won't, just get off before it's detected!"

Eve didn't hesitate. She tore open the release strap and gripped her sword tightly before crouching and hopping off the drone frame with her legs bent to her body in anticipation of a drop from height and the resulting requirement to roll out of the landing.

She hit the ground after dropping all of three feet, then she heard the drone take off again and skim the top of the wall before landing heavily on the other side and going silent.

"Spud's battery is drained," Jonah reported without any hint of jest despite his words.

"Okay, Eve, we've got you," Rebecca said. Eve resisted the urge to look up, as if she could see four thousand feet in the dark, until her vision flickered and appeared brighter as if a full moon had suddenly risen.

"Enhancement online, Eve? You getting it?"

"What is it?" she asked.

"Light enhancement feature in the glasses. Is it working?"

"Yes, why have you only just turned it on?" she asked back in an annoyed hiss, earning a response from Rebecca.

"You wanted to see where you were when you were in the air?"

Eve ignored the question as she most certainly would not have enjoyed being able to see more while flying.

"Didn't think so," Rebecca said. "Go north west now. No patrols heading your way for a mile."

Eve went, picking her way effortlessly through the low buildings as she headed for the right location. Twice she stopped, asking which way she was going to check the direction against the mental picture of the compound that she referred to.

"You're doing fine," Rebecca told her. "Just... just hold there for a minute..."

Eve waited, hearing what had sparked the concern in Rebecca's voice before she was given any more instructions. She moved low, ducking between two water barrels attached to the guttering of a long building, and waited as the sound grew louder.

"Eve, get into cover! Two guards are... oh," she said, stopping as she turned her attention back to their operative, who was evidently hiding as Rebecca couldn't see her on the display.

Eve waited, watching as what looked like two bouncing beams of blue light moved along the path ahead of her. She knew it wasn't really blue, but the light enhancement gave the dark world an ethereal glow that distorted all but the shapes of things.

She waited, listening to their boots hitting the ground in step, waiting until that sound faded away into the distance before she resumed her path towards the centre of the facility.

"Almost there," Rebecca muttered in her ears. "Can you see three residences in a row together?" Eve could. She moved towards them slowly before the next words forced her direction to change.

"Mobile patrol," Rebecca warned. Eve heard it after she'd retreated and sought cover under the shadow cast by an overhanging roof of another building. The transport stopped in front of the target's house and a single figure stepped down from the rear doors before thumping the body of the vehicle with his flat hand.

It pulled away, leaving the street empty except for her and the man heading straight for the front door.

"That's him," Eve whispered, rising from her hiding place to watch as he opened the door and went inside.

"What's happening?" Rebecca asked nervously. Eve ignored her and watched as the man passed through the ground floor, turning on a single light at the back of the house.

"I'm going in for a closer look," Eve reported, slipping out from her hiding place and glancing both ways before sprinting across the road to slip down one side of the house. She stopped at a fence of solid metal railings and gave them a tentative pull, ensuring that they weren't loose and they wouldn't sound an alarm if she climbed them.

They stood firm, and she slid the sword into the elasticated slip on her back before jumping and scaling the barrier noiselessly to drop down into the shadows of an enclosed rear yard. She crouched under the window bathing a concrete area ahead of her in a warm, yellow light and rose carefully to peer inside.

She saw Horrocks, sure that it was him from his posture and the shape of his wide, sloping shoulders, pouring something from a bottle into a glass, then standing still, both hands resting on the counter. He turned around, leaning his back against the side and hesitating with the glass halfway to his mouth before he took a large gulp of it.

"Confirm target," Eve reported in a whisper.

"You're sure?" Rebecca asked. "One hundred percent?"

Eve watched the man, certain he was her target.

"Confirmed," she whispered back, looking up at the windows to find the best way inside.

She didn't have to worry, as Horrocks finished the drink with another big gulp, refilled the glass and walked out of sight to the door opening up to the rear yard. She watched as his shadow blocked out the weak light from inside the building and heard the click of locks being turned.

The door swung inwards, only ten feet from her, and Horrocks walked out still holding the glass in one hand as he stepped down onto the concrete and let out a sigh of exhaustion.

He was dressed in dark, military-style clothing but with badges of rank that she could see. Ignoring the possible reasons for that, she drew one of the small daggers from her right thigh and made tiny adjustments to her body position, ready to take him down.

Her foot crunched with a faint sound, amplified impossibly loud in the darkness, and Horrocks' head snapped to her position with a hunter's accuracy.

She stood, right hand already cocked back ready, and launched the knife before his body could fully turn towards her. She heard the faint whistle it made flying through the air before the gasp and thump of it hitting him.

She'd thrown enough knives and killed enough people in her life to know the sound of a successful strike made by steel entering flesh.

She arrived just after the impact, just as Horrocks began to fall, and in time to intercept the falling glass as it dropped from his hand. She kicked it in mid-air, sending it off its trajectory towards the hard concrete and instead onto a patch of grass where it landed with a soft thud too quiet to wake anyone else and raise the alarm.

Horrocks gagged and croaked, as he fell into Eve's arms. She cushioned his fall to the ground to keep the noise profile low as his right hand fluttered for the knife protruding from his neck and his left hand tried awkwardly to reach across his body for the gun holstered there.

Eve dropped onto him, her knees driving the air from his lungs and the fight from his hands as he yelped in pain. She clamped her left hand over his mouth, seeing into his eyes in the low light and finding nothing but savage anger.

"It has to be this way," Eve whispered to him, unsure why she spoke to him at all. "Too many people would die if I d—"

Horrocks smacked her hand away, freeing his mouth to snarl his last words to her as her right hand brought another knife to his throat.

"I won't bow to their rule," he hissed, panting for breath under the weight of her body and the pain of his life pumping out past the cold steel. "Why can't you just leave us alone to live in peace?"

"Peace?" Eve hissed angrily, pressing the knife harder against his throat without breaking the skin. "You think attacking the Citadel brings peace?" Horrocks, in spite of the pain he was in, smiled.

It was a sad smile, full of pity and irony.

"Is that what they told you?" he asked, adding one last word before doing something she didn't expect for one second.

"*Fool!*"

He snatched the knife embedded in his neck and tore it free, dragging it sideways to open up the wound and end his suffering. Blood ran out from the wound in huge, hot gouts as his body pumped it through the ragged wound to leave him convulsing weakly, gasping for a few seconds before he went still.

Eve didn't move. She was so surprised, so shocked by his final act that his final words hadn't really dawned on her yet.

"Eve!" the radio crackled in her ears. "Report!"

"Target down," she said woodenly. "Moving to exfil."

"Negative," Rebecca told her, hesitating before giving another order. "Check the house for his family and detain them for questioning."

CHAPTER EIGHT

DAWN RAID

Inspector Black, formerly *Captain* Black of the Citadel quick reaction force, was impatient. He was unhappy that he had to wait for clandestine forces to do their underhand dirty work when he had a dedicated force of trained and motivated people ready to get the job done.

He accepted that other departments had other ways of dealing with problems, but the real problem with that was that his way was always the fastest and most efficient way to get anything done.

He looked at his watch, turning his wrist so the face on the inside came to life in a dull green glow to tell him there was still at least an hour and a half until daybreak. Sitting in the lead vehicle, ready to be part of the first wave of his unit into trouble as was his style, he glanced at the other soldiers – *officers*, he corrected himself – and saw their mixed expressions that seemed to sum up every part of doing their particular job.

One man had his head back, his eyes closed, but Black knew the man wouldn't be asleep and only resting his eyes.

A man beside him jigged his right leg constantly, the

nervous tension keeping him alive and wired, ready to work.

A woman next to him, eyes open but unfocused, likely imagining every way the situation could go, mentally rehearsing her reactions.

Almost half of his people had been former Party soldiers, and those who hadn't been under what remained of his previous command had all earned their acceptance through almost daily raids to execute search orders and detain people who posed a threat to their new democratic society.

"Sir, comm from the escort team," a man to his right said. "They're confirming that the asset reported target down."

"Confirm that," Black snapped. "I want a definite target down report." The man muttered into the radio again, speaking to the members of the escort team deployed with the covert assets before he came back with a nod of certainty.

"Confirmed," he said.

"All units, this is Delta One," Black said into his radio. "Execute. Execute. Execute."

The whine of the transport's engines hitting the power band filled the air as the officers of the DRT were rocked from side to side under hard acceleration on the uneven road.

"Time to target, two minutes," a report came over their channel.

"Deploy drones," Black ordered, knowing that inside the last vehicle in his convoy, the technical support wagon, drones would be triggered to take off from the roof of all of their vehicles and accelerate ahead of them to attack the gate. The second wave of drones carried explosive ordnance which would be remotely dropped onto the gate ahead of their arrival.

"All units, check IR strobes active."

He checked his own, reaching to the top of his helmet to ensure that the switch was pulled all the way to the left to activate the infrared strobe that would prevent any of their drones from targeting them in the assault.

His people knew their jobs, so he knew he didn't have to repeat himself. To remind them of what was expected now would show weakness. It would betray a nervous disposition that he didn't feel and it would undermine their confidence and their ability to perform.

He kept quiet, not reminding the support vehicle to wait outside of range and for the fourth transport to stop inside the soon-to-be-destroyed gates to secure that area, while his transport headed directly for the control centre and the others fanned out to their own strategic locations.

The drones flew over the gate, bursts of gunfire taking out the visible sentries as the first wave split off to follow their manually controlled flight leaders and cut off the relief troops.

The second wave, weighed down by their explosive payloads, dropped targeted munitions onto the gate to blow it open ahead of the lead transports to allow them to crash through the wreckage. One drone, however, manually controlled by an officer in the support vehicle acting on a very different set of orders, made straight for Eve's location.

———

Eve hesitated for a few seconds until Rebecca transmitted again to demand an acknowledgement of her orders.

She said nothing but stepped inside the house. The

light blinded her for a second before the glasses adapted and killed the light amplification ability to allow her to see where she was going, and also allow her to see the bright red footprints she left on the white tiled flooring.

She searched the few downstairs rooms fast before heading for the stairs, stepping lightly to the outer edges where there was less chance of her finding a creaking board to alert anyone upstairs enough for them to arm themselves before she could reach them. Her glasses activated again, amplifying the light from downstairs to give her a better view of the dark house.

Three doors were closed, and she put a hand on the first after twirling the knife in her right hand to hold it in an overhand grip better accustomed to fighting in a confined space. Busting in she found an empty bed with tidy sheets unslept in, then spinning away and repeating the same routine on the second room.

Empty.

Gearing herself up for the last door, she opened it, finding a bathroom instead of a bedroom. She paused, checking the rooms again before looking in the wardrobes and cupboards for anyone hiding.

"There's nobody here," she reported.

"What? No, check again," Rebecca told her.

"I'm telling you there's nobody here," Eve hissed, feeling as though she was overstaying her welcome.

"Is there a loft space?" Mouse asked. "I'm getting a faint heat signature from the house."

"You're sure that's not me?" Eve asked, annoyed.

"Not unless your suit suddenly isn't working," he told her. She bit her lip to stop herself from saying anything stupid and looked up at the ceiling, finding a small loft door set into it by the bathroom.

She heard the distant sound of muted explosions and

rattling gunshots telling her that the main assault had begun ahead of schedule.

Sheathing the knife, she stood beneath it and jumped, throwing her feet out to either side and bracing her slender body between the wall and a doorframe. She caught her balance and reached up, sliding back the opening just enough to take a firm grip with both hands, and swung once before pulling herself fast up into the void.

She looked around, glasses amplifying the light again, but with very little ambient glow she saw more shadows than anything else.

"Nothing," she reported. "There's a water tank."

"Dammit," Rebecca said. "Okay, get out of th—"

The radio went dead.

"Rebecca?" Eve said, still standing in the void before she figured out what she was being told and dropped back to the landing and crouched to soften the fall.

A light outside the bedroom window to her left flashed brightly to almost blind her, followed immediately by the sound of breaking glass and a shattering, thumping noise of gunfire.

She rolled, running for the stairs as the thin interior walls erupted in plaster dust and noise. Reaching the top of the stairs, she paused out of sight of the drone whining as it hovered outside and she saw the light illuminate the foot of the stairs ready for her to appear.

She didn't hesitate, running back into the bedroom and opening a window to drop down to the concrete outside next to Horrocks' body. She ran for the same spot in the fence where she'd got in, leaping up to vault it with no sense of stealth but driven by a need to put distance between herself and the killer drone no doubt activated as a defence protocol and assigned to Horrocks.

"Your intel didn't say anything about a drone!" she

snarled, unsure if anyone back in their transport could still hear her.

Broken words came back to her, none of them making sense as she ran in a straight line just to gain some distance from the scene of the killing.

"…Eve?…filtratio…now!" the radio in her ears barked, making her angle her run to the right on instinct as her sense of direction steered her back to the western gate.

Lights were coming on in all the residences now, the occupants startled by the sounds of gunfire, and more than one motion-activated light flared to illuminate her running form, while the intermittent whine of a drone reached her ears.

She ran. She had no other option. She had to get out of that compound before it was overrun, acting on some base survival instinct driving her to move faster than she ever had before.

After maybe half a mile of weaving between buildings the terrain changed back to the long, low buildings which she guessed were part of the agricultural setup and she paused for breath.

The whine of the drone was gone but she didn't feel safe. She wouldn't feel safe until she was back on the other side of the wall and with her friends again.

"If they really *are* my friends," she muttered angrily to herself. Her mind raced to search for the betrayal but the urgency of her situation forced those thoughts aside. She searched the dark sky pointlessly for the invisible drone, wondering which of her 'friends' was operating it.

She took her bearings, looking up at the sky until the right path presented itself to her and she set off again at a run. Before she'd even made it another hundred steps the whine came again – loud and growing rapidly louder as if the drone was dive-bombing her – until a beam of harsh, bright white light nailed her to the spot.

The gun chattered again, tearing up the ground where she stood a second before she threw herself to one side and took cover behind a building. The drone banked sideways, gun silent but search beam slicing the ground in an effort to cut her off on the other side of her cover.

But Eve didn't run around the building. Instead, she hopped to place one foot on a water barrel and jumped to grasp the sloping edge of the roof and pull herself up. Her left hand dropped to her thigh and came back bearing one of the small cylinders given to her by Jenna.

The drone hovered at her level, searchlight roving along the ground ready for her to appear there, and she pulled the pin to toss the crunch underhand to time it perfectly.

It bounced off the edge of the roof once before denotating with a muted thump and a crackle of static electricity. Just as the drone's searchlight blinded her and she felt three massive impacts to her chest.

CHAPTER NINE

COLLATERAL LOSSES

"Eve? *Eve!*" Rebecca called into the radio before turning around to the others. "Why isn't this working?" she demanded. Her voice was strained. Stressed. The others shrugged, all of them hitting buttons and switches on their own terminals.

"My drone's down," Mouse reported, tapping furiously at the keys.

"I've lost connection to mine but I've still got telemetry," Jonah offered. "No control though – it's just hovering."

Jenna huffed, breaking open the rear door to begin berating the first uniform she encountered to ask what was happening.

"They've started the assault early," she reported, stepping back inside the transport.

"What? Why?" Rebecca asked, shaking her head as she realised she was the one who was supposed to be giving the answers and not demanding them. Changing the station on her radio, she called up the assault team.

"Delta One, Delta One, Echo One, over." No response.

"Delta One from Echo One, over," she repeated more forcefully.

"Echo One, stand by," a voice that didn't belong to Black answered. Rebecca, trained into a life of military servitude, didn't press it and adhered to protocol, waiting as she was instructed. With the doors open, they could hear the distant battle, and all four of them craned their ears to try and make sense of it.

"Try her again," Rebecca ordered, hearing Jonah use the radio for Eve. He turned after his third attempt and shook his head.

"Delta One from Echo One," Rebecca snapped crisply into the radio. "Friendly asset not recovered, repeat asset is still inside the complex. Received?"

"Echo One, Delta Four," came the response after a few seconds. "All received. All Delta units, all Delta units, covert asset is still in play. Check fire. Check fire."

The various fireteam leaders acknowledged the order over the radio but it all sounded somehow *off* to Rebecca. She ordered her personal escort to start the transport and drive to the northern gate, but after a delay she demanded to know why they weren't moving.

"It's the escort unit, Ma'am," the man responded. "They won't let us move. They say we have to wait here until the compound has been cleared and secured."

"Fuck," she yelled, banging her hand against the terminal in impotent rage.

———

Black, after a brief and bloody firefight with the trapped reactionary force still inside their building, called for gas to be used. Canisters fired through the glass windows shattered by the exchange of bullets to force the survivors out into the open where a combination of drones and rifles took them down.

Nearby, under the leadership of his second in command, the control room was stormed and taken with few casualties to the attacking side.

"All units, Delta One," Black called into his radio. "Confirm objectives secured."

One by one they came back to him, reporting a successful raid on the compound. Each team leader reported their casualties, of which there were a handful of injuries and three killed, before their commander gave them their next phase orders.

"Round up all civilians," he instructed. "Anyone found with a weapon or anyone in uniform is to be treated as hostile."

They knew what that meant. Buildings were stormed and people of all ages, both male and female, were dragged outside and corralled. Those buildings were searched and anyone found to be hiding a weapon was rewarded with a burst of gunfire to their chest and head.

Men and women were lined up against walls as impromptu firing squads worked endlessly to eradicate any possible resistance to their might.

This went on far into the morning as the sun rose to warm the green valley the facility lay in. Drones scoured the perimeter, killing those attempting to flee, until a few hundred traitors were all held in a single storage barn, ready to be processed.

People sobbed, some wailing at the loss of their loved ones gunned down by the small army that had come in the night, and in spite of the assurances given in the planning phase of the operation, the death toll was high.

Rebecca, finally permitted inside the compound via the

northern gate, told the former resistance members to stay inside the transport as she walked, *stormed*, towards Black with her two escorting officers flanking her.

In an unwinnable game of posturing, six armed members of Black's Direct Response Team shadowed them for what was described as 'their safety'.

"What the hell happened?" Rebecca demanded, finding Black sitting in the former control room with his armour hanging over the back of the chair and his feet on the desk as he sipped something from a cup. The room stank of chemical smoke and the bullet holes striping the walls told a tale of their own.

"Inspector!" Black announced loudly as though greeting the unexpected arrival of an old friend. He swung his feet down from the desk and stood, towering a full head over her with a beaming smile that was more predatory than friendly.

"Welcome to agricultural zone three-two!"

"Save it," Rebecca snapped. "What. The. hell. Happened?" Black's smile faded and he spoke a few words loudly.

"Clear the room."

As far as demonstrations of power went, his was an impressive one.

Officers busy searching and repairing key systems wordlessly stood and filed out to leave the two inspectors staring one another down until they were alone.

"*My* asset got the job done and *you* had to go and jump the gun. Where is she?" Black breathed in through his nose and held it, nodding slowly before letting it out.

"Our reconnaissance element discovered that the traitors were expecting an assault. I made a judgement call and went in." He stepped back, holding his arms out to his sides to both demonstrate their success and intimidate her with his size. "As you can see, we were successful."

"Lot of gunfire for successful," Rebecca answered with a sarcastic huff. "Where's Eve?"

Black at least had the decency to look dismayed if not apologetic, sitting down and rubbing his face with both hands before tapping at a keyboard to bring up a file and wave her around to see it.

Rebecca looked, seeing the green hue of night vision optics fill the display as Black hit a button and the image moved.

"One of our drones captured this," he explained, pointing at movement on the screen which Rebecca had to lean close to in order to make anything out. "We think that's your asset."

The screen flashed with what she belatedly realised was gunfire, and the dark shape dropped as a flash obscured the view.

"Whatever that was," Black said as he hit more keys and showed a daylight view of a burned building, "it torched the place. There's no sign of her. I'm… I'm sorry."

Rebecca staggered backwards two steps before her legs hit a desk and she sat back on it, scattering damaged equipment as she did.

"I…"

"As for the rest of the operation," Black went on with no trace of the empathy he'd just shown, "it was a total success. We took far fewer casualties than expected, even though the resistance was… *spirited.*"

"I brought her back," Rebecca whispered, not hearing his words. "I convinced her to do this…"

"A number of the traitors tried to fight back, and their losses have been higher than anticipated."

"How? I thought the defence systems were inactive."

"We can only surmise that the drone was on some kind of automated program protecting Horrocks."

"I need to search the area," Rebecca said, standing and coming back to the present again.

"I assure you the area has been thoroughly searched. You're officially stood down, with orders to return to the Citadel."

"No," she argued, "I need to recover her body at lea—"

"It wasn't a suggestion, Howard," Black snapped. "This is an order."

"You don't give me orders, *Black*," she answered, mirroring his hostility.

"No, but I do," a deep voice said from the entrance. She turned to see Chief Inspector Garrett, their senior officer advising the Prime Minister, walk in wearing a tactical uniform that was so newly issued it looked shiny. The gun holstered on his right leg looked so uncomfortable on the man that she worried he'd likely shoot himself if he drew it.

"Sir, I—"

"Will return to the Citadel as ordered?" he asked, cutting her words off.

"No Sir, my asset is—"

"Confirmed dead, I believe. That means you will return to the Citadel."

"But Sir, I have…" she glanced at Black, not wanting to show her hand in front of him but having no choice. "I have another asset, a covert intelligence source, in the compound."

"I am aware of this," Garrett said stiffly. "And when they are processed accordingly to maintain their cover, they will report back to you."

Rebecca looked between him and Black, sensing a

deeper conspiracy than she suspected there was, and knew she was powerless to fight the system.

"My assets. *Mine*. You can't do this to them." Garrett smiled out of one corner of his mouth.

"Yes, I can," he said happily. "I'm the Chief Inspector."

Rebecca ground her teeth together to prevent her jaw from opening and saying something she wouldn't recover from, career-wise anyway. She glared at Garrett for as long as she dared, wondering if the rot went up as far as him or further. All the way to Helen, perhaps?

Defeated but still owning just enough decorum not to sabotage her own career, she left the room and met the soldiers who escorted her back to her transport, and all the way to the Citadel gates.

CHAPTER TEN

BACK UNDERGROUND

Eve woke, instantly gasping a noisy breath in as her chest and ribs exploded in fiery agony.

Hands reached for her, holding her down. In spite of her pain, she lashed out, slamming the heel of her right hand into an unseen skull before bringing her left knee up into a soft part that elicited a grunt of pain.

"Hold her!" a male voice growled in the darkness. More hands piled in to defeat her with sheer body weight as a sharp sting in her thigh made her cry out in impotent rage. She thrashed, squirmed and tried again to break free as her limbs slowly began to feel heavy and the fight took too much energy to maintain.

She felt herself slowing, fading, not into unconsciousness but into a kind of deep lethargy that left her entire body too heavy to lift off the flat surface she was lying on. Her head felt light and her mind wandered. Unfortunately for her, it wandered back to the lowest levels of the Party headquarters building where she was imprisoned in the not so distant past, and while her body was useless, her mind raced as she replayed images and sounds that tortured her.

She was free, she told herself. She was stupid to go back to this life, back to the darkness, and all for the promise of saving a life when all she'd done was take life and almost lose her own.

As the grotesque irony seeped into her soul to leave a bad taste in her mouth – metallic and fuzzy – she passed out.

―――――

When she woke again, she fought down the urge to cry out in pain as she had before. Her brain was still spinning, with fog clouding the edges of her thoughts, and her body was still racked with so much pain that she could barely breathe.

Images flashed to her mind, as if her brain was rebooting like a computer and recalling the last images recorded.

Horrocks' body. His confusing final words. His missing family. The drone.

Her hands fluttered to her chest where her fingers discovered a soft, thin linen covering in place of the flexible plate armour she'd been wearing. Her hands moved fast to her legs in search of a blade, of anything she could use to defend herself, but her legs were bare from mid-thigh.

She closed her eyes and lay still, breathing in small, shallow gasps so she didn't aggravate whatever terrible injuries she'd suffered and went into herself to utilise the other tools still under her control.

She breathed in through her nose, rolling the smell of the room around until she could make out details.

Damp. Still air. No breeze. Underground.

At the same time she was assessing the scents around

her, her hearing reached out to every corner of the dark chamber, listening to the muted sounds and echoes outside.

When she had learned all she could, she checked herself, feeling the centre of her chest and the left side of her ribs explode in an agony that radiated outwards until her breath caught and her fingertips tingled with numbness. She gasped, her breath fluttering randomly as her eyes prickled with tears brought on by the pain.

Noises, muted by walls and distance, turned her attention outward from her injuries to focus on the sounds. Her concentration made them into words intermittently, but the mass of sounds rolled into one indecipherable rumble. One part of that rumble was louder and deeper than the other, and it was the higher tone she could make out more clearly.

"...don't *know* what she knows... ...need her..." The lower rumble cut the speaker off then, the noise not translated into words she could track, before the sound of locks being opened outside her door clacked and banged.

The door creaked open, tentatively as if the person doing so were fearful that she was free and dangerous. A head peered inside through the gap before the owner straightened, seeing her still flat on her back. Eve slowed her breathing and closed her eyes, waiting for an advantage.

"She dead?" the bass voice said. Now that the speaker was closer to her, Eve could tell that the depth of the voice matched the amount of air the man displaced. He was big, she could sense that, but she didn't think he was all that healthy, given the acrid wave of sharp body odour coming from him.

"No," the other voice answered, annoyed at the man for saying something stupid. "See her chest is rising and falling? We call that *brea-thing*."

"Prick," big man muttered, not even attempting to speak under his breath before huffing a derisive noise. "Not much of a chest anyway," he added.

Eve kept her features still and her breathing steady, rhythmic, like she was sleeping. If the comment was designed to goad her into showing she was awake, it was pretty weak as far as goads went.

The other man unzipped something on her left side, holding her bare arm with one hand and speaking like he was concentrating on something. "There's more to life than that," he said. "we just nee—*agh!*"

He yelped as the arm he was holding rotated, the hand gripping his wrist and crunching the joint to make him drop whatever he had been holding.

Eve recalled the gestures performed in her past when she'd been injected with chemicals and didn't want to repeat the process. She rose off the hard bed, the grip on the locked wrist not relenting and she forced the man down to the ground with another cry of pain, as her momentum transferred through his arm to double the pain he felt.

A grunt of surprise behind her warned of the fat man's delayed reaction. Without looking, she threw back her right heel, lifting it up and over the bed, but for his assumed size and poor fitness, the man moved with a speed she didn't anticipate, stepping back quickly enough that her heel only caught him a glancing blow.

She adjusted, turning to her left as he was scrambling around the bed from the other direction to get to her, forcing her to release the vice-like grip on the smaller man's wrist to face the bigger threat. She hopped back a step and took a stance ready to exchange blows with him, already anticipating the feel of her numb hands hitting him in the soft places where his nerve clusters would be vulnerable.

As if knowing this, or maybe playing to his only advantage of size, he didn't stop to fight her but rushed her like an animal and slammed his sweat-stinking body into hers to flash a resurgence of pain all across her chest on impact, then again as both of them slammed into the wall together.

She broke her arms free of his grip, writhing like a serpent, and used her feet to climb him where she rained elbow strikes down on his skull and neck. Immediately she felt his grip weaken but he continued to lean into her and keep her trapped against the rough surface of the wall, shouting for guards to rush into the cell and help him.

Her breath abandoned her as the pain in her sternum and ribcage robbed her of the ability to breathe deeply enough to supply her muscles with the oxygen they needed. Digging deeper, she dropped a gear change into fighting dirty and jabbed the fingers of her right hand into the man's eyes to force his head backwards and followed with two savage, short-range blows from her left forearm into his windpipe.

He staggered backwards, dropping to one knee but still fought to contain her, even if he was unable to yell for assistance any longer. Eve found the space she needed and brought her right knee up into his jaw. He froze, toppling backwards so slowly, like a tree being cut down was just beginning to submit to gravity. Eve slumped, her hands on her knees as she croaked and fought to breathe, as the door burst open and three men in black uniforms rushed in, their eye wide with fear and adrenaline.

Eve sucked in a breath and held it to keep her chest rigid, standing up and letting the first one come to her, readying the stun baton in his right hand to zap her. She let him make his thrust, turning her body to avoid the crackling tip of the weapon and seize his wrist before slamming her right elbow into the bridge of his nose to drop him with a crunch, but the other two were fast.

Not as fast as she was, not if she could breathe, but fast enough to touch the tips of their batons to her body and send enough voltage through her to turn out the lights.

CHAPTER ELEVEN

ABOVE YOUR PAY GRADE

Rebecca said little on their journey back east, speaking only when the drivers called out that the gates of the Citadel were in sight. She and the others had kept their mouths shut since the little remaining space inside their transport had been filled with two of Black's direct response team troops who said nothing but cradled their weapons with purpose.

"Unpack the gear and write a debrief," she told them as if the conclusion of the mission didn't warrant any serious discussion. "After that you can stand down."

They acknowledged her, all three of them exchanging subtle glances as if to say they'd hold their own debrief when safely back in their own environment.

"Go ahead," one of the DRT members said, leaning his head down slightly and showing a partially vacant expression as he listened to whatever he was being told over his earpiece.

"Inspector Howard," he said respectfully, looking back up to her as if joining them again. "Request from

Command that you report to the control floor and give an immediate mission summary."

Rebecca nodded, her facial expression giving nothing away but inside screaming at the unexpected turn of events.

When the transport stopped, pausing a second before reversing back into the vehicle bay at the headquarters building, she stepped out to find the same two men fall into what was outwardly an escort position just behind each shoulder, but she took it as a clear and deliberate message that she was being *brought* to Command to give her answers.

Choosing to go with the flow until she knew which way this was going to go, she surrendered her short-barrelled rifle to one of her own team and stripped off the tactical vest so she went looking less like she was expecting significant trouble.

Still with a gun on her thigh, and half expecting to be told to remove that also, she walked to the elevator at the centre of the building and scanned her eye to activate it, with both of Black's men still hovering in her blind spots.

She ignored the obvious intimidation, reminding herself to act the rank and station she'd been awarded for her part in the overthrow of the Party, and not be the frightened girl she'd been when Nathaniel and the Resistance had both manipulated her.

The elevator arrived and she stepped inside, half expecting the escorting men to follow, but they stood still and stared at her.

"Not coming up?" she asked politely, feigning ignorance of their tactics. One shook his head, still staring at her as the doors closed and the floor jolted lightly against her feet.

She let out a sigh, fighting back the threat of tears

through stress and fear, and leaned over a little. Recalling the fact that every elevator – especially *this* one – had cameras, she stood straight and forced an appropriate expression of annoyance at the way the operation had turned out for the benefit of anyone watching.

She fought another urge then, telling herself to hit the button for any other floor so she could double back and go to her own offices and speak with the others before reporting to Command, but she knew that any deviation now would raise suspicion where it wasn't warranted.

The doors opened onto the control level and she strode out, scanning through security confidently like she belonged there, because she did, despite how Black made her feel. Walking to the offices where her superiors were usually located, she was stopped in her tracks by Black, who stepped into the corridor ahead of her, still dressed for war but without the rifle, and smiling and laughing with someone behind him.

Rebecca watched the doorway, seeing the smaller frame of the Prime Minister walking behind him and sharing whatever joke they'd enjoyed before she arrived.

Rebecca fought the urge to imagine any number of ways that joke could be at her expense and nodded a greeting at their leader.

"Ah, Inspector Howard," she said with a wide smile. "Inspector Black was just filling me in on the success of the mission."

"Success?' Rebecca blurted out, unable to stop herself.

"Yes, what else would you call it?"

The tantalising lure of telling her side of the story almost won through, but she retained just enough sense of self-preservation to stop herself from letting fly about Black and his actions.

"Ma'am," she said instead, "I lost my asset, Eve. She's

gone. And my embedded source is as yet…" she glanced pointedly at Black, unable to stop herself that time, "… unaccounted for."

The Prime Minister's face fell into cold professionalism, turning to face Black to silently demand an explanation.

"It's true, Prime Minister," Black said, feigning some kind of empathy for the loss of life. "I've personally checked the list of captured traitors and, sadly, he isn't there." Rebecca bridled, her nostrils flaring at the gender assigned to her source, which was something she hadn't divulged to him, which meant that Garret probably had.

"He wouldn't be using his na—"

"I've cross-referenced identities through visual ID also," Black interrupted, talking over her to the Prime Minister. He held his hands out, palms up, pretending to give a shit. Rebecca held her tongue as she recognised being on the losing end of an argument quickly enough.

"Inspector," Helen said smoothly, "thank you for a job well done. Please pass on my congratulations to your officers?"

"Of course, Ma'am," he responded. "And my condolences to the injured?" Helen smiled, nodding slowly.

"Yes, please." Black drew himself up and took his dismissal, walking past Rebecca and treating her to a wolfish smile of triumph. She returned his look with a glare before returning her attention to the Prime Minister, seeing the woman's cold look of disappointment.

"Follow me," Helen said, turning on her heel and walking down the corridor.

Not walking… strutting. Helen strutted, like a woman riding high and enjoying her power. She wore it well, but Rebecca couldn't help imagining her compared side by side with Nathaniel and coming a distant second in the competition of who wore their power better.

She shook her head to clear the unexpected thought away and followed her to a busy outer office which the Prime Minister walked straight through. Rebecca followed, not feeling as if she should wait for permission to enter.

"Close the door," Helen said, spinning her chair and sitting down to regard the tired woman standing in front of her. Rebecca did as she was told, clasping her hands behind her back and fighting the urge to sway a little. Until then, she hadn't felt the combined sting of a night spent awake, the travel and the mental stress of events.

"The operation was a success," Helen said flatly.

"Prime Ministe—"

"The operation," she said again, more slowly this time in case Rebecca wasn't following, "was a success."

"I understand the end goal, Ma'am, but th—"

"Do I need to tell you again, Inspector?"

Rebecca stifled a sigh of exasperation and kept her mouth shut.

"No, Ma'am."

"Good. You may not like some of the things that happened or the way they went down, but we need to show a strong, stable, united front to the people. The operation was a success, say it with me."

"The operation was a success," Rebecca parroted as ordered.

"The armed traitors resisted us, they were convincingly beaten, and we have liberated an agricultural zone to bring it back under the protection and leadership of this government," Helen said, sounding very much as though she were giving Rebecca lines to rehearse.

"Yes, Ma'am," Rebecca said woodenly.

"As for your assets," Helen went on, tapping a key on her terminal to wake the screen, "as ever, the risk of collateral losses is not insignificant. It's regrettable, but it's life.

Now, I don't need to remind you that we have other covert intelligence sources and other assets with the particular skills you—quite rightly—believed were necessary for this operation. So, congratulations on a job well done. I think you'll probably need to take the rest of the day off to rest, so I'll see you tomorrow morning. Dismissed."

Rebecca smiled as genuinely as she could manage and turned for the door.

"One more thing, Inspector?"

Here we go, Rebecca thought as she turned back and restored the false expression.

"Black is a man on the rise, as they say... it probably doesn't pay to pick fights you can't win."

Rebecca fought down the first three things her brain lined up for her to say out loud, the first being that Helen had so recently been a woman on the rise and the implications of what that meant for men like Black.

"Thank you, Prime Minister," she answered, resuming her exit and telling herself that picking a fight with Black was precisely what she wanted to be doing.

CHAPTER TWELVE

PRISONER

Eve regained consciousness for the second time, her breathing turning rapid and deep for two breaths before the pain lanced through her again. She was angry. Angry at being defeated, angry at being caged and not knowing where she was.

For a young woman only so recently accustomed to freedom and life above ground, to be back behind a locked door without the precious gift of sunlight – denied her for her entire life – all this forced feelings to the surface where they bubbled over to make her feel vulnerable and childlike all over again.

She sat up, gasping and wincing in pain, with both hands clutched to her chest as her breath hissed between her teeth. She wasn't sure if it was the original injury or if she'd been hurt again fighting, but the pain seemed intensified from before as she swung her legs painfully off the edge of the bed.

Her feet touched the ground, sending feedback of the cold floor back up to her brain, but she could barely concentrate past the agony of breathing. She was sure she had broken bones because no muscle injury she'd ever experienced before had hurt like this.

A metallic grating noise jerked her attention from her body in a second, making her head snap to the door like an automated gun system coming online.

"You're injured," the voice said. "You need pain medication and… and I need to examine you. I'm a doctor."

She recognised his voice as belonging to the man who was going to inject her the last time she was conscious. The man whose wrist she'd almost snapped.

"I promise you," he said, "I'm not going to hurt you. Can you do the same?"

Eve wanted to laugh at him. She wanted to insult and threaten him, but she didn't have the capacity or the energy in her current state. She knew it was only a matter of time before she passed out again anyway, and whatever they were going to do to her, she knew from bitter experience that they'd do it by force if she didn't comply. Deciding to tip the balance of the scales in her direction, she nodded and gestured for him to enter the cell with a weak wave of her hand beckoning him.

Muttered voices exchanged a hushed but brief argument outside, and she guessed the man who claimed to be a doctor was going against the advice of whoever was out there making sure she didn't cause another ruckus.

The door clunked as a bolt was drawn back and it opened only just wide enough for the man to be thrust inside before it was banged shut again. The slit in the door was filled with two wide eyes watching her, ready to react violently to any wrong move she made.

Eve had already told herself she wasn't in a good enough way to start anything then. She was weak, she was in a massive amount of pain and she wanted some facts.

"Hello," the man said nervously as he skirted to the outer edges of the room. "My name is Doctor Michael Hegarty. I won't hurt you, but you have some quite severe injuries I need to take a look at to make sure you aren't showing any signs of internal haemorrhage."

"How?" Eve croaked. Hegarty looked confused for a moment before answering, making his already small and sharp features seem even more birdlike.

"Oh, well… I'll need to see the injuries…"

"How did I *get* the injuries?" she asked again, gasping with the effort of speaking.

"We found you wearing some form of prototype armour with what appears to be three high-calibre bullet impact injuries to your chest," Hegarty told her. "As to the how, we were rather hoping you were going to tell us…"

"Drone, *ungh!*" Eve said, grunting as she leaned back to slowly lie down on the bed again. "One of your drones shot me," she finished, logically assuming that she was in the custody of the enemy and still inside the complex.

"We don't…" Hegarty began before shaking his head and taking a step towardss her. "I'm sorry about this, but I'm certain you know where the injuries are…"

Eve breathed out through her nose, making it sound like a sigh of either annoyance or resignation but nodded her assent anyway, before lifting a finger and pointing it at the door.

"Tell whoever *that* is, that they better look away." She sensed Hegarty turn his head, imagining him frowning at the door before speaking.

"If you don't mind?"

"Your funeral if she decides to snap your neck," the reply came, sounding amused at the prospect of her killing him.

Hegarty waited until the sliding sound ended in a

resounding *clack* before turning back to her, rubbing his hands together. "Sorry, always did have cold hands," he apologised as his icy fingers touched the sore skin around the massive bruise in the centre of her chest. He explored that wound, checking the other two on her side before placing his left hand on her abdomen and tapping it with the fingers of his right.

"No internal bleeding then?" Eve managed to say before the pain forced her lips to clamp shut once more.

"Doesn't look that way," he answered, his mind on the task of examining her. "Any breathing problems? Shortness of breath?"

"Only when I breathe," Eve grunted in response, earning a satisfied and amused noise from her visitor. He covered her up, laying the open sides of the loose shirt she wore over her and stepping back.

"As I suspected, it appears that you have fractures of the sternum and... well, most of the ribs on your left side. Frankly, I'm amazed you could even move, let alone..."

"Yeah," Eve said as she sat up slowly. "Sorry about that."

"Not at all," Hegarty answered, chuckling lightly as if the attack were all water under the bridge.

"What's going to happen to me?" Eve asked him, seeming for everything in the world to be the frightened young woman she intended to portray.

"That's not exactly up to me," he said sadly. "Other people make those kinds of decisions and I just patch people up." He gave a self-deprecating shrug and allowed his face to drop, adding, "if I can."

"Listen," Eve said. "You could just let me go. I wo—"

"I can't!" Eve recoiled at his sudden flare of anger bursting out in the words. "And it's no good pretending to look frightened... we... we know who you are."

Eve dropped the pretence of being vulnerable and, again in spite of the pain it caused her, she swung her legs down off the bed and advanced two paces on him with her gown hanging open like she didn't care.

She did, because being naked was an additional vulnerability she could've done without, but she decided to use it unashamedly on him to get answers.

"So, you know why I was there? You know why your drone did this to me?"

Hegarty recoiled, pacing away until his back hit the wall and brought his hands up to ward off another brutal assault.

"We don't have any drones," another voice barked deeply from the doorway. Eve froze. So intent was she on her one target that she'd failed to even hear the door open. She turned slowly, realisation dawning on her that she'd recognised the speaker, to see Mark.

They were never close, not like she and Cohen had been, but Mark had trained her with weapons and about the Party systems he'd once used before he'd switched sides. Looking at him now, she guessed that switching sides was something he made a habit of.

Before she could speak, he held up both hands to ward off whatever she was about to say. If she'd been able to breathe better, her words would already be out now, echoing between the bare walls of the windowless cell she was being held in.

"It's not what you think," he said, "these people aren't the enemy."

She stopped. Whatever fire had risen inside her was extinguished then – snuffed out in a heartbeat at the realisation that she already suspected that.

Eve staggered, the pain and disorientation too much for her. Hegarty stepped close to support her even though only seconds before, he'd been afraid of her, demonstrating to her that he was unable to stop himself from offering aid, regardless of the risk to himself. She recognised that bravery, that calling, and relaxed as he took some of her weight and helped her back to the bed.

"Talk," was all she managed to say.

"Okay," Mark answered. "Let's be hypothetical for a minute… let's say you were told that Horrocks was leading some kind of Party rebellion against Command, and let's say that you believed what you were told…"

Eve lifted her head slightly to catch his eye and her expression told him he wasn't wrong yet.

"And we can assume that your coming back was a personal favour… Howard?" She allowed herself to give the smallest nod of agreement.

"And you did what you thought was right, only it went wrong straight after."

"Drone," she answered, still unable to make full sentences.

"She's in pain, let me administer—"

"In a minute," Mark snapped, not taking his eyes off Eve. "That drone wasn't ours. It was *theirs*. They planned to take you out all along, just as soon as you'd dealt with the target."

"Why?" Eve asked weakly, still dwelling on his use of the word 'ours'.

"That part I'm not certain of, but I can tell you this place wasn't what you were told it was."

"Tell me," she managed, struggling for breath and fighting the urge to lie down and pass out.

"This is no rebellion. This is… this is a *secession*. We never wanted to take over the Citadel, we just wanted to live our lives here in peace, to govern ourselves and live free. The exact same reason the Resistance planned to get rid of the Party in the first place."

Eve's head swam with the information, with the guilt and shame of her actions and for being played like an idiot.

"Enough's enough," Hegarty said, leaning Eve back to lay her down. "She needs painkillers and she needs sleep. Talk can wait."

CHAPTER THIRTEEN

STRIVING TO SECEDE

Mark visited her later that day with food. He told her it was later but for her it might as well have been two days later as she woke from a drug-induced sleep that left her dehydrated and rolling the taste of tin around her mouth.

She ate – a simple broth that tasted salty and made her thirst intensify – and drank before he started to speak.

"I was sent here four months ago as part of a team checking out why communications had gone dark," he told her as he took a seat and rubbed his tired face with both hands. "We were expecting Party remnants like a few other times. Holdouts who either weren't in the Citadel when it all went down or others who'd escaped and were running around the country tearing into abandoned sites. This place was—"

"Wait," Eve interrupted, "we're still in the complex?"

Mark shook his head.

"Sorry, didn't mean to confuse you. We had an escape route set up ready for when this happened. We're a few miles south in an old underground grain store that they stopped using when the facility got a rebuild years ago. It was blocked off but there are other entrances."

"And how did I get here?"

"We'd evacuated some people – key personnel mainly – but we had no chance of getting the others out with how fast they attacked." His face darkened at the memory, at his impotence about it all.

"Weaponised drone attacks against civilians?" he asked rhetorically. "I guess Helen's really worried that the idea of freedom will catch on."

"Back up," Eve said. "So, the facility wasn't a militarised camp and there's no plot to overthrow the government? Again." Mark shook his head in apology.

"Sorry, just let me tell the story. I'll get to it. Anyway… the place wasn't under guard, not properly at least, and we met with the top guy, Horrocks. He was the detachment Captain here when it went down, and the people wanted to stay here. You know, live their own lives and make their own decisions. The way most people saw it outside of the Citadel was… was like it didn't really bother them. It wasn't their fight. Conditions here weren't bad, and they were allowed a lot more freedom than in the city."

"So, you went back and told them that, and they came up with the story about armed rebels coming to snatch power away from Command?"

"Yeah. Kind of, but not at first…" Eve's questioning eyebrows asked for a little more clarity than he giving her.

"Sorry," he apologised again, "I haven't slept much in the last few days. Horrocks gave us a tour of the place, gave us free reign to go anywhere and talk to anyone, so we knew he wasn't giving us people with their lines learned ready, and the place was… working. It was more than that, it was happy."

"Happy?" Eve asked, voicing a word not many people had ever used around her.

"Happier than the people in the Citadel and happier than they were before. A lot of soldiers came back with us, and a few had already left because they didn't want to deal with a new reality or something, but I went back and reported it all to Rebecca, although she's *Inspector* Howard now, and a few days later we turned around and came straight back to start talks."

"About what?"

"About how it would work. Would they be a separate state? Would they expect anything from the Citadel?"

"And Helen didn't like the idea of that," Eve stated flatly.

"She was all for it, at least it seemed that way. She sent one of her guys, Harvey, with us to talk. Only Horrocks spoke for the people, but we found out that was what they'd asked him to do. They kind of adopted him as their spokesperson and he doubled up as their protector too."

"And his family?" Mark stiffened, whether at the interruption spoiling the flow of his recall or at the mention of them specifically, she couldn't tell.

"I was sent here as an escort for Harvey, only I was wearing two hats." Eve's eyebrows crinkled and rose together pointing above her nose. Mark saw the expression and shook his head again.

"I mean I was doing two jobs at once, you know? I was wearing my 'I'm here to escort Harvey' hat and another one. I was collecting intelligence... anyway, I... well, Harvey fell in love with the place. So much open space and greenery and the people were happy to all work together and get along. Horrocks was... he was unhappy that his family were still in the Citadel and he formally asked for them back, like we were holding them hostage or something. The man was really cagey about it and I couldn't figure out why back then. Turns out he was right."

"About what?"

"About Command not being willing to just let it slide and hand over their nearest food production site to a bunch of people with no leadership and wanting to make it on their own."

"So, you came back here with his family and stayed to spy on them," Eve surmised, skipping to the end of the story that was already taking too long for her headache to be happy with.

Mark nodded.

"Harvey stayed here, and a few soldiers requested to come back…" he shrugged. "Horrocks wasn't the die-hard Party man they made him out to be; turns out he was just torn between wanting to be with his family and worrying that hundreds of people would be at risk if he left them unprotected."

Eve gave in and lay back on the bed, waving away his offer to leave her to rest.

"So, you came back here with his family, made out like you'd switched sides to keep feeding intelligence back, and what did you think was going to happen?"

"Communication went dark almost four weeks ago," he told her. "I was sending it out, but nothing was coming back. I knew something was coming then, but with too few soldiers and not enough resources, we'd be vulnerable to any kind of attack. We smuggled a few people out when we got wind of the convoy leaving the Citadel but we… we didn't expect this."

He told her, in detail on her insistence, what the attacking force had done. Mark was close to tears when he spoke, either through upset or anger; she couldn't tell which one without seeing his face, but she suspected a mixture of the two emotions.

The attack had been brutal, with drones blowing the gates and cutting down innocent people whose only crime was wanting to live free and rule their own lives. Did that make them so different? So dangerous?

"Black," Eve said. "The man who led the attack was a guy called Black."

"Black? From the DRT?" Mark evidently knew of the man and Eve confirmed with a noise.

"He was brutal when he was QRF, and last I heard he'd been arrested for trial. How did he not end up with a war crime sanction?" Eve shrugged, regretting it instantly as she imagined the rib bones under her left arm crunching with the movement.

"I guess they kept a couple more trained attack dogs for themselves than I thought."

Eve breathed slowly, asking herself the question a few times over in her head before summoning the courage to say it out loud. Once she said it, there would be no going back if she didn't get the answer she wanted.

"And Rebecca?"

Mark hesitated before answering, just long enough to cause Eve deep concern.

"I don't know," he said finally. "In my heart I don't think she'd be a part of it, but she wouldn't be the first person to turn on their beliefs for a better life."

"Meaning what?" Eve asked, imagining that he meant her leaving the Citadel as if she hadn't earned a retirement from a life of violence.

"Meaning that others have been seduced by privilege and power."

"But not you?" she asked, if only to gauge his reaction.

"Not me," he said to her with so much honesty it had

to be the truth. She didn't know Mark well, but Cohen had. And if Cohen trusted him, then she felt obligated to do the same for so many irrational and logical reasons.

"You think we just swapped one dictator for another?" she asked quietly, looking for her own culpability in all of it.

"Maybe," Mark answered. "If not a dictator, then we just got rid of one corrupt leadership for another. From what I see, little has changed in the Citadel – people still have to go to work to get fed, only the armed guards wear a smile instead of black face plates."

"So none of it was worth it," Eve muttered darkly, knowing that the pain of her injuries was making her mood worse. "None of the death and none of the risk was worth it, because we helped people take control who are too frightened of losing it to be any different from the last bunch."

She balled her fists until the pain in her ribs was too much to bear. Everything they'd done, everything they'd been through to fight for what they were assured was a better life, all led to a woman in control who hadn't even earned the chance to be considered. Not like Cohen had...

"I hope not," Mark said. "But having lived under both rules back there and having lived here, I can tell you I don't want to go back."

CHAPTER FOURTEEN

KEPT IN THE DARK

Mouse returned to their underground lab without saying a word as the twins bickered quietly between themselves. The larger elevator they rode down in carried their remaining drones, the others unrecovered, or more accurately they hadn't been permitted the time to recover them, so they'd only brought back one of their prototypes. After storing them in the secure parking level, the three of them returned to their small, personal headquarters.

"I say we reach out," Jonah argued. "Get in contact with Jasmin—"

"Samaira," his sister corrected. In truth, as far as rank went, the woman they were referring to went by neither of her former ranks and instead was in a civilian capacity of leadership to unite and govern the northern facilities and ensure that the materials required for manufacturing kept coming.

"Whatever," Jonah said irritably, "I say we contact her an—"

"And what?" Mouse asked. "Ask her to come back and stop people in charge from telling us what to do?"

"Get it into your head," Jonah said as he rounded on him. "This isn't Command in charge, and we aren't Resistance. They've become *them*."

"Dangerous conversation to be having," chided a voice from the darkness of the lab and instantly silencing their argument. Jenna stepped forwards to activate the motion sensors and illuminate the entire lab, and the lights flickered on to reveal the room, which was empty with the exception of Rebecca, sitting at a desk with a glass in her hand and her feet up. She was leaning back as if relaxed, but in reality, her body language spelled out an exhausted resignation instead.

"He's right," Rebecca went on, squinting as the bright strip lighting flooded the room white. She leaned forwards, dropping her boots off the desk with a thud to put the glass down. She looked like a woman who hadn't slept in two days but then neither had they, so her exhaustion was likely caused by the additional mental stress she was under.

"What's the plan? Tell someone else that the government – the one *you* directly helped install – is taking away your rights? Grow up," she spat with more venom than they expected. "You can't go crying to anyone, because there isn't anyone left to tell, because there's no Resistance."

"What are you saying?" Jenna asked as she pulled up a chair beside her. Rebecca could only have been there a little while – long enough for the motion lights to go off – but she'd evidently drunk enough of the contents of her glass to be speaking as recklessly as they were.

"I'm saying this is what it is," she said with a slight slur of tiredness to complement the alcohol. "We made our bed, and now we have to lie in it."

"What happened upstairs?" Jonah demanded, venting

his anger at her, which earned him a reproving glare from his sister and a cold look from Rebecca.

"I got told that Eve was 'an acceptable loss'. I also got reminded that we aren't running anything down here and that I should watch out for that bastard Black. He's 'a man on the rise' apparently."

"What the hell does that mean?' Jenna asked, her anger clouding her judgement along with her ability to comprehend.

"It means that we aren't running anything down here," Rebecca told her flatly. "Command has obviously decided on an approach with anyone not falling in line and…" she trailed off, leaving the others to glance at each other.

"And what does *that* mean?" Jonah asked quietly.

"It means," Rebecca said with a sigh, "that all we've succeeded in doing is replacing one rule with another."

"You mean the Party were no better than Command?" Jenna asked.

"She means that Command are no better than the Party," Mouse muttered as if speaking out loud to himself, oblivious to the fact that the others could hear him. His fingers rattled over the keyboard he sat in front of as his eyes flickered along the display of the terminal he was working at.

"That's the same thing," Jenna told him.

"Not necessarily," Mouse went on in the same distant tone as his fingers danced over the keys. "I mean that Command wanted to overthrow the Party and bring freedom to the Citadel—"

"Only they don't want freedom here, because they won't have enough people left to do the work," Rebecca finished. "So you know?"

"I'd guessed," Mouse answered. "The people we

attacked this morning weren't really going to fight us, were they?"

"What do you mean?" Jenna asked him, shaking her head angrily as if too many conflicting pieces of information were fighting with one another for her attention. "You saw the intel – Horrocks was a soldier and he was coming back here to re-establish the Party."

"Horrocks was a soldier, yes," Rebecca said. "Only there was some intelligence to say that he was just trying to defend some people who wanted to live on their own."

The four of them sat in silence punctuated only by Mouse's incessant key clattering.

"But your intel… from Mark…" Jenna asked, still confused. She glanced at her twin brother, who sat in silence to put all the pieces together.

"Was cut off weeks ago," she told them. That silence stretched out again until Mouse made a small noise of triumph and spoke.

"Ha! It did, but only to you." Rebecca sat forwards.

"Meaning what, exactly?"

"Meaning he was still sending reports, only they weren't reaching you. There was no blackout," Mouse told her, leaning back to show a screen filled with characters in random formations as if it meant something to her.

"What am I looking at?" she asked, hiding her annoyance at the man who just never seemed to understand social interactions, no matter how many he had.

"Here, see?" he said, pointing at a line of code.

"I see," Rebecca answered him with as much patience as she could muster, "but I don't speak computer."

"This is a divergent code splice," he explained, as if his words made anything clearer to them. "They intercepted the transmissions and didn't report them to you. Normally this works the other way around so that nobody else gets our transmissions, only it's been turned around against us."

"We can do that?" Jenna asked.

"We've been doing it for months," Rebecca answered. "But it looks like we weren't the only ones. Can you undo it?"

Mouse made a noise as if to say it was beyond even his capabilities.

"Rotating random algorithms are hard to beat," he said sadly. "And this one is… well, it's *beautiful…*"

"Fascinating," Jonah said, snapping out of his funk. "So we were on the good side which is now – *potentially* – the bad side, they've just used us to assassinate someone who may or may not have deserved it and none of that helps us one bit because we've still lost Eve and Mark and all we can do is smile and go along with it or we'll be… what? Shot for treason?"

The looming threat of punishment for crimes against the ruling regime was ever-present, and almost all of those deemed guilty of treason were already long dead.

"We do nothing," Rebecca said firmly. "We go to sleep, we get up, we do our jobs and other than that… We. Do. Nothing."

Blank stares returned her words as if they were waiting for her to say more.

"That rotating thing," she said to Mouse. "Can you make it work for us?"

Mouse considered the request for a second, blinking rapidly and looking at the arm of her chair instead of her face as he answered.

"I need some time, but yes."

CHAPTER FIFTEEN

TRUST IS EARNED

The complex was small, Eve could tell that much from the way people were crammed in on top of one another and supplies.

The underground complex had a temporary and hushed feel about it, as if everyone there were quietly waiting in a building for the monster upstairs to fly away, and when Eve was invited by Mark to leave the cell she was in, she saw the way people eyed her nervously and gripped the handles of their weapons in case she turned on them.

"Friendly bunch," she hissed at Mark as they walked beside one another. She hissed from the pain caused by the effort of moving and couldn't understand why the pain of her injuries had worsened overnight.

"People are scared," Mark told her, "with good reason to be. Plus, you know, you did kill one of their leaders."

"I never confirmed that," she answered in a quiet voice. Mark chuckled at her answer, as if anything could be funny in that strange time.

"There are probably two people I know who could've

infiltrated the base and got away with it," he told her. "And the last I saw of one of them, he was on a boat heading west."

"Have you heard from Adam?" Eve asked, full of concern and hope that he and his cat-like bride would return to save them again.

"No, and I don't expect to. When he left the Republic, everything was fine, so why he'd come back ready for a fight he doesn't know is happening is beyond me."

Eve sagged, partly at the disappointment and partly due to the pain she was still in. Leaning a hand against the cold, damp wall, she steadied herself and took a few breaths. She'd gauged the exact amount of inflation for her ribs not to feel like they were cracking apart again, but that left her short of breath if she did anything other than lie down.

"Listen," Mark said, taking his opportunity to speak when she was unable to answer. "A lot of people here never lived in the Citadel. They only heard stories about what it was like, so when the brave leader of the Resistance – the one who killed the evil dictator – comes here to kill their people, they get a little confused."

"I…" Eve gasped, "don't blame them… they'd trust me… less than they trust… you."

"That's another issue," Mark said quietly as he leaned in closer to her. "They don't know I was sent here. They think I decided to stay by myself."

"But you *are* on their side… right?"

"I am now, because I see what they're trying to do is right and what happened back there…" his features darkened as his mind wandered back to the atrocities he'd described as being worse than anything he'd seen Nathaniel order. "What happened back there is *wrong*."

"We agree on that," Eve said, standing up straight once she'd recovered her breath.

Mark led her slowly through the complex, Eve learning about the few hundred people they had there and seeing people who were clearly farmer and workers holding weapons with all the comfort she felt wearing a skirt. There was a small army down there, and she shuddered to think what would have happened if these people had stayed to fight trained and organised soldiers above ground.

It was happening all over again, only this time the lines of right and wrong – or at least who was bad and who was good – were more blurred than ever.

He led her through increasingly busy areas, with people almost frantic in their activity, until they reached what was obviously the temporary headquarters of their group. Eve had seen enough setups similar to this to know when she'd been brought into the nerve centre, watching as younger men and women came and went, carrying and bringing messages with them.

One man at the centre of it all seemed to be doing three things at once, and one of those things was taking hurried slurps from a metal mug. The aroma of the contents reached Eve's nose and her body seemed to react by forcing a craving for the sugary drink.

"You're back," the man said to Mark. "Good."

Eve recognised him, even in the poor light with dark bags under his eyes to complement the short beard he'd grown since she'd last seen him.

She wanted to stand tall to meet him, to not show any weakness, but her injuries still robbed her of breath and forced her to lower herself slowly onto a pile of crates.

"Just to be clear," the man said, still not looking at her but busying himself with things arrayed along a folding workbench, "you're still alive on Mark's word, so the consequences of any hostile actions you might be inclined towards will fall on him also."

"You're Harvey," she said with a hint of accusation in her words. "You were part of Command when I was their prisoner, weren't you?"

Harvey shot a glance at Mark, who gave no response or acknowledgement to his look.

"I was," he answered, "yes."

"So what happened?'

"What do you mean, *what happened*?" he asked, distaste fighting with shock on his face.

"When I left the Citadel, everything was going fine. The Party gave up, people were free, everything was going to be sunshine and whatever... so what happened?"

Harvey's face dropped into a smirk that tried to look annoyed but failed.

"I forgot you left straight afterwards," he said. He sighed and pulled up a crate opposite her. "It took weeks to clean up the city. There were pockets of soldiers and officials everywhere, although most of them were just too frightened to surrender after what happened to some people... anyway... Command took over, power was redistributed, and the world had to keep turning."

"What does that mean?" Eve asked, trying to ignore a fresh stab of pain from her fractured chest.

"People still needed to eat. Materials were needed for the factories we had to reopen. Just because the military rule ended, it didn't mean everyone could stop working. How would they eat? Who would keep everything clean and running as normal?"

Eve contemplated his words, realising that the reason she hadn't thought of those things was because she'd never lived in a world where each facet of society had its own role so that everyone had what they needed.

She'd been kept underground, existing in a perpetual cycle of training and indoctrination until released into the world above ground where all that training was translated into blood and fear.

"So…" Eve winced as a stab of pain radiated down her left arm to punish her for breathing. "My question still stands."

Harvey stared at her, not blinking, as if prolonged eye contact could break through whatever lies he suspected she would tell. She didn't know what he hoped to achieve but attempting to stare her into submission was as effective as trying the same thing on a cat.

Up close, she could see how tired he was, like it was an illness with physical symptoms. She hadn't known him before, but she'd met him, and the man in front of her now could have been his much older brother.

He sighed, leaned away and gulped the last dregs of his drink by holding it tipped up to allow the froth to find his mouth. Lowering it with a sigh, he stared at the ground and started to speak.

"The Party soldiers were gone. Locked up or dead or they'd just run away. Many of them were released, swore an oath to serve the people and abide by the rule of the government, and that allowed us the safety to start reorganising things. We needed them, you see? Our own people were running wild, killing Party members and their families… their *families*… I suffered their rule like others, not as bad as some had it and harder than others did, but…" He trailed off, shaking his head. Eve knew this already, but she'd learned enough to let a person tell their story at their own pace.

"We had no choice but to keep a lot of them in the positions they currently held, only with new leadership in most cases. Still, there were more allegations every day, and people had to be stripped of their weapons and taken off duty... when I heard about this place, I came to try and get them to surrender, you know? I couldn't stand to see any more lives lost."

His eyes came back up to search Eve's face for her reaction.

"And it wasn't what you were told it was?" she asked, prompting him to go on.

"No. Not one bit. This wasn't a military faction. They weren't looking to take over anything, they were just... they just wanted to keep living their lives in peace and most of the soldiers here guarding them decided they wanted that too. Horrocks was... he was a good man, deep down. He could've left, could've gone back to the Citadel and from everything I know, he'd have been vetted and returned to duty. Nobody ever accused him of anything, so he..."

Harvey sighed from exhaustion. Eve guessed that exhaustion was more than just tiredness and had a lot to do with his inability to understand the inherently violent nature of humanity.

"Why didn't you tell me any of this before?" Eve asked, her eyes searching Mark's face for the truth. "Why did you let Adam and Dren go away if you knew the fight wasn't over?"

"It *was* over," Harvey said, speaking for Mark. "It was *all* over, until it wasn't..."

"Eve," Mark said in a low, controlled voice. "Command were running the city until they agreed to adopt a new kind of legitimate government. After that... well, let's just say Command members started to melt away."

"Call it what it is," Harvey told him stiffly. "Command started to disappear. And now, we have this situation..."

"I acted on information I was given, by someone I trusted, and I was wrong," Eve said quietly. "I did what I did because I thought I would save more lives than the one I took. I'm sorry."

Harvey looked at Mark before he turned back to face her.

"That doesn't matter now," he said. "What matters is what you'll do next."

CHAPTER SIXTEEN

LAYERS OF LIES

Rebecca left the underground lab where her department was primarily based, heading back up to return to her plush apartment where she stood under a hot shower for so long that it was beginning to grow dark outside her windows when she got out.

Walking through the rooms in a robe, her bare feet swishing through the thick carpets, she stopped outside the spare room where Eve had stayed. Hesitating before she stepped inside, Rebecca half expected to see the place how she last saw it, with the covers of the bed messy and unmade by the young woman who probably tossed and turned there, unable to sleep in a soft bed.

She expected to find the piles of clothes Eve left still crumpled in a heap, but walking in and seeing her shining black outfit folded neatly on the end of the bed made everything somehow so much worse.

She walked out of the room and closed the door behind her, her hand resting on the handle for a moment, her eyes closed, before she shook both hands in front of her and blew out her held breath making the shape of an O with her lips.

Stepping into the open living space, she walked straight to the fridge and poured herself a glass of something from a clear glass bottle. She gulped it down and walked to her own bed where she set an alarm for the following morning and cried until she passed out.

———

Inspector Rebecca Howard, the recipient of the People's Hero medal, survivor of the Resistance's plan to overthrow the Party and a woman who had a personal stake in the success of that night, walked out of the elevator on the command floor of the headquarters building.

She walked with purpose, her black uniform fitted and looking as proud as she was, with her hair tied up neatly and a perfect face of subtle makeup, and strode into her office ready to make the day her own.

In her chair, however, and with his dirty boots resting on the edge of her desk sat Black.

"Glad you could make it," he beamed arrogantly, implying that she was late to her own office to run her own department.

"What do you want?" she asked, careful to make her voice sound bored and disinterested by his annoying presence instead of betraying the jolt of fear he caused her to suffer.

"A report on all current cases," Black said, still smiling and not even having the courtesy to take his feet off her desk. "Along with a full rundown on all covert sources."

"Fuck off," she replied in the same casual tone he'd used to demand information so far beyond his scope that she wanted to draw her weapon and shoot the man.

Still smiling, Black rested his hands together in his lap and used his legs to swing the chair gently from side to side.

"You misunderstand me," he said wolfishly. "I wasn't *asking*, I was *telling*. I'd like a report on all of your open investigations, a full run down on your covert sources, and while I'm here, I may as well take a look at your intelligence files."

Rebecca ignored him, walking to the cabinet on the side where she picked up a coffee cup and poured some from the pot, which was already a third empty. Realising that he'd been there long enough to have at least two cups made her think there wasn't a single filing cabinet or drawer in her office which he hadn't searched.

Hating herself for the unconscious self-betrayal, her eyes flickered to the locked filing cabinet where the files of all covert agents were stored so as not to be accessible to anyone with computer access. Black saw the glance, as fleeting as it was, but said nothing about it.

Sipping her drink, Rebecca sat down at a chair on the wrong side of her own desk and tried to look equally as relaxed as he did when she spoke.

"Why are you here?" she asked. "Other than to demand information you're not authorised to have."

"You're right on one thing there," he told her. "I am demanding it."

"And you're not having it."

Black shrugged as if it suddenly made no difference to him whether he got what he wanted or not, which made her think he was just there to mess with her.

"I'm also right about you not having the authority to even see what you're asking for, unless I decide to disclose it to you," she told him. Her words were calm and patient, as if she were explaining something simple to a child who was intentionally being obtuse. "There is no Special Operations any longer, you realise? You don't get to pull your little thing out and wave it around. The world's changed."

Black smile widened at the mention of him waving that part of his anatomy about, but his confident demeanour stayed resolute.

"*You* were part of Special Operations though, weren't you? How come *you* didn't find yourself put up against a wall?"

At the accusation in his words, Rebecca bit down on the explanation she'd given so many times as to why she was recorded as having access to that level of shady Party activities. He wagged a finger at her knowingly and grinned, making her give up on any kind of response at all.

Black dropped his feet off the desk in a rapid movement and leaned forwards.

"Have dinner with me tonight," he said, startling her with such an unexpected change of subject. He laughed at her expression of shock rapidly becoming revulsion and leaned back again.

"Or don't, it's up to you."

"I'd rather cut myself and shower in salt," she told him, making him smile wider at the confirmation that he was well and truly under her skin.

"Your loss," he said as he stood and straightened his uniform. "I thought I'd offer you a chance to do it my way, but I guess you insist on having *your* way."

She tried not to. Tried with every fibre of her body but her mouth stabbed her in the back and opened anyway.

"What's that supposed to mean?"

Black paused at the door behind her and she could just imagine him smiling at getting her to bite. She stiffened as he leaned down and spoke so closely in her ear that she could feel the heat of his skin on her cheek.

"We all know how you got to a position of power, and I wanted the chance to try out the goods... like the Chairman and his right-hand man did."

Rebecca's teeth ground together and the muscle in her cheek bulged with the effort of not launching an elbow strike back into his smug nose. She knew it would be pointless to cry her innocence or throw accusations back at him, because she knew that all he wanted was a chance to see her upset. She let out her breath, forcing the sound to become one associated with boredom and not tears of anger.

"You finished being a prick?" she asked in a jovial tone. "Because I prefer to let my breakfast go down before I start dealing with morons." She stood, forcing him to take a step back before her shoulder caught him under the chin.

"Get the door on your way out," she ordered, not looking at him but pointedly taking a tissue from a box and wiping down the desk where his boots had been.

"See you soon," he said, opening the door to the outer office where the chatter of her department's discussions quietened at his appearance.

"So, my place at nine tonight?" he asked her loudly from the doorway with the childish intention of undermining her authority among her own people. "Okay, great, see you then. Wear something... *nice*."

Rebecca sat down after the door slammed behind him, fighting the urge to scream and throw something across the room.

His message was clear; he was coming for her, and he wanted access to the restricted information she held the key to. What she also knew was that a man like him, if he couldn't bully her into giving it to him, then his next recourse would be to threaten her or something she held dear. After that would come the undermining of her position, perhaps even an intentional failure of some form which could be attributed to her, and maybe even using his control over others higher up her particular food chain to get what he wanted.

And what he wanted was the information she'd amassed on every potential threat to the new leadership, every covert operative in every location and in every walk of Citadel life, and most of all, the intelligence files she kept off the computer system regarding the former Party members now aligned to their new government. A government which, when she really thought about it, worried her just as much as he did.

She snatched up the phone, hitting a button to direct dial the workbench where her three former Resistance fighters – all of whom proudly sported the lack of scar at the base of their skull like a medal – but as the call was picked up on the other end she slammed it down.

If she were Black, or at least if she were trying to get some leverage on him, and she had who knew how long alone in his office, then she certainly wouldn't be leaving in possession of everything she'd entered with.

Standing, she lifted the entire telephone set and traced the wire back to the wall before pulling it out with a sharp tug. Carrying it into the outer office, she dumped it on the desk of one of the uniformed analysts, telling him to dump it and get her a brand new one.

He didn't question her orders, mainly because the instruction was so bizarre it probably didn't pay to know the reason why and stood to take it away.

"Nobody," she said loudly, "and I mean *nobody*, enters that office without me present. Is that understood?" A murmur of affirmation rolled around the office.

"Good," she said, as the remainder of the positive mood she'd forced on herself that morning evaporated, and she left for the elevator to take her downstairs to ask Mouse in person if he had a device to check her office for any kind of bug.

CHAPTER SEVENTEEN

BUSINESS AS USUAL

Rebecca stood on the podium behind and to the left of the prime minster who, standing at the forefront of the stage, spoke into the microphones to deliver the public press release.

"Citizens of the Republic," she announced proudly. "I'm talking to you today to keep you informed of events outside the Citadel walls. Too long did we toil in the darkness, denied information and ruled over by others who put themselves above us: *the people…*"

All over the city, the screens that had once looped the propaganda material and indoctrinated the Party's subjects showed her face as she spoke earnestly.

"Two days ago, our brave protectors in the Republic security forces dealt with a threat from beyond the city; a threat posed by former Party soldiers and officials who planned to return here in force and seize control back from you – the people – to take it for themselves."

Murmurs rippled through the gathered crowds, made up from those enjoying time off from their work assignments, which was one of the more welcome changes in the city.

"Our forces were forced to take military action against these people who, in spite of our attempts to reach a peaceful solution, insisted on a different path. That path was violence, and our only recourse was to meet that threat with the same brute strength."

She paused, looking down to turn the page in front of her with a thumb that she dabbed on the tip of her tongue.

"A large agricultural complex to our west was seized by these people, all of them traitors to the people, and I can tell you now that they have all been brought to justice... but that's not all of it..."

Rebecca's eyebrows crinkled without her meaning them to move, betraying to anyone watching her facial expression that the Prime Minister was going off-script. She straightened her face and stood resolute, portraying the unified front of important officials everywhere so that the people could see their faces and know there were people looking out for their interests.

"As before, when we liberated the city, we need your help. We need volunteers, people to step up and do what's needed to make sure we all succeed together. We need people to move to the agricultural zone and begin work to ensure our supply of food is unaffected. We will offer those volunteers incentives and reward their hard work, so if any of you are strong enough, brave enough to do what is needed, talk to your workplace supervisors and put your names forward."

She paused again, looking down at the papers, which made Rebecca realise she wasn't off-script at all. Looking up, her face genuine and concerned as if she were the loving mother of everyone watching her, she stared directly into the lens of the drone hovering ten feet away in perfect stillness to transmit her image via the control room to every screen under their control.

"We will protect you, have no fear of that. I will personally be sending a protection force to maintain the safety of all brave volunteers, so be assured, we will look after you. *I* will look after you all. Thank you."

Applause broke out among the small crowd gathered, and already Rebecca could see people pushing through the crowd to reach the front through the press of bodies. She scanned those faces, checking every single one for any sign of hostility and resting on a man whose expression was less than friendly.

Snapping her fingers for her two-man escort's attention she took a fast pace to her right and singled out the man by pointing at him.

"Stop him," she called out, earning the unwelcome attention of Helen as her head whipped to the side to find out what was happening. Her hand dropped instinctively and drew the gun from her right hip as the crowd began to split apart amid screams and shouts of fear.

The drone flew straight upwards, controlled by a person in a control booth many floors above where they were at ground level, to get a better view of the area as Rebecca's team dropped off the stage and barged their way through to land on the man and bury him on the ground under their combined body weight.

"Get her out of here," Rebecca yelled, pointing back at the Prime Minister, who was already being surrounded by uniformed men and women who ushered her off the stage and obscured her from sight.

"Back!" an officer screamed at the nearest members of the crowd as he brought his weapon up into his shoulder and leaned into the stance. "Get back!"

The barrel twitched from person to person, all of them

desperately trying to escape the immediate area of the detained man but prevented from doing so by the others behind them.

"I didn't do anything," grunted the man from underneath Rebecca's two men as the crowd cleared and he was spun over onto his front and handcuffed before he was searched by rough hands.

"He's clean," an officer told her.

"Get him up," she ordered, stepping back half a pace as the man was hauled painfully upright to stare wide-eyed at her. His panted through a combination of fear and exertion, his lower lip split and bleeding from contact with the concrete, and his face told the tale of everyone who had ever had a run-in with the Party.

She felt a stab of shame then. For herself. For her actions and the actions of the men and women who had followed her orders to spread panic and fear through the crowd.

"Check him," she demanded, waiting as a chip reader was produced and the base of his neck was scanned.

"Alan Hollis," said the female officer who had scanned him. "Fifty-four, resident of block three, work allocation in chemical plant H."

"What were you doing, Alan Hollis?' she asked, her tone softer but still authoritative, having started the whole incident and needing to see it through.

"I…" he stammered, still out of breath and shaking, "I wanted to shake the Prime Minister's hand," he admitted. "For… for all she's done for us… and I wanted to volunteer personally."

Rebecca swallowed, feeling her body deflate slightly at his story, which was so naïve, so pathetic, that it had to be true. Had his file possessed any markers or intelligence, the scan would have directed her to that, but he was clean.

"You understand there are still people here who would do her harm, right?" she asked, trying to work her logical way around the apology she wanted to blurt out and run from the steps in shame. He nodded fast, like he was demented and would agree to anything she said just to try and avoid punishment.

"You understand why pushing your way through the crowd to get to the Prime Minister looked like you posed a threat, don't you?"

"Yes. I'm really sorry… please don't… please don't arrest me. I wasn't going to do anything, I swear."

Rebecca fought the urge to drop her head or to rub her face with her hands and try to force out the sick feeling infecting her for what she realised she'd become.

"Are you injured?" she asked, seeing a look of confusion on his face at the words. "Are you hurt?"

"I'm not injured," he said suspiciously, waiting to see where the trick was and fearing that if he said he was, his trip to a medical unit might become a one-way journey.

"Good," said Rebecca with a sigh. "There's that at least. Let Mister Hollis be on his way and give him my contact details in case he wants to discuss what just happened when things have calmed down."

Hollis looked even more suspicious then, as if the very concept of raising a complaint about the misunderstanding was even an option, and that was the moment Rebecca saw it.

It was her epiphany. Her personal 'oh shit' moment when it all sank in and locked into place in her mind.

While she had *been* the Party before, this was supposed to be different. For the people, like Hollis who believed he'd just narrowly avoided execution, the change in government had made no difference to them at all. They were still subjects, still ruled over by the elite, and the addition of promises and a whole two days off a week instead of one didn't change their mindset.

She told herself that it was just habit as she walked up the steps to return to her office, that the people who had lived under rule their entire lives knew no other way to be, but the fear in that man's eyes confirmed it in her mind that they were – *she* was – just as bad as the ones before.

She kicked herself mentally for allowing her ideals to be blinded by the good fortune which had rained down on her since the revolution. She'd been a nobody before, elevated by circumstance of timing and sheer luck, and that position had seen her capitulate out of fear to help the side who had eventually won.

She saw the cowardice in her past, saw the self-serving nature of her actions, and now that she'd been living well of the proceeds of privilege, she felt more complicit than ever.

CHAPTER EIGHTEEN

HAZY

Eve suffered terribly throughout the night. The painkillers Hegarty had given her allowed for undisturbed sleep but when that prematurely ended after only five hours, the pain lancing through her torso was unbearable.

The pain made her gasp for breath and breathe harder, made her heart beat faster, but that only served to worsen the agony until she let out an involuntary cry and doubled over on her side in the bed.

One of the guards posted outside her door, nominally for protection but there nonetheless to tell her that she was still very much a prisoner, opened the door and reluctantly asked if she was okay. She sobbed, unable to answer or even draw in enough breath and hold it long enough to speak, but the guard read her inability to communicate as a strong negative response.

Minutes later, not that she was keeping track of time as her eyes leaked tears to soak the thin pillow she lay on and plaster her hair to her face, the door opened again and the bent over figure of Hegarty fussed inside to start talking to her. She still couldn't answer, having worked herself up into a state of near panic through the pain she felt, but his hands moved fast as his lips uttered the words, "sharp scratch".

Eve barely felt the needle pierce her skin, not in any kind of way that would register as a pain response at least, but her breathing began to slow and the pain ebbed away ever so slightly with each breath out.

"Thank you," she managed. "I wa——"

"Shh!" Hegarty interrupted her. She opened her eyes to see him with a pressure cuff wrapped around her upper arm and a device stuck in both ears. He wore a look of focus as small hissing sounds reached her brain before shaking himself out of the deep concentration he'd been in a second previously.

"All seems fine," he said, putting his equipment away and checking his watch. "Four in the morning," he told her. "I'll need to give you more at eight, but until then just try to lie still, okay?"

Eve nodded weakly, too exhausted from the tears and the pain and feeling oddly as though she were floating and detached from the world and her injured body. Hegarty rested her head back on the pillow and tucked the sheets up over her gently before tiptoeing from the room.

Eve watched him go as if viewing something on a television screen that showed herself lying there, feeling her eyelids grow impossibly heavy until she could no longer summon the energy to lift them again.

———

She woke again, feeling no pain but experiencing the same kind of panic as before. She swung her head to her right side, feeling the movement to be sluggish and requiring too much effort for such a simple gesture. Her hearing was muted, like she was underwater, and her eyes blinked as nothing were truly in focus.

"It's okay," Hegarty said soothingly. "You're okay…"

———

Twice more she woke like that, and each time the room was different somehow. On the most recent occasion she overheard a conversation between two men and recognised one of them to be Hegarty, but the other was shrouded in abnormal darkness, like a shadow had come alive and moved out of the room's corner to intentionally hide the speaker from sight.

"How long?" he asked, Eve hearing only a snippet of their conversation over the impossibly loud sounds of her own breathing. His words were distorted, like the conversation was happening above water and she was somehow below the surface.

Hegarty's reply was similarly muffled, but she could make out some of what he said.

"Impossible to tell… serious internal… could be weeks…"

"…need to debrief…" the voice of the hidden man asked. "Up-to-date intel…"

Eve spoke clearly in her own mind, lending credibility to the guess that she was watching some replay of a closed-circuit recording, telling them that she had no up-to-date intelligence because she'd left this life behind. She laughed to herself, the sound totally at odds with the sluggish paralysis in her body and the warped sensory input she was watching.

She told them that she'd been totally isolated, happy even, and was on her own with no idea the people she fought so hard for, almost died to free, were straight back to tearing one another's throats out like wild animals looking to take the top spot and keep it.

Hegarty turned to face her, stopping the man in the shadows mid-sentence to bend down to her and ask her what she said.

Eve tried again, telling him that she lived alone on the coast and enjoyed it that way.

Hegarty looked pitifully at her and smoothed her brow, which she realised for the first time was slick with sweat. He turned away and issued orders she couldn't make out because they were still on the other side of the water's surface to her, and she was powerless to say or do anything as she was lifted and moved for clean sheets to be wrapped around the mattress for her.

The man left, and Hegarty made more sounds that could have been words. They must have been, because other people – the people connected to the hands that had moved her – did so again, only this time they removed her thin gown and forced her floppy arms into a clean one before tucking her back in as she drifted back into unconsciousness.

CHAPTER NINETEEN

BEING THE BAD GUY

Rebecca was in her office when the summons came. She was busy using a device made by Mouse, scanning the small box and thin aerial over every square inch of her office until she was certain that no listening device had been planted there.

Her brand new phone sat on her desk, not plugged in as the thought of a wiretap somewhere else to that line plagued her.

As her own telephone wasn't connected, the summons came via a knock on her door.

"Come in," she yelled from her position on the carpet under one corner of her desk. She saw shoes and ankles sheathed in fine stockings walk in before they froze, no doubt the result of the owner of those feet wondering what the hell she was doing.

"Erm... telephone call from the Prime Minister's office," the woman reported. Rebecca began wriggling her way out at the news.

"I'll take it," she said.

"They're not holding," the woman informed her, "it

was a request for you to report to her directly at your earliest convenience."

When the Prime Minister gave anyone the leeway of responding at their earliest convenience, it categorically meant that they should drop whatever they were doing and go there immediately.

Rebecca stood, smoothed down her shirt and reached out to snatch up her black uniform jacket. Swinging it in a movement that might look flamboyant under different circumstances, she slipped her arms into the twirling garment and shrugged her shoulders, fastening the buttons as she moved away from her desk.

Walking out into the busy corridor where so many heads of department and their administrative teams had offices, Rebecca walked confidently down the carpeted walkways until she reached the secondary security station designed to keep out unscheduled visitors. She was waved through, telling her that the officers had been briefed that she was coming, or else her standing had somehow been elevated, which she felt was doubtful.

Ordinarily, such a summons would provoke a healthy amount of fear but given what she'd been involved in over the last week, it was too long a list to start guessing which particular incident she was being called to account for.

A secretary with a bent back and older than most of her contemporaries stood slowly to get the door for her as she approached, but Rebecca waved her back down to save her the trouble. Knocking at the door twice in short, sharp raps that sounded like they came from a person with no time to waste, she waited for the summons from within and twisted the handle.

"Ah, Inspector Howard," Helen said through a wide smile. "I didn't expect you immediately."

Rebecca knew that was bullshit, but she didn't know

whether to be impressed at the feigned humility or annoyed that the woman felt the lie necessary.

"I was in between a few things when you called," she replied, lying just as smoothly as Helen had.

"Fortuitous," the Prime Minister answered. Her voice held no genuine interest, which Rebecca took to mean she had more important matters to contend with than the small-talk she ended. She gestured for Rebecca to take a seat opposite her and resumed her position behind the expansive wooden desk.

"Do you know why I've summoned you?"

Straight to business, Rebecca thought. She decided on total honesty.

"Not entirely, Ma'am. It could be something to do with the operation, the incident during your speech or the three other things since."

Helen smiled, almost predatorially, as if she had expected the much younger woman to attempt a line of bullshit on her or just feign ignorance.

"All of the above," she said, "but I only have one incident on my list since the speech. Care to begin there?"

"Early hours of this morning, Ma'am," Rebecca reported. "Fourteen of the citizens' ID chips went offline. It was reported as a system signal error and left until the next system backup scheduled for tomorrow night, but the same fourteen people were reported as absent from their work placements shortly afterwards."

Helen frowned and picked up the tablet on her desk to swipe over it in an attempt to find the reports.

"I don't have that," she said. "Why don't I have that?"

"One is a routine maintenance log being raised and the other is buried in the work placement non-attendance lists. Neither, I imagine, you would be given unless the dots were connected."

"They were," Helen shot back. "By you. So why don't I have the report?"

"If you'll excuse me, Prime Minister," Rebecca said, "that should come from the intelligence department, not counter-intelligence."

"I understand the difference," Helen told her coldly. "I'll revisit that shortly. Tell me about the other incident."

"A disagreement between a group of soldi— ...a group of officers and three citizen workers. Seems there was some kind of disagreement over curfew."

"Curfew? Since when did we re-introduce a curfew?"

"*We* didn't, Ma'am. It seems from the accounts given that the officers took it upon themselves to order the workers to clear the streets and used a curfew as their rationale..."

"This concerns me..." Helen said, pausing in thought before scribbling a note in front of her. "The official report shows that three citizens were taken into custody for non-compliance and disorderly conduct, but here you are telling that there's more to the story?"

"One of the men detained was former Resistance," Rebecca said, waiting for the flash of hostile recognition on the Prime Minister's face.

"In what capacity?"

"Very minor, from what I understand. The Party knew about his involvement and evidently decided he was a small fish so let him keep swimming. It's better to know something about your opposition and them not realise it than h—"

"Thank you for the lesson in covert politics," Helen said, her features blank and impossible to read. She was making the point that she'd *been* the leader of the Resistance, and Rebecca felt the words 'for all of five minutes' on the tip of her tongue before biting down to prevent them from reaching the air in the room.

"Sorry. I have one of my officers going to debrief them, just to see what they say in case they believe the rebellion is still happening or any su—"

"Excuse me?"

The interruption wasn't loud, the voice not angry, but the severity of the question tore through the room.

"What I mean, Prime Minister, is that it's our job to ensure that the old ways of the Resistance aren't being hijacked by terrorist elements." Helen relaxed, evidently pleased with the explanation.

"Send me your report when completed." Rebecca nodded her agreement before Helen went on. "Which leads us to the incident at the speech…"

"Prime Minister," Rebecca said formally, trying not to sound too defensive. "I submitted my repo—"

"I've read it," Helen interrupted. "I wanted to thank you."

Rebecca couldn't hide the shock she felt from reaching her face, which made the Prime Minister laugh lightly.

"Ma'am?" Rebecca asked uncertainly.

"I wanted to thank you," she said again. "That kind of loyalty, that kind of *instinct*, doesn't come easily. You saw it when nobody else did."

"But I was wrong."

"This time," Helen said. "Who knows? Next time you might not be."

Rebecca stuttered, learning forwards to try and explain a dozen thoughts at once but Helen stopped her with a raised hand.

"That's all I'll say about it. Now, have you come to terms with what happened at the facility yet?"

CHAPTER TWENTY

WITHDRAWAL

Eve came around again, waiting for the crippling pain to break through the cloud of lucidity like it usually did, but instead only a dull ache gripped her chest and ribs.

She tested it out with a deeper breath to find the limit of her new reality and found that the pain was bearable, so she slowly swung one leg at a time over the edge of the bed and sat up.

Resting there, hands gripping the frame as her toes wiggled just above the cold floor, she waited for the pain to come but still it didn't. What her senses did pick up, however, was the smell of her own body.

Her hair was thick and greasy. It clung to her head, sticking to the skin of her cheek which was gritty and tacky to the touch. The gown was similarly tainted, and she stood carefully to peel it away from her skin where it touched before risking a stretch.

Slowly she extended her right arm to her side before attempting to raise the left and stopping a quarter of the way there as pain flared in her chest. She went with her instincts, lifting both and finding the range of movement increased and the pain of the movement lessened until she reached a point when the stab of agony made her feel faint.

"Bad idea," she grunted, bent over at the waist and panting until the agony subsided.

"You're up?" Doctor Hegarty said as he walked towards her wearing a smile and carrying a metal tray. "Let's get you back to bed."

"No," Eve said, waving him away. "I ache all over, I need to move around."

Hegarty tutted, making it obvious that he disagreed but was letting this one slide as he put the tray aside and helped her back upright.

"How's your pain? Would you rather have some more painkillers and lie down?"

"I've lain down enough," Eve told him. "I'll get cramp everywhere." She shivered and gently rubbed her arms which she tenderly hugged to her chest. She shivered again, feeling hot and cold at the same time and not enjoying either sensation.

"I need a shower," she said.

"We can do that," Hegarty told her, earning a quizzical look from Eve. "The windfarms generate power for this facility too, so hot water is easy enough. You'll need some help though…"

Eve leaned over again, feeling weak and shivering, as Hegarty waved over one of his own people and sent her away with instructions to collect the things Eve would need.

"And some real clothes," Eve added, hearing the request passed on before he asked her to move with him slowly and led her to a bathroom.

"Shout if you need anything," he told her before turning the taps to start the water flowing and walking away, leaving the female outside the door, no doubt to protect Eve's modesty should she require assistance.

Eve peeled off the gown and discarded it on the floor as the water ran hot. She stepped under the flow, gasping as the heat stung her skin and made her breathe faster until she acclimatised to the change. She still shivered, still felt cold and hot at the same time, and her stomach cramped painfully.

Letting the water wash away the dried residue of sweat, she tried to understand how the pain could have grown so much worse since she first regained consciousness. Lathering up soap in her hands, she washed herself, moving slowly and carefully so as not to aggravate whatever healing process had begun, and repeated the process until her skin felt clean.

She did the same with her hair, awkwardly reaching up as far as she could manage, making sure she raised both arms together and not just on one side; that was more comfortable, she had discovered from her earlier experimentation. Very carefully, she massaged her scalp until the worst of the grease was gone. Standing under the flow for much longer than she was accustomed to, her mind wandered back to the last time she'd been held captive and the first time she'd taken such a long, hot shower that the steam fogged the room entirely.

She'd been underground that time too, but at least then she'd known who the enemy was – at least she thought at the time that she knew – only this time she could barely even think straight.

Her heart raced. Her breath felt rapid and ragged, which threatened to bring back the pain, and that caused her anxiety to soar in anticipation of the renewed agony. In the battle raging inside her body between feeling too hot and too cold, heat won and she fumbled to kill the water and carefully towel herself dry without pressing on her ribs.

Dressing slowly, twice having to summon the breath to answer the woman outside who annoyingly kept checking if she was okay, Eve re-emerged into the room looking like a new woman, even if she still felt just as wretched as she had before.

"Time for your medication," Hegarty said cheerily, bringing the tray back to the bed, which had been changed and the fresh sheets folded neatly over the sagging mattress.

Eve sat, holding out her arm robotically until something inside her, some voice yelling and banging on thick glass at the back of her mind, suddenly broke through.

She pulled back her arm, tugging down the sleeve too fast and gritting her teeth at the flare of hot pain in her ribs.

"What's wrong?" Hegarty asked. "Aren't you in pain?"

"I am, but…"

"This will help," he said as he reached for her arm again. "Trust me."

Once more she pulled back her arm, feeling some resistance from the man who didn't seem to want to release her.

"I said no," she told him firmly, fixing him with a look that she hoped would recall the memory of her hurting him. He backed off, holding up his hands to show he had no intention of using the hypodermic needle on her.

Eve wanted to ask if there was anything else she could have, anything except the chemicals he had been pumping into her for days, but she knew she wouldn't trust whatever he gave her in place of it.

"I just need to rest," she said again, leaning back to slowly lie back on the fresh bed.

———

With no daylight showing through a window, when she next woke it was hard to gauge the time of day but with far fewer people around, she guessed it was later in the day when others were resting.

Seeing only two other people in the large room, she sat up slowly, still feeling almost feverish, and shivered when her bare feet touched the cold floor again. Her body hurt all over and she felt tense and aching with an overriding sense of nausea.

The two spoke to one another in low tones, no doubt keeping their voices down so they didn't wake her, and both had their backs turned to her, which made slipping out of the room simple enough when they walked away.

More people moved around out in the subterranean walkways, making her re-evaluate her initial thoughts on it being late at night. The clothes she had been given included a sweatshirt with a hood which she pulled up over her hair on instinct as she moved slowly through the shadows and worked at being invisible.

She moved slowly, bent over slightly because of the pain she was experiencing as well as hoping that anyone noticing her would see an older woman worn down by age.

Like Cohen.

The thought struck her so hard and so unexpectedly that she almost stopped walking. It was as though her mind had turned a blind corner in the dark and she'd run headlong into something she didn't expect, because she hadn't thought about the woman who'd raised her for a long time.

It wasn't that she did this through a lack of care, but more that her memories of the small woman and her claims of invisibility were painful to recall because she missed her and still felt responsible for her death.

Those memories, coupled with the fever and the pain dulling her senses, led her to a place she didn't recognise and forced her to stop and turn back so she didn't find herself in a crowded area she should've sensed a mile away.

She turned, stopping and looking up into the amused eyes of Mark.

"Going somewhere?" he asked.

"I was hungry," she lied.

"And nobody was in the hospital to ask?"

"I didn't want to bother them," Eve said, sticking to the lie. Mark watched her for a minute before letting out his breath and relaxing.

"Come on, kid," he said. "You shouldn't be on your feet. You look like hell."

"I *feel* like it," Eve answered honestly. "Hegarty, you know him?"

"Of course I do."

"No," she said, "I mean do you *know* him?"

"What are you asking me?" Mark said, eyes narrowing suspiciously.

"The drugs... they... I don't feel right..."

"Then don't take them, but I've seen no reason not to trust him. You on the other hand..." Eve rolled her eyes which still somehow hurt her ribs no matter how small the movement was.

"I know, it's just... it's just like I'm feeling like a prisoner and I don't like it."

"You *were* a prisoner," Mark explained, "and you're not one now because I vouched for you, so sneaking around like this could get us both killed. You want that?"

"Not really."

"Good," Mark said. "Me neither." He hesitated,

pausing as if he was going to say more before deciding on it.

"Most of the people are leaving in the morning to go to another agricultural facility that wants to break alliance to the Citadel."

"Most?" she asked, sensing that was the more poignant part of what he said.

"I'm going south to the Nocturnals. I'll ask for their help, but…"

"But you want me to come with you."

CHAPTER TWENTY-ONE

NORTH

Minister Samaira Nadeem expected her return to the northern mining facilities to be awkward, but the sad and brutal truth was that so very few of those she had worked with when masquerading as an acting captain in the Party military still lived.

Unlike in the Citadel, when the Nua and the Nocturnals descended from the night to overrun the perimeter fences and storm the guard posts, the workers in the northern parts of the Republic rebelled in an instant and took up arms against their oppressors without hesitation.

Tools became melee weapons. Machinery was turned on their guards to crush them and tear down their defences. The frightening invaders butchered almost all of the rest.

When the brief, savage conflicts were over, the attackers flowed on to the next facility in turn to destroy that, leaving behind the bewildered citizens unsure of what to do next.

Unlike in the Citadel where the Party forces were afforded the opportunity to surrender and face the fair judgement of trial under a democratic government, the men and women in the outposts were cut down. Some had the sense to drop their weapons, to take off their armour and seek safety among the citizens, but many of those chose a worse death by attempting to save themselves.

Days afterwards, when envoys arrived from the Citadel bringing food, medical supplies and – most importantly – news from the capital, they took time to take in their new reality.

When she walked in, she expected, *hoped*, to see at least one friendly face. When that didn't happen, she looked for any face she recognised but found none. When she addressed the crowd to tell them what had happened and that she was the representative of their new government, instead of the cheers she hoped for, she was met with more sullen anger.

"You want us to go back to work then?" a woman shouted from near the front, her bravery in speaking up stoked by the cries of agreement.

"Yes, but not like it was before," she told them. "Now we will al—" Her words were cut off by loud yelling and jeers, prompting the men and women assigned as her protectors to ready their weapons nervously and step forwards. She waved them back, feeling the hostility of the crowd swell dangerously, and held up her hands, hoping they would afford her the opportunity to speak further. When they eventually quieted down, she told them of the plans for their return to work.

"Your shifts will be shorter," she promised, "and you'll only work five days a week." That gained some positive reaction from many, but the majority still saw her arrival as just another overlord in place of the last ones.

"Rations will be increased, and medical care will be better and more accessible than before," she went on.

"What if we want to leave?" a man asked, his eyes earnest and pleading.

"If you want to leave, you can. You can travel back to the Citadel and get work there. You can go to the farming facilities in the west, and whatever you choose, you'll still only have to work the same hours and the same promises will be made and kept… this is how things will be from now on. We don't want to sacrifice the health and happiness of the people for productivity, but without you working here, others will have to come so that everyone can enjoy a better life than before."

The arguing and pleading went on for hours, and only when she announced that work wouldn't recommence for another week did the crowd calm and begin to lose interest in the display.

When Nadeem learned that not all of the Party soldiers and supervisors had been killed or fled, and that many were being held prisoner, she gave up on the idea of resting after a long journey and a stressful encounter and demanded that she be taken to see them.

She hoped to find the kindly Major Bentley or even Second Lieutenant Baxter, but none of them were among the captured. They were mostly mining and construction supervisors, low-level Party members, and the handful of soldiers who survived were injured, which led her to believe they were found still alive after the fighting had finished.

She knew she was largely responsible for their deaths, being not so naïve as to think they'd escaped the fighting, as her report on this facility had allowed the Nua and the Dearmad to rush in and storm the place quickly.

She knew at the time that there would be loss of life, but when she was caught up in the final throes of the

Party's downfall, she realised she hadn't given the individuals a moment's thought.

Until now.

Ordering her own guards to take over duties and keep them safe, she ensured that more rations and medical care was given to them.

In time she would check each person to hear any complaints about their actions, and any of them deemed to be worthy of standing trial would be sent back to the Citadel under guard. Those who made it through this stage would find themselves offered a chance to abandon their Party ideals and embrace the new government, whereupon they would be allowed to return to work in whatever role best befitted their skills and experience.

"Captain?" croaked a young man sitting on the ground near the door to the dark storeroom they were being held in. "Captain Blake?"

Samaira knelt down beside him to see his face, not recognising the man but unsurprised that he recognised her. She hadn't served there long, but as usual, she'd left a lasting impression on anyone who had met her.

"I'm a Minister of the new government now," she told him as she unscrewed the cap from a bottle of water to hand it to him. He held the bottle but stared at her uncomprehendingly.

"The Party is no more," she explained. "There is a new government now, formed from the leaders of the Resistance, and I'm a part of that."

"How?" he croaked. "How can you switch sides to be with those traitors?" He still hadn't drunk the water, but his shaking hand told her that he wasn't coming around to their new reality quickly.

"I'm one of them," she said. "I always was."

His face contorted, cracking the dried blood between

his top lip and his nose, and he squeezed the bottle until water flowed over the top and spilled on his filthy hand.

"Please," she begged, "you should drink tha—"

He tipped the bottle to pour the contents onto the floor between them, making Samaira stand and move back so she wasn't touched by it.

"Keep your water, traitor," he snarled, turning his face away so he didn't have to look at her face. Samaira sighed, knowing the fate of the young man long before he would discover it, and left the room after reiterating her orders that the prisoners were to be treated with dignity.

———

For weeks she barely rested, travelling from compound to compound until all of the salvageable facilities in the north were returning to work and managing their own business.

Each place was as difficult as the last, and her answers to the same questions became almost robotic when faced with them over and over.

Finally returning to the largest facility, the one she had been posted to after changing her identity and falsifying the transport records to smuggle Adam out of the Citadel, she took up residency as the senior government official in the northern reaches to monitor productivity and handle the problems that others wanted solved for them, often by agreeing to the good ideas they reluctantly presented.

That was the thing she found most annoying about command, about leadership, that most people knew what to do but were too frightened of an adverse outcome to make the decision to take action themselves.

Such was the culture of fear and blame that they had all grown up with, had all been born into, and the sadness that accompanied the realisation that such attitudes would take generations to fix saddened her even further.

She didn't return to the Citadel, even if she was required to check in daily and speak with the new Prime Minister at least weekly, so when a private communication marked as confidential appeared on her terminal, she was excited at the chance of a break in the monotony of making sure everything stayed the same as it had in their new world.

CHAPTER TWENTY-TWO

GOING AROUND

Mouse was silent about it as was his way, happy to keep his eyes down on some complex but unimportant task as others talked around him. He only joined in when he was forced to, or when one of the speakers presented a distorted fact or incorrect information, so when he was put on the spot about his recommendation, he sighed tiredly before speaking.

"I don't see what the point is," he explained. "What would you gain?"

"If we call Jasmin," Jonah said with condescending patience.

"Samaira," his sister interjected, and was promptly ignored.

"Then she can say whether this is happening in the north or not."

"And what would that prove?" Mouse asked, still not looking up.

"It would prove that the government is doing what the Party did before," Jonah finished almost triumphantly, as if he'd forced them both to come around to his way of thinking by repeating it ad nauseum.

"And if she says yes," Mouse told him, "and isn't doing anything about it, then we have to assume she's okay with it and you'll be reported to the government. If she says no, that it isn't happening there and she isn't aware of it, then what's the first thing she'll do?"

Jonah paused, waiting to be told the answer and not realising the question was rhetorical.

"She'll either contact the government to ask if the rumours are true, or she'll say it was us asking, or she'll try to find out *if* it's really going on and that will bring too much attention to her, which will lead them back to us," Jenna said.

Mouse, still looking down at his task, lifted one hand and snapped his fingers to end the gesture in a pointed digit aimed at his female companion.

"So it's pointless?" Jonah asked. "Doesn't matter anyway, I doubt you could manage to get a message through without setting off some trigger anyway."

Mouse stopped working, eyes still cast down, and rested the electronic box he was tinkering with gently onto the desk.

"I know what you're trying to do," he said quietly. "If you think you can taunt me into proving that I can bypass not only the security screening programming, but the comm traffic logging algorithms, then you're wrong. I can do both, but there isn't any need to."

"Thought so," Jonah said as he stood. "He can't do it."

"Can't do what?" a voice asked loudly from the darkness beyond their sea of light in the dark office. The three of them froze, waiting to see who emerged from the gloom. They all recognised the voice, but the question remained as to whether that individual had come alone or not.

"That he can't make an automated machine that makes hot drinks," Jenna said curtly. "What do you want?"

"Want?" asked Fly with amusement as he took a step and activated the movement sensor lights. "Can't a man simply drop in on his friends without wanting something?"

"Not you," Jonah said. "You always want something."

"This again," Fly said with a bored tone, lowering himself into a seat as if expecting the cheap materials to give way under his weight which, in the months since they had last been on good terms, had grown through better nourishment and access to weights. All trappings of the government lifestyle he'd chosen instead of the path they had taken.

"Maybe I don't want anything this time," Fly said as he leaned forwards to intentionally flex and bulge the muscles in his shoulders. "Maybe I just wanted to catch up and find out how you were doing."

"Three types of people," Mouse muttered as if he believed nobody else could hear his words.

"Excuse me?" Fly demanded, startling Mouse and making him twitch his eyes at nothing on the floor between them.

"I said there are three types of people who ask how you are."

"Meaning what, exactly?" Fly said coldly, leaning over further to put his head close to Mouse's and gripping the underside of the chair for balance.

"Three types," Mouse mumbled. "One asks because they care, one asks because they're being polite and one asks because they need the intelligence on you."

Fly leaned back and let out a derisive bark of laughter.

"Ha! Weird as ever, I see. Well, you got me. I ask because I want to know. You didn't like how things went down on the operation, you got Eve killed, an—"

"*We* didn't," Jenna snapped.

"You think our government did?" Fly asked, shock coursing through his words like lightning, making him sound almost believable. The other three said nothing, knowing their words would be reported.

In truth, they had sided with the government, but the government they had allied themselves to were the Resistance, and none of them felt that the ideology of that organisation had survived the changes, especially after recent events. Fly had taken to life above ground in a position of power with a concerning ease and had split away from them without a moment of hesitation to become... something else.

"That's what I thought," Fly said as he leaned back in the chair and relaxed. "You three stay down here, cowering underground like you always did... the war's over, you know? We won."

"Did you want something?" Jenna asked acidly, bringing them all back to the original question.

"I wanted to see how you were doing, but I see I can expect more hospitality from the rats in the sewers."

Fly stood, leaving the heavy connotation of his final words hanging in the air like a bad smell before walking away shaking his head. They waited until he'd left the room, then even longer until they heard the elevator doors open and close, and only then did Jenna speak.

"That piece of shi—"

Mouse snapped his fingers to get her attention, holding the index finger of his other hand to his lips. He stood, carefully turning over the chair Fly had been sitting on to reveal a small box with a flexible wire aerial snaking out of it stuck underneath. Carefully, he set the chair back down and stared at the other two waiting for them to catch on.

"Screw this," Jonah said. "I'm done for the day. You two coming?"

"Might as well," Jenna answered. "That arrogant bastard spoiled my mood anyway."

Mouse nodded at them both before following them to the elevator and waiting until the doors shut behind them.

"How did you know?" Jenna whispered, mindful of the camera and microphone in the metal box with them.

"Black left one just like it in Rebecca's office," he murmured. "Meet at the usual place in an hour?"

CHAPTER TWENTY-THREE

RECOVERY

Eve spent another two days in pain, only now it was constant and didn't come with the waves of vomit-inducing nausea to accompany the cramps, muscle aches and cold sweats.

She'd refused the medication Hegarty had offered, saying some more than unkind things to him about keeping her drugged, and when he offered her a lower dosage of another medicine in tablet form, she slapped the metal tray away from his hands, forcing Mark to step in.

"What the hell's the matter with you?" he demanded.

"He's poisoning me," Eve growled, sweat sticking her hair to her forehead as she ground her teeth together.

"Doc?" he said over his shoulder. "Are you poisoning Eve?"

"Of course not! I… I would never…"

"See?" Mark told her, picking up one of the pills she'd scattered and popping it onto his tongue to swallow it dry and show her his empty mouth afterwards.

"Take the pills or don't," he ordered her, "but don't be a bitch."

She accepted the pills, gulping down water with them as she fought the urge to throw up. She still sweated and felt so on edge all the time that she was on the verge of panic, and that was an unwelcome new sensation to her.

The pain was still killing her every time she breathed and the only time it didn't hurt was when she was asleep, only then she had twisted dreams that tortured reality and her memories into a phantom beast comprised of Shadow, Host, Nathaniel... sometimes the beast wore a mirrored black visor, and sometimes under that visor the beast had her face, even if she never saw it.

The reprieve from these horrific nightmares came at a price, because the pain in her ribs and chest stabbed at her until she wanted to claw at her own skin, as if she could tear away the damaged flesh and start anew.

The tablets helped, only instead of washing away the pain in a fuzzy haze of surreal thoughts, they simply took the edge off it so she could at least breathe without wanting to die.

The bruising between her breasts and down her left side was livid, with pale patches of skin ringed by lurid purple circles that dissipated outwards to turn yellow at the edges before the colour melted away to merge with the more healthy looking skin, which had tanned since she had been living on the surface.

Her thoughts came in a confused jumble; out of sequence and so chronologically disturbed that she connected to the sensations of those memories from months and years before.

The first time she smelled the damp night air. The sight, sound and feel of her sword blade's first fatal strike as she cleaved the head off the body of a guard just for walking down the wrong alley what felt like a thousand years ago.

Cohen, chiding her for chewing her long hair and telling her stories as she cut the long fingernails she hadn't chewed, only this time she knew the stories weren't just stories but were meaningful lessons about what kind of person Eve should grow up to be.

She cried, tucking herself into a foetal position and hugging her damaged body as she recalled with perfect clarity the lines of Cohen's face and the sad, sweet smile she wore as though the world could do no more to hurt her.

Eve had hurt her. She had been responsible for her capture, for her death, and in another of her nightmares she saw herself as the one who kicked in the door of the old woman's cell and gunned her down with an automatic rifle.

She hated herself for doing that, felt the bloodlust rising in her, but when her dream-self surged forwards to attack Cohen's killer, she remembered that she was only a small girl, unable to take a life or even lift the long, heavy sword to protect Cohen and save her life.

"Eve!"

The little girl in her dreams stood and cried as the older version of her, the one holding the smoking gun, laughed at her for not being able to pick up the sword. That older version shouted her name again, reaching forwards to shove her in the shoulder.

"Eve!"

She snatched at the wrist of the hand reaching out to shove her again, throwing her right leg up and over the pinned arm to drive her left elbow into her attacker's jaw.

"EVE!"

Her eyes opened, blinking into focus and fixing on the red face of Hegarty with his glasses knocked sideways and his eyes bulging under the pressure of her knee across his throat.

Mark yelled again, knowing it was useless and wherever the girl's head was didn't matter, because her body was about to dislocate the small bones in the doctor's neck with one more ounce of pressure.

Using a trick he'd employed on Adam for all of the young man's life, Mark bent his index finger to drive the knuckle into her ribs on the left side. She yowled and shrieked in pain at the touch and released her near-fatal hold on the man trying to help her.

She fell back, gasping and crying in pain as Mark stood over Hegarty and checked him over.

"You good?" he asked, receiving a wide-eyed and shocked nod in response before turning back to Eve, who sobbed and rocked from side to side on her back.

"Sorry kid," he muttered. "You back in the real world now?" Eve nodded, blinking away her tears of pain and shame.

———

The next time she woke, Eve looked around her, making sure the things she saw matched up with the last time she was lucid in the makeshift hospital room. She didn't trust herself not to concoct a dream that matched reality so closely that she could kill a real person.

She tested out her pain levels, feeling the limits of her movements before committing them to memory so that she didn't overreach and injure herself. She stood, stretching slowly as far as she could allow herself, and walked out of the room in search of something she hadn't thought of for days: food.

Her stomach, instead of feeling ready to void the bile it

held, grumbled in protest at not being given any work to do. Walking out into the main room, she stopped, her eyes locking with Hegarty's and recognising the fear in them. She held up her hands in front of her, wincing and leaning down slightly to her left.

"I'm sorry," she said, her voice weak and raspy courtesy of her bone-dry throat. "I... I..."

"You were hallucinating," Hegarty said, relaxing. "Understandable, given the circumstances."

"What circumstances?"

"Hard to say without tests, but my best guess is that you have an increased sensitivity to opiates." He watched her blank stare until it sunk in that he was talking a different language to her.

"Because your injuries were so bad and the pain was unbearable, I gave you an opiate drug called morphine. It appears your body is highly sensitive to it, and addiction can happen in a very short timeframe if—"

"*Addiction*?"

"Yes, it's naturally a very..." he paused, seeing that she wasn't in the mood for a complex medical description. "It makes your body crave more, but it can kill you if you have too much. I wasn't... I wasn't poisoning you, I was trying to help you."

"I know. I'm sorry I..." she trailed off as she mimed choking herself.

"Don't worry," Hegarty said, appearing distinctly uncomfortable for a moment. "I imagine you're rather thirsty?"

"And hungry," Eve admitted.

"Well, if you can refrain from attempting to break my neck, I'll sort something out for you."

CHAPTER TWENTY-FOUR

THE LONG ROAD

Eve sat hunched over, wrapped in a heavy blanket over the layers of clothes she was wearing, to try and ward off the cold that seeped into her bones and wouldn't budge. She remained still, chewing slowly on the dry bread she was dipping into a salty soup..

"The Doc says it could be hyperalgesia," Mark explained. He sat opposite her, his eyes ringed with dark circles and a cup of coffee held in both hands. Her eyes lifted to meet his in silent question. "It means you'll feel pain more as a side-effect of the drugs you had."

"It'll go away though, right?" she asked hopefully. Mark nodded, only without much conviction. Her ribs itched and her chest burned but she forced herself to embrace the pain to fight the side-effects her exhausted brain tried to understand.

The coffee and food helped, giving her something else to focus on instead of her injuries and the residual emotions brought on by her drug-induced nightmares. She changed the subject to distract her further.

"What's the plan?" she asked him. Mark took another gulp of his drink before answering.

"The plan for who?"

"You. Me. These people…"

"They're moving to another facility to the south, hoping to find somewhere to start again," he told her.

"And you?" Eve asked, knowing there was more he was reluctant to say.

"Well, that depends on you, and what you want."

Eve frowned, chewing and swallowing before she spoke. "What do you mean?"

"I mean," Mark said patiently, "that what I do depends on what *you* decide. Do you want to go home and forget about everything or do you want to help us fight it? I wouldn't blame you one bit for wanting to go… I know I would if I had the chance."

Eve finished her mouthful and rested the crust of bread down beside her bowl.

"I think," she said after a pause, "that we should go back to the Frontier and ask for their help."

Mark hid his smile but the small tells were all over his face. That was the answer he'd secretly been hoping for, but Eve wanted more from him before she agreed to anything. She wanted to know more about his suspicions, about what the new government she'd been instrumental in installing were doing and she wanted proof that she was picking the right side this time.

They spoke for another hour, with Mark detailing his concerns from the very beginning and repeating the information he'd already explained, leading up to the assault on the facility.

"It's the same as the Party, only this time people were promised freedom. None of these people aren't prepared to work, ask Harvey about the proposed trade deal. We were happy to keep the same output and send food to the Citadel in return for the manufacturing goods we needed. That was laid out plainly, but their answer came in the form of you…"

He trailed off, sensing that his words sounded harsh and critical, but Eve understood. She was angry that she'd been used, and the betrayal by Rebecca and the others stung her the most. She counted no friends still inside the big city any longer, and that loneliness brought her an acceptance that she needed friends, no matter how much she'd enjoyed the break from reality living alone by the sea.

She longed to be back there, living in peaceful safety, but she knew her conscience would keep her restless if she went back there now.

"So how do we go about it?" she asked.

"We?" Eve raised her eyebrows to convey that Mark should answer the question and not get ahead of himself. "We have to show the people what the government did. If it's truly a democracy we have to call for a vote, let the people decide after they know the real facts, and when the leaders step down or are removed, then we elect a new Prime Minister and start afresh."

"And what happens to Helen?"

"She'll face trial for what she ordered," Mark told her in a flat tone that meant he was hiding his emotions from her.

"What about the people who followed those orders?" Eve asked, making Mark shift uncomfortably in his seat.

"That's a difficult one," he admitted. "It depends if they acted with the full knowledge or not, because just following orders isn't a good enough reason to commit murder, sanctioned or otherwise."

"Would you have followed those orders?" she asked

quietly, seeing Mark's features darken and set into a resolute mask.

"It won't be easy to achieve, but we have to find a way of broadcasting that information to the people. That's only the half of it, because we'll still need to force Helen out of office until we can hold an election."

"I thought you wanted to live separately." Eve asked. "Isn't this just getting involved with the Citadel again? Why not leave them to deal with their own problems?"

"Because their problems are our problems. Because they won't allow us to make our own decisions. Because they think anyone outside of their control is a threat."

"But you are," Eve said softly. "Aren't you?"

Mark let the question hang in the air, affording it the appropriate respect and not answering quickly to dismiss it.

"We are, but we didn't start this and they won't stop coming after us until something changes… you need to rest now. The others will be leaving soon, but you're not ready to travel yet."

———

Eve went back to bed and stayed there for half the day, drifting in and out of sleep as before, only this time the pain was more of a constant ache and the dreams didn't torture her mind.

When she woke, sensing somehow that the day was drawing to a close, she got up and tended to her personal needs before hunting down more food, which her body was crying out for now. Finding a lot fewer people around, she confirmed her guess with Mark, who told her that a large group of people had set out that afternoon and that the remainder would follow the next day.

"Too many people moving at once could catch their attention," he told her.

"But we're not going with them?"

Mark shook his head.

"You need to heal before we can move," he said as he reached to his side for something propped against the wall beyond her sight. Coming back with her sheathed sword, he turned it in the air before offering it to her in both hands ceremoniously. "Build your strength back up slowly," he warned her. She didn't hear his instruction, only felt a warmth from being reunited with the missing part of herself she'd believed lost.

"My armour?" she asked, hoping that it had survived with her blade.

Mark shook his head again slowly, giving her the sad news in silence. Eve nodded her understanding; given how badly bruised her body was, she could only imagine the destructive damage the armour had taken on her behalf.

"I'll get you the right clothes for the journey," he promised, "but like I said, you need to rest before we go anywhere."

CHAPTER TWENTY-FIVE

PICKING SIDES

Mouse, Jenna and Jonah all met up at the place they kept secret even from Rebecca. Mouse was already there, with the twins arriving within ten minutes of one another, having covered each other's passage through the dark streets in their symbiotic way.

As Jonah dropped down into the underground chamber, his sister quipped at him about being late. Jonah, for once, let the jibe go and concentrated on the question that had been eating him up ever since they'd left headquarters in frustrated silence.

"Why the hell would Fly plant a bug on us like that?" he demanded.

"That's the second question," Mouse said. "Not the first question."

"So, what's the first question, genius?" Jonah shot back, not in the mood for any of Mouse's peculiarities.

"The first question is whether they're following us too," Jenna cut in, proving yet again that she was sharper than her twin brother. Mouse spun the chair he sat at and rattled at the keyboard with both hands to bring a small bank of monitors back to life. Knowing what they were looking at, the three of them watched the hacked street surveillance camera feeds showing the access on both ends of the blind spot where they had all disappeared.

It didn't take long before the two men appeared on the screen, dressed similarly in rough work clothes but giving themselves away by not walking with the resigned trudge that came with the outfit. Both men walked upright and alert, and both had the same stride and tempo which marked them out to their covet observers as military.

"I didn't see them," Jonah admitted.

"Don't blame yourself," Jenna said as she tapped at another terminal and twisted the monitor to show the others. "Observation drone at height," she told them, one finger pointing at an icon on the display.

None of them panicked about their hiding place being discovered, as when they had entered the camera blind spot they had moved through a disused factory building yet to be demolished or repurposed after the manufacturing inside was moved to a newer building.

Once in there, they went below ground into the network of tunnels that were once their entire world and then to a backup site that wasn't on any Resistance map because it was one created and used solely by the three of them.

Since Fly had left them, since life above ground had become fraught with agendas and internal political struggles, they had been feeling less and less connected to the people they'd fought so long for, and this place, along with the need for secrecy in accessing it, became their only private arena.

"Can you ID them?" Jenna asked Mouse, who wordlessly opened up a new dialogue box and began typing. Jonah knew what he was doing, at a rudimentary level anyway, as he was able to do the same thing, only much more slowly.

"Blocked," Mouse reported, explaining that he'd found the two ID chips in the bodies of the men above them but access to their personal details was firewalled.

"Since when did that ever stop you?" Jenna enquired sweetly, but Mouse was already typing with blurring fingers to find a route around that wall.

Sometimes when it came to such walls, there was a door that he imagined himself standing in front of. Sometimes the door was locked, sometimes it wasn't, and sometimes it didn't exist at all. At times like that he either created a door, tunnelled underneath the wall or just broke it down. As they had to be careful about what they were up to, Mouse took his time and walked along the imaginary wall, brushing his fingers along the brickwork until one of them shifted under his light touch.

He pushed on that one brick, swinging a section of the wall inwards just enough for him to look through and view the records of the men following them. He stayed just long enough to memorise their assigned residence addresses and names before he stepped back through the wall and allowed it to swing shut as if he'd never been there, returning to the real world and withdrawing his imagination from the computer.

"Both former Special Operations," he said.

"I thought they were all rounded up." Jonah asked. "Except Rebecca, I mean."

"You think there weren't others?" Jenna challenged him. "You think every one of them who committed crimes against the people was caught?"

"The Resistance issued pardons to hundreds of soldiers to get them back on the streets with new supervision,"

Mouse offered, wondering why they were arguing over such common knowledge events.

"So who sent them?" Jenna asked. Her brother sat forwards and leaned closer to Mouse, who was still tapping at the keyboard.

"You said Black did the same to Rebecca? He left a listening device in her office?"

Mouse didn't respond, earning him a jab in the ribs from Jonah.

"What? Oh, yeah. Same device. I told her how to deactivate it so it didn't look like she'd tampered with it."

"So, what are we going to do?" Jenna asked them both.

"Working on it now," Mouse said, fingers still dancing over the keyboard.

———

Rebecca, still wearing her uniform shirt but without the tight trousers, boots and jacket, padded around her apartment with the same device Mouse had given her, checking every conceivable place where a bug could've been placed.

She checked each room, working over every wall systematically and checking every vent, fixture and fitting in the place before finishing and sitting down to think. She got back up after a few seconds, going to the fridge to pour herself something alcoholic, then started the process again from the beginning until she was certain that her home was clear of any covert surveillance.

When she'd finished her second search and her third glass, she picked up her personal tablet and logged in with her biometrics, pausing before she accessed anything as she realised the computer pad would be the easiest of all ways to check up on her activities.

Turning it off, she went to her room and dug out her old one, the previous model which she hadn't returned in the confusion of the government changes and logged in under her old credentials as an adjutant corporal of the Party. To her surprise and delight, the systems showed as active, even though she couldn't access any of the databases.

Staring at it, trying to figure out what to do for the sake of doing something, a message icon appeared along the top bar and flashed. Dragging her finger down, she opened it, seeing the sender was marked as 'undisclosed', and tapped her finger on it.

Under surveillance by former special operations soldiers. Fly placed same listening device in counter-intel offices under a chair.

She read it twice over, knowing it could only have come from Mouse as nobody else she knew could circumvent the computer systems as he could, and then she tapped the icon to respond.

It was a risky move but if discovered, it was one she could explain, given the shady dealings of certain officials and their pets, and if it came to it, she told herself she would gather the proof and report it to the Prime Minister directly.

Residence clear. Unsure if I'm being followed. Sit tight and speak tomorrow.

No response came as none was asked for. She guessed

that if there was anything else relevant, the original message would have contained that, but as she was about to hold down the power button to kill the tablet, another icon flashed up.

Drone watching you from outside – zoom lens.

She understood the pause then. Mouse was checking the drone deployment against the routine security patrols and found the anomaly of the stationary unit watching her through the large windows overlooking the dark city below.

Casually she stood, picked up the remote and turned on the screen to select something, anything, from the very short list of available programs and drew the tall curtains across the windows before returning to her tablet and finding another message waiting.

Still watching you on thermal. Don't do anything.

She didn't know what anyone expected her to do as she had no clue what she *could* do herself. Instead, she poured herself a fourth glass and savoured the effects of the first three to sit and watch a new movie created by the government's media branch, who weren't much better than the Party propaganda team at spreading the narrative they wanted the people to live by.

She stared at the screen, not really watching the badly filmed content, until her sixth glass was drained and she walked unevenly to her bed to crash out until her alarm went off in the morning.

CHAPTER TWENTY-SIX

WE WALK

Eve felt well enough to forego the pain killers entirely unless she was intending to sleep. She walked around in between naps and forced her aching body to remain active, no matter how much it yelled at her to lie down.

Every so often she would stand and slowly run through the poses of one of a dozen sword dances in her mind, each time feeling her senses and composure return to her a little more. She still felt pain, still doubled over in agony if she moved too fast or too strenuously, but the tablets left by Hegarty before he left with the second group were sufficient to both wean her off her body's dependence on painkillers and keep the pain in check long enough to heal.

Eve had always healed quickly, no matter what the injury. Numerous times in her childhood she'd been too ambitious in training and had twisted a joint or torn a muscle by overstretching herself. This time was worse, because even though she'd never broken a bone before, to break one that moved when you breathed made it difficult to isolate the movement.

The tablets were holding the worst of the pain at bay

but if she went past the time she was due to take them, she had to stop whatever she was doing and rest until the medication took effect.

When Mark came to tell her that the time to move was upon them, she reluctantly stood and tested out her range of movement before giving him a nod to signify that she was ready.

She was excused having to carry anything, that task being undertaken by the five others who had stayed with them. Eve spoke to them in passing as they were the only few people left in the underground facility, but none of them seemed willing to share anything about themselves.

"Three are former Party soldiers," Mark explained to her as they walked through the long access tunnel leading them back up to the surface. "And two were agricultural workers. They're all freedom fighters now, I guess."

Eve said nothing to that last remark, feeling that the lines were too blurred to make sense, considering how her enemies had become her friends and now some of those friends were her enemies. The truth was that she didn't know which side of what fence she belonged on, but she knew in her heart that if people were being oppressed like they were before, her conscience wouldn't allow her to do nothing about it.

"How do the guns work?" she asked before qualifying her question in case it was taken as a very basic one. "With the chips, I mean."

"That entire system got shut down when we took power," Mark explained. "Mouse scrambled it so our people could use the weapons we broke out of the armouries and it never got put back together... at least that's what I understand."

"So anyone can use any gun now?" she asked, having spent a lifetime knowing that the destructive technology was denied them. Her head swam with all the rumours that she found out weren't true, along with her initial disappointment that the feared and anonymous Party soldiers were very human and very easy to kill.

Except the few monsters that Nathaniel had kept in the bowels of the Citadel headquarters and unleashed on her own, pure born team.

"Here we go," Mark said, pulling her from her private reverie as the low light of dawn showed ahead of them through the open tunnel access doors. "We move south west," he said, calling out for the benefit of the others. "Avoid high ground and don't get skylined or find yourself too far from cover at any time."

Eve gripped the sheathed sword tighter in her left hand and moved out with them, her mind spinning and her senses alert for the small sounds that might betray an attack or a drone monitoring them.

———

She was out of breath, sweating and in pain by the time Mark called the first stop in the small shelter offered by a large rockslide so old that trees had grown upwards between the jagged boulders.

Eve's shaking hands fumbled with the tablets, almost dropping one which she caught by slamming her thighs together to trap it before it could hit the ground and disappear. Retrieving it and pushing it onto her tongue with the other in her hand she struggled with the bottle cap before managing to swill the tepid water into her mouth and swallow them down.

She lay back on the rocks and gasped for breath, her eyes screwed shut against the pain in her chest, until Mark sat down beside her and spoke in a hushed voice.

"Are you okay to keep moving?"

"I will be," Eve gasped, determination overtaking the weakness in her words. "Just need a few minutes."

"You can have ten," he told her. "Any more than that and people risk pulling muscles."

The pace was set intentionally fast for so many obvious reasons, and Eve, in spite of her youth and injuries, kept up through sheer determination and a competitive streak wider than the roads they avoided using.

Only once did the woman leading at the front, a slender woman easily ten years older than Eve with harsh expression permanently fixed to her face, call out a warning to seek cover and that was followed a minute later by a passing drone high overhead.

"Did it see us?" a young man asked after it was gone from sight and sound.

"It wasn't on a search pattern," the woman at the front replied, betraying with her knowledge that she was one of the former Party soldiers. "And it was moving too fast to be looking for anyone."

"It could be casting ahead to try and cut us off," Eve whispered to Mark nearby, not from any need to keep her voice low but because she was still in pain and struggling for breath.

"Switch direction," Mark called out to all of them. "Head directly south for the rest of the day, then we'll cut back west in the morning."

They continued, avoiding the path of the drone in case it was linked to them in any way, and by dusk they were searching a rocky valley for cover to spend the night under. Finding a small cave system, Eve sat and panted after forcing more tablets down her dry throat and watched as a small fire was made in the depths of the dark, damp cave to keep them warm.

Eve glanced between the cave mouth and the fire, guessing that the distance was sufficient that a drone would have to fly into the cave mouth to detect them and that would mean it would likely be manually controlled, which would be difficult in the wild landscape they occupied.

Before the sun dropped, Eve saw miles and miles of rolling hills and valleys on either side of her, broken only by the brooding western horizon of much higher ground that, even at such distance, looked treacherous to cross.

With the sinking sun came a much lower temperature and a howling wind picked up so that nothing beyond the mouth of the cave was available to her senses. Ordinarily that would bother her, as trusting anyone else to keep watch invariably led to her being more on edge than if she were standing sentry herself. But with the pain and exhaustion of a day spent exerting so much energy, she willingly wrapped herself in a thick blanket and curled up in a softer crevice between two rocks to close her eyes and grip the warm wood of the sword's sheath in her left hand comfortingly.

———

Morning brought with it a crippling pain assaulting her on all fronts, from the cramp in her bunched and tired muscles to the renewed pain of her injuries. She rolled into a sitting position, rocking back and forth as she breathed through clenched teeth to push away the agony, and stayed there until Mark crouched down beside her to ask if she was okay.

She didn't answer, knowing it was an obviously stupid question, but when he insisted on getting her to speak to him, she lashed out with words.

"Get off me," she snarled, twitching her hand on the

sword to make him recoil as though she were venomous. The thought arrived directly in her brain that even the distance he had retreated would be pointless if she chose hostility, because the sword could flick out to triple her natural reach and skewer anyone within reach.

She chided herself privately for the thought, knowing that there was no way she could hurt the man who was so closely entwined with her own upbringing that the two shared a bond without having interacted for most of her life.

She saw the look on his face then, saw the wide eyes of a man who had feared his own death for just a split second, and she cried.

She cried from the pain, from the fear of everything turning so suddenly upside down again, and she cried from the shame of making Mark fear her.

"It's alright," he said softly, reaching forwards again and wrapping his arms around her small, huddled frame. "It's going to be alright."

"Is it?" she sobbed quietly. "When? When will it be alright? When will everything stop?"

He said nothing, just soothed her and held her like a father would have done if she had ever been graced with one.

She hadn't. She'd been born in secret, taken away from an unworthy or unwilling mother, and raised in the darkness to become a killer. To exist in the space between darkness and light, to be a shadow with a blade and to help overthrow the tyranny that made them all exist in fear.

She wanted their sacrifices, their losses and their blood, the time she had spent as a captive, all to *mean* something. If it didn't, if they were just going to change the name on the door of the office that ran the Citadel, then what was it all for?

She'd spent the months alone contemplating all of these questions, telling herself that it had been worth it to end the violence and the bloodshed and the fear, and the only reason she ever agreed to return there was to try and prevent more lives from being lost – lives of people who couldn't do what she could.

"I..." Eve sobbed into Mark's chest. "I miss her. She died because of *me*."

"Shh," Mark soothed her, stroking a hand over her messy hair to smooth it down. "I know, I know... I miss Cohen too. None of this would be happening if she was still here."

She sniffed again, trying to stop the tears and failing, so she wept quietly into his shoulder.

"What have I done?" she asked in a small voice.

"You didn't do anything wrong," he told her. "You did what you thought was right, what would save lives, but you were lied to."

"Like I was lied to before?" she accused him, angry at the world. "Like Command lied to us just so they could become what we were supposed to be fighting?"

"It isn't... It's not... it's not like that," he said. "Things got turned around. Power does that to some people."

"Not me," Eve answered. "Not you."

"No. Which is why we have to make it right."

CHAPTER TWENTY-SEVEN

THE APPEARANCE OF NORMALITY

Rebecca returned to work, conducted all her usual tasks and spent less time in her office than she usually did. She told herself it was staying busy with tasks that kept her moving but in quiet moments she admitted that it was because she felt that the internal power struggles of the command level in the headquarters building were waters too dangerous to swim in.

She managed her assets, relayed intelligence wherever necessary and fought a constant battle against Black and others he ordered to do his bidding in an attempt to get access to information she had a duty and responsibility to keep secret.

Lives would be at risk if he gained the knowledge of the identities of the agents reporting to her department, and every one of those men and women trusted her to keep their positions safe from such prying eyes as Black's; and she simply didn't trust what he would do with it.

In the days since the assault on the agricultural facility, an assault she deemed to be a failure in its method rather than the accomplishment, tensions among the senior levels in the Citadel were running high.

Her anxiety had been quadrupled since Mouse and the twins had reported their run-in with Fly and his attempt to plant a listening device in their underground lab; magnified now by her own problems with a senior leader trying to conduct a hostile takeover of her department, things were worrying.

When the message came through from one of her agents established in the main western distribution and storage facility that a large group of survivors from the place they had assaulted had arrived with tales of a government takeover, her initial feeling was one of elation until the consequences dawned on her fully.

"Inspector," one of her analysts called to her as she passed through her office only to collect some paperwork before heading back out.

"What is it? I'm a little busy."

"I think you'll want to see this," he told her with a serious expression. She hesitated a second before dropping the report she was holding on his desk and she leaned over behind him. The file on his screen was marked only with an agent identification code and the heading 'urgent'.

"This came through our secure communications server?" she asked anxiously. He nodded, hitting the keys in front of him to transfer the file to her tablet as he searched a drop-down menu to find her details.

"No," she interrupted him. "Send it to a spare unit. In fact, hardwire transfer it so it doesn't pass through the system."

"Ma'am?"

"Trust me," she said with a smile of confidence she didn't truly possess, bluffing the man. He complied, rising from his desk to pick up a blank, unassigned tablet used for secure briefings and isolated from the main system. He plugged it into his terminal, dragging the file and waiting as the progress bar filled up until it showed as complete.

She snatched up the tablet and walked fast from the room, taking it wordlessly to the bathroom in the corridor and locking the door behind her.

She put down the seat and perched, then selected the file, tapping her foot as she waited impatiently for the text to show up. She knew that her agent, from memory a man placed in that facility as one of the first wave of volunteers to leave the Citadel and extend the reach of her eyes and ears to every corner of their domain, must have risked his life to send the message but thoughts of his mortality were outweighed by the intelligence.

She read his report on the number of people arriving, realising that Black's assessment of the numbers captured and killed must have been grossly overestimated, and searched for any mention of Eve.

She found none, other than confirmation of what she already knew in that Horrocks was killed by a covert government agent prior to the attack.

Rebecca searched the rest of the short report for anything that expanded her understanding, finding that Harvey, a former member of Command in the dying days of the old Resistance, had turned and spoken to them.

[PRECIS OF SPEECH GIVEN BY HARVEY] she read. [STATED THAT GOVERNMENT OPPRESSION IS EXTENDING AND WORSENING, THAT CONTROL OVER ANY SETTLEMENT WISHING TO DECLARE INDEPEN-DENCE WOULD BE ACHIEVED BY LETHAL FORCE. SUGGESTED PLAN TO CHOKE OFF ALL FOOD SUPPLIES TO CITADEL BY BLOCKADE OF DISTRIB-UTION CENTRE UNTIL PEACEFUL RESOLUTION IS FOUND]

"What the hell does that mean?" she asked herself. Deciding that there was no way she could keep this from the Prime Minister, and to do so would be treason, she worried what response the woman would order unless a better solution were presented alongside the problem.

Sitting there, racking her brain for the answer, she tried to formulate the words in her mind in a way that could present such an answer without showing weakness, capitulation to terrorist demands or leniency.

CHAPTER TWENTY-EIGHT

WATERWAY

Eve was beyond exhausted by the time their small team reached the lower ground where the distant mountains swooped low to the wide river.

There, as though acting on information given or received without her knowledge, a boat awaited them. It was a wide, low craft not designed for the open ocean but instead the sheltered inland waters. As soon as she saw the hooded, shrouded figures manning the vessel, she knew instantly who they were and where they were from.

"Head back to the distribution centre," Mark told the others. "Move like we have and stay out of sight." They nodded their agreement as they were eager to use the last of the daylight and make good progress, turning back north to leave Mark and Eve to make the final mile over open fields to meet their transport.

"You remember your lessons about the Nocturnals?" he asked her as they walked slowly. Eve struggled; walking bent over slightly with her left arm hugged to her chest as if keeping pressure on her fractured bones could prevent them from exploding outwards with the pain. Her right hand still gripped the sword and Mark wouldn't think of offering to take away even that small burden.

She'd been separated from that sword before, and it pained her still if he knew the young woman at all.

"Don't make them angry, don't show disrespect, call their leader King and bow," she grunted as she walked stiffly. "I know them well enough," she added, annoyed that Mark hadn't recalled how close she lived to their territory.

"That'll do," Mark answered, figuring that he could handle the finer points so long as she didn't sabotage their negotiations.

They walked the rest of the way to the banks of the river, watched all the time by the small figures.

"*Gorhemynadow, koweth,*" Mark said, stumbling over the difficult words and bowing his head respectfully. "*Skoodhya nei–*"

"We speak your tongue," one of the hooded figures said with barely an accent. They stood, drawing back the hood to show a man who was tall for a Nocturnal, standing at close to Eve's long-legged height with slicked back black hair and wearing the darkened goggles they needed to be anything but blind in the daylight. "We received your message and came."

"And you have our gratitude," Mark told him.

"I am Helghor," the Nocturnal introduced himself, "and you are... you are hurt?" Mark looked to Eve who was leaning over further and gasping for breath now that she had stopped moving.

"She was injured days ago," Mark explained. "Her armour stopped heavy calibre bullets, but her ribs and chest bones were cracked."

Helghor turned to another of his people and hissed

something so rapid that Mark couldn't even make out a single word of it. The man leapt lightly off the boat's gunwale and onto dry land where he scooped her up gently to turn and pass her down to the others waiting. Many hands moved her as gently as possible but any movement caused her unbearable pain after the exertion of travel.

She was rested at the prow of the boat on a soft pile of sacks before being covered to keep her warm. Not one of them tried to pry the sword from her hand as if they understood on a cellular level how inseparable she was from it, and when Mark stepped down onto the boat, adding to the weight of two Nocturnals and feeling the craft dip and wobble in the water, they rushed to take up oars and push them away from the bank.

"We go fast," Helghor said. "She needs our healers."

————

The journey was fast and silent, much in the style of the Nocturnals themselves, and the boat seemed more to glide over the surface than it did plough through the tidal waters, as the river mouth opened up to become a miles-wide stretch of open water overlooking the sea between the mainland and Ireland in the invisible distance.

Helghor, steering the boat expertly from the stern, hugged the southern edge of that river mouth to keep to the shallow water of the coast. Seeing Mark looking around, he intuited what the question would be and answered it in advance.

"Our draught is too shallow to risk deeper water," he explained. "We stay in shallow water near land. It is slower but safer." Mark nodded his thanks for the explanation and returned to his tense wait in silence, watching Eve sleep, unable to rouse herself even when the cold, wet spray of the frigid sea showered her hair.

As the day began to fade into darkness and Mark's visibility was reduced to only two dozen paces ahead of them, the Nocturnals removed their dark goggles, allowing them to use their genetic advantage to the full.

By the time Mark saw the moon showing over the watery horizon, Helghor turned the boat sharply inland up another river so overgrown by trees hanging down as to obscure the rocks either side. Mark panicked slightly, showing no outward fear but not enjoying the tension he felt inside with the dump of adrenaline coursing through his body.

A pace either side of them in places were jagged rocks sharp enough to damage their boat, and after the third time he was struck by low branches, he was forced to retreat to cover beside Eve in the prow where his skull would be safe from damage.

"We're almost there," he whispered to her reassuringly. "Won't be long now."

Eve gave no response, proving to him that she was more unconscious than asleep and worrying that he had pushed her too hard on the journey. He knew she was physically capable enough, even with her injuries, but he suspected that some of her exhaustion was due to the emotional strain she'd been experiencing, coupled with her body's reaction to the painkillers and injections she'd had.

"Almost there now," he told her again, hoping it was true.

CHAPTER TWENTY-NINE

BEARER OF BAD NEWS

Rebecca waited outside the Prime Minister's office under the watchful gaze of two uniformed guards and a secretary so overbearing that she doubted even Nathaniel could have intimidated the woman.

A buzzer sounded on her desk, but no words were spoken, prompting the secretarial equivalent of a shock trooper to raise her judgemental gaze to Rebecca and speak.

"The Prime Minister will see you now, Inspector Howard."

Rebecca stood, smoothed down her shirt, which was so crumpled by the time spent sitting in a chair desperately trying to figure out what she was going to suggest – or more appropriately *how* she was going to suggest it – and she wished she'd put on the jacket to cover the creases, as if her appearance made all the difference to what she would say.

She walked in, giving the door a cursory knock as she entered to announce her presence, even though she'd been summoned, and stood smartly in front of Helen's desk.

"Inspector," she greeted her warmly, acting as though she didn't realise Rebecca had been waiting outside her office for close to half an hour before she called for her. "Take a seat. How are you?"

"Fine, Ma'am," Rebecca answered hurriedly as she sat, eager to get to the heart of her reason for calling for such a short notice meeting with the head of state. "And yourself?"

"Wonderful," she answered, smiling as if only she knew the punchline to the joke she was about to tell.

"Prime Minister," Rebecca said, launching into her practised report. "A short while ago I received a secure transmission from an agent in one of the main western distribution centres responsible for a large amount of food transportation to the Citadel. It appears that a former senior member of government is now there, having fled the assault on the agricultural facility. He is calling for negotiations with a government representative to discuss terms."

She sat back, looking at the older woman to see if her words had taken effect. Helen merely stared blankly at her, showing no reaction to the news.

"That message," she said in a conversational tone, "was received at the Citadel over three hours ago and says more than you've just informed me of."

She spoke in facts, not asking questions, and Rebecca knew in that instant that her authority to run the counter-intelligence department had been circumvented in spite of her attempts to keep the circle small.

"That report," Helen went on, "threatens terrorist action against the people here unless demands are met." She sat forwards in her chair and leaned on the desk with both elbows to make sure Rebecca could see the determination and anger on her face.

"We will *not* negotiate. We will *not* be dictated to. We will *not* capitulate to these threats."

Each statement was emphasised with a stab of her right index finger onto the desk.

"Furthermore, I am concerned that this report wasn't brought to my immediate attention, forcing me to learn of it from another source. A source, I might add, *not* dedicated to the relaying of vital covert intelligence such as this."

"Ma'am, I—"

"I'm certain there are good reasons for this, you understand," Helen went on as if she hadn't spoken, "which means that the delay was probably caused by you being overloaded with a current workload beyond the capabilities of your team, which is why I am removing this case from your workload effective immediately."

"Ma'am, please, if I can just—"

"Just what?"

"If I can explain both the delay and the suggested plan for dealing with this?"

Helen stared, saying nothing butallowing Rebecca to proceed at her own risk.

"The intelligence came to me earlier. However, I had to corroborate certain facts with other sources and what we already know to authenticate the intelligence. After that I researched the people involved, the facility and all other information relati—"

"And the plan you're going to suggest?" Helen interrupted, tired of Rebecca's corporate language excuses.

"I suggest we send people to negotiate, someone neutral perhaps and not an immediate representative of the Citadel but someone who can be seen as a mediator of sorts. I suggest we allow them to stay at the facility so long as all scheduled food deliveries are maintained alongside the key performance indicators, and in the meantime we can establish further links to the facility and grow our intelligence network inside their group."

Helen said nothing, leaning back and frowning in thought. Rebecca began to think that she might actually go for it, might not hand over control of a political negotiation to make it a military action, but her bubble burst with crushing disappointment.

"You suggest a weak approach, effectively offering a slow-burn protocol to undermine a dangerous terrorist threat, when they hold a boot to our throats as leverage for their independence from state." She sat up again to pick up a piece of paper and read the headlines to Rebecca.

"The Citadel holds twenty days' worth of produce, with another supply convoy due in eighteen days. If that doesn't come, then you know what will happen here? Disorder. Public disobedience. Riots. Everything we fought so hard to prevent, and you want to play into their hands by showing them a weak response and *asking* for what is ours? No. The people require action, and they will receive action."

"Ma'am, I apologise for not making myself clear, I'm suggesti—"

"Your suggestion is noted and refused. I have another incident I wish you to take care of in one of the northern facilities and I doubt your subordinates up there can handle it. Take a personal escort with you, but I will require the remainder of your team to continue work on all other projects in your absence."

Rebecca sat and gawped with her mouth open, unable to respond to the carpet-bombing of bad news her mind had just endured.

"If I can ask who is covering my department?" she enquired quietly, fearing that she already knew the answer

"I am temporarily promoting your senior sergeant to cover your duties," Helen answered diffidently. "I'll have orders drafted for you immediately, so you'll excuse me?" Her eyes went to the door and Rebecca stood, feeling insignificant and thoroughly, resoundingly beaten at her own game of subterfuge and secrets.

Leaving the office, she almost walked directly into Black, showing the bright white of an additional star on his rank badge to denote that he now outranked her. He smiled, which she tried her hardest to ignore, and scurried back to her office knowing she was beaten.

Inside the office where Black walked in and sat without invitation to do either, the Prime Minister smiled at him.

"As you expected," she told him. "Our counter-intelligence department seems more interested in negotiation. I prefer force, and you have eighteen days with which to achieve the goal. Good day, Chief Inspector."

"Good day to you too, Prime Minister," Black answered smugly, before walking out of her offices and heading for the elevator to take him down, deep underground, to where he now held the authority to unleash a weapon previously denied to him.

CHAPTER THIRTY

SWALLOWED PRIDE

Rebecca found her orders on her desk, printed and signed by a newly minted chief inspector simply to rub salt in her already open wounds.

She read them twice, trying to see between the lines for where the real mission was until she realised that the simplicity of her task was yet another slap in the face. She was being sent to conduct interviews with suspected dissident members of the northern facilities' workforce with a view to corroborating certain intelligence matters reported by the senior government officials there.

"This is bullshit," she said to herself, turning the paper over for more and searching the plain envelope in the hope that there were unofficial orders hidden inside. "This is fucking *bullshit!*"

A knock at the door startled her. Turning, she saw Mouse holding a laptop terminal under one arm and appearing as much like a nocturnal prey animal out during daylight.

"Just need to update your operating system," he said, with his eyes locked on her to make his attempt at nuance so obvious she was glad nobody else could see him.

The fact that he spoke loudly and looked directly at her was so out of character for him, but then she realised that of all the people he'd have seen on his way up here, none of them knew him well enough to recognise that.

"Of course," she said casually. "Please come in."

Mouse entered the office, closing the door behind him twice as he didn't like the way the handle clicked on his first attempt.

Rebecca looked at him, saying nothing and holding her hands out questioningly as she cast her eyes over the walls.

"Oh no, the room's clear," Mouse said confidently. "It was your personal communications they were monitoring. I haven't changed that, I just wanted to give you this." He set the laptop on her desk and opened it up, pressing two keys on either side of the keyboard to make the panel pop up. Removing it, he produced a new tablet identical to the model she was issued.

"Simple work-around," Mouse said, eyes down and muttering as if rehearsing what he wanted to say instead of actually saying it. "Any communications you want to be kept private go through this application," he turned the tablet around and showed her an unfamiliar icon. "And anything you don't mind other people reading, just do normally. It's replaced your old tablet on the system," he added, holding out a hand for the tainted device which she gave over and watched him hide inside the dummy laptop to be taken away.

"How?" she asked, meaning so many things by the question that she sat back and waited to pick the relevant information out of the rambling she expected to come her way.

"Just a similar protocol to the secure communications

network from the assets, only this can't be intercepted. I've used a coding system that disguises incoming and outgoing transmissions as diagnostic speed tests – that won't be detected because I set up a similar process on all systems to do the same."

Rebecca sat back and assimilated the information he'd blurted out, happy that he'd anticipated her needs.

"I have to go away," she said, sighing in exasperation as there was no way she could see to avoid the orders.

"I know, and those orders allow you to take a technical team and an escort. I'm on the technical team."

She stared at him, making him look away and smile to himself as he was evidently pleased with his actions. She was pleased, she realised, not to be going alone without anyone she trusted fully.

"What about the others?" she asked, meaning the twins and having to explain that when Mouse looked confused.

"They'll stay here. They can communicate with us the same way, and they'll be able to keep us up to date with what's going on."

As he spoke, Rebecca's new tablet flashed up a message through the new system. She tapped at it, waited a few seconds for the content to load, and widened her eyes.

"What is it?" Mouse asked, concerned.

"Jonah. He's been given orders to dispatch with a team to enter into negotiations with Harvey and the other faction."

Mouse's face fell, his mouth dropping open as his eyes flickered back and forth with the effort of thinking fast.

"What about Jenna? Is she going too? Who's making him go?"

"No, it doesn't look like she is, and I don't know… but I'm pretty certain I can guess."

———

Four hours later, after hurriedly packing and changing into the tactical field uniform, Inspector Howard, Mouse and two of her detail boarded a transport to set off north under the watchful gaze of Black.

He waited until the transport was out of sight, smiling darkly before he turned and gave a junior rank an order.

"Order the advance team to be assembled and ready in two hours by the western gate." He waited for confirmation of their understanding, waiting another few seconds for the sound of their boot steps to fade away before speaking again.

"I need another transport organised to accompany the DRT leaving twelve hours behind. I need the Erebus asset and the necessary support team in place for that, along with a full complement of assault support. Drones, replenishment, prisoner handling and tech support to repair any systems damaged when we take that place back."

"Are we…" a sergeant assigned to his personal detail asked, quailing under Black's intense gaze but refusing to let it go. He swallowed, cleared his throat, and tried again. "Sir, are we not seeking a resolution first? With the negotiations, I mean?"

Black took a step closer to him, looming over the man, who held his gaze and refused to back down.

"You have an issue with my orders, Sergeant?"

The man swallowed again, a fear response as Black saw it, but didn't recant his question. He was one of many in his unit who weren't initially from the Party quick reaction forces, and as such, Black still saw him as an outsider.

"Let me guess," Black went on. "You know someone there. A cousin or a friend perhaps?" His facial reaction gave Black the answer he needed.

"So you're concerned for an individual among hundreds, possibly thousands, who represent a risk to the safety and security of the Citadel. Who are intent on challenging the government for power. Do you have any idea, Sergeant, what will happen to every other place outside these walls if we negotiate with these terrorists and give them what they want? Do you know what will happen *inside* these walls when words gets back here? The government will be done. It may not happen overnight like the last time, but it will infect the people like a wound turned bad and that infection will spread until the body dies, and what then?"

The sergeant stared at him, not offering an answer, so Black provided one for him.

"Then it will all fall down," he growled in a low voice only inches from the man's face. "It will all. Fall. Down. No more rules, no more order, just these idiots, these *animals* running wild. Where were you the last time someone succeeded in doing that?"

Again, the sergeant said nothing, and Black's smile told him he knew exactly where he'd been – locked inside a barracks surrounded by an angry mob.

"Go and give the orders for the Erebus asset," he snapped, waiting until the sergeant had left before giving his final order.

"Redeploy that man elsewhere. I don't want him on this operation if he doesn't have the intelligence to understand it or the stomach to get it done."

CHAPTER THIRTY-ONE

HEALING

Eve's consciousness fled her in the bad weather, so she didn't witness their arrival in the territory of the Nocturnals. She had lived a few miles from their land before but on the softer landscape to the east, instead of the harsh, rocky outcrops and cruel coastline that this part overlooked.

When the watery part of their journey ended, Mark picked her up carefully and stepped ashore with her in his arms, her sword still clutched in one hand, seemingly unable to let it slip from her grasp even when unconscious.

From there, Helghor showed him the way with a small burning torch which none of them needed but Helghor was aware that the outsider, the large man from another sub-strand of their shared species, was all but blind in the darkness they so thrived in.

Eve was laid down in the soft bed of a cart that was too small for Mark to sit with her, so instead he sat in the one behind as he saw how all the carts were linked front and back to others.

"It's a train," he breathed in wonder.

"It runs underground for many miles, *koweth*. It will lead us through many paths if we desire, but for now we will travel to our centre *hware*."

"Straight for the King's chamber?" Mark asked, hopeful that he was correct as he knew the layout and many of the people there. "To the *Myghtern*?"

"He is gone from these lands," Helghor said quietly. "He is in *Talamh dearmadta*, and his brother's son sits in his place."

Mark stiffened, partly at the words and how Helghor said them and partly because the small train began to move with a jolt and a squeak of metal on metal. The speed soon picked up until they were hurtling through the underground tunnels. He gripped the sides of his cart and turned to face the man sitting behind him. The cart lurched, sending his eyes wide with fear until Helghor spoke.

"*Kosel, Kowr-den,*" he said with a playful smirk of amusement at Mark's discomfort. "This man, our *Gwithyas*. The man is in charge in place of the *Myghtern*, but he is not as our *Myghtern* is. He does not see a way that our two people should be united." Mark took the warning in his stride, showing no reaction to it other than to give a knowing nod, but inside he feared for the consequences of what those words meant.

The train hurtled along, chilling his face and hands as the air current slowly froze him. The journey gave him time to think, to play through the possible outcomes of asking for the help of the Nocturnals once more after their bond was broken by peace when the Party was overthrown.

To ask for help again, this time to combat an enemy of their own making, made him worry deeply. That worry, combined with the rhythmic movement of the underground train, lulled him into an exhausted semi-sleep where his mind raced and none of the outcomes he imagined were positive.

———

Mark was so drained from fleeing the facility, from missing so much sleep since then, and from the arduous journey across rough terrain that he had to be shaken awake by Helghor when they arrived. Climbing stiffly out of the cart, he found Eve awake and sitting up, watching him with the same kind of concern he felt for her. He nodded to her, telling her that he was fine and asked how she felt.

"Like I've been beaten up," she gasped, climbing out with difficulty and more stiffness than Mark had shown. She was pale and short of breath, both of which symptoms caused Mark great concern.

"She needs to get to the healers," he told Helghor insistently. "Now." Helghor nodded, muttering orders to his fighters.

"This way," he told them. "The *medhek* will be expecting you."

Mark half carried Eve who still gripped her sword as if her life depended on it. She faltered with every other step, which told Mark that he was wrong to have moved her in the condition she was in and more certain than ever that her injuries had suffered complications, or else Hegarty was wrong about his initial diagnosis.

They were led to a chamber, lit from a single light source high up in the domed ceiling, and Mark lifted Eve onto the bed, making her groan and whimper in agony. A small person, minute even by Nocturnal standards, lending them the appearance of a child, asked questions of Helghor, who turned to Mark to translate.

"He wants to know what happened to her."

"She was shot. Three times with a heavy calibre weapon at close quarters. She was wearing bulletproof armour which stopped the rounds going through, but..." he gestured to the girl, who brought her knees up involuntarily in pain. The tiny Nocturnal fussed him away, muttering words he barely understood but was certain that he was being insulted on a racial level in some way.

He moved back, turning away abruptly as the man cut away her clothes with a tiny, hooked blade that seemed sharp enough to slice through steel. Seeing her bright white, pale skin before he looked away so as not to see anything she wouldn't want him to, his mind flashed back to the last image his eyes had captured of the lurid bruising contrasting so terribly against her now pale flesh.

He'd seen the bruising before, only what he saw now was far worse, which meant that her injury had grown more serious since they'd left their hiding place.

"There is nothing more you can do here," Helghor told him kindly. "You must eat and rest. Trust us to take good care of her."

Mark allowed himself to be led away, to stoop low through the familiar surroundings of the underground city, until he was shown inside a chamber with furs on the floor and a bed just large enough to accommodate his size.

Hot water was brought to him in a bowl to wash with, followed by the doughy pastry-wrapped meal of meat and vegetables roasted slowly which made his mouth water and his stomach recall the taste of them with anticipation.

He sat on the bed and ate first, gulping down mug after mug of crisp, cold water to wash down the heavy meal, then stood to strip and wash his body with the tepid water before falling into the bed and collapsing into the soft covers where he lay awake and seemed unable to stop his mind from racing.

How had things got this bad so quickly? Was this what it was like in the beginning, when the Resistance was first born? Did they fight for the first Party government, only to find out that they'd created a monster to spell their own doom?

He hated himself for his part in what was happening now, for the loss of innocent lives at the hands of people he had been with and supported fully. He told himself that he couldn't have known this would be the way things would go, but the more he thought about it, the more he knew that they had all acted without considering the slim chance that they could actually win.

That chance had been all of nothing, with a heavy expectation of nothing, and most people had joined their revolution thinking that death was a better ending to their lives than the one they could already expect. When they had won, the need to grasp some kind of order and hold onto it had forced them to take actions they hadn't considered, and that meant putting a military force back on the streets to stop the mob rule and killings of anyone in Party uniform. The people, so long trodden down under the bootheel of the soldiers, turned on them like animals and it took days to bring the Citadel back down to earth.

In hindsight, he knew, that initial control measure set the tone for the way Command would run the city, would control the people, and it became the easiest path to take to keep the same tried and tested methods of oversight and control.

They could restructure as much as they liked, could turn the soldiers into a police force and call themselves different things but Mark saw it all for what it was then.

They were just the same, only they didn't have the self-awareness to admit that they were doing it.

Mark was certain, or at least he hoped he was certain that Helen, the meek, bewildered leader of Command after the reign of James and Cohen was burned down, meant well. He was also certain that there were elements of her senior advisory level of officers who were promising one thing and delivering another through means she either wasn't aware of or didn't want to know about. In his book, turning a blind eye was as big a crime as doing whatever it was you chose to ignore, so as much as he wanted to believe that their democratically appointed Prime Minister was innocent of such crimes, he knew in his heart then that he couldn't forgive her for allowing them to happen on her watch.

A bang on his door dragged him out of his semi-lucid thoughts and back to the present with a jolt.

"I'm coming," he called out, searching the floor for something to put on and cover his dignity. Pulling on pants, he opened the door to see Helghor leaning on the tunnel wall.

"*Medhek* says she is stable," he told Mark. "Says she was bleeding inside – not much but enough that she would die if he had not stopped it."

Mark's face fell. He realised he'd known it as soon as he saw the pallid tone of her skin. Internal bleeding was no joke, and to treat it would require the level of medical care only available at the largest of the western outposts, if not the Citadel itself. Thinking that his need to put the mission first stung him in that it had almost cost Eve her life.

"Thank you," he said breathlessly. "And thank your doctor for me?" Helghor bowed his head respectfully in acknowledgement.

"I will take you to her for now," he said. "It will soon

be time for the morning meal. I will get you before then."
He took Mark back to where he'd left Eve to the ministra-
tions of the *Medhek.*

He left the room, leaving Mark sitting beside Eve, who
breathed gently but was otherwise perfectly still.

"Damn them," he said softly, reaching out to hold her
hand to comfort himself. "Damn all of them."

CHAPTER THIRTY-TWO

WITH US OR AGAINST US

Jonah was given his orders in person by the one person he would hate the most for telling him what to do. Mouse had left the twins in their underground workshop laboratory tinkering with the wiring of a communication device hardwired into a suit of armour much as Eve's had been, and his awkwardness at leaving them was obvious.

They were all careful about what they said, given their knowledge of at least one listening device in their place of work, but to say nothing of the mission and their orders would raise an alarm to anyone eavesdropping, so they said their farewells and made no mention of their concerns.

When Mouse had left, sent to the northern outposts with Rebecca, brother and sister sat apart from the few others working there, saying very little until the elevator doors opened and Fly walked in, flanked by two uniformed officers in tactical gear not often seen in the Citadel, now that their role had transitioned from enforcement to peace-keeping.

"Bad news coming our way," Jenna muttered to her

brother, who looked up and frowned at the approaching men.

"What can we help you with, Fly?" he asked, still concentrating on his work without looking up, only knowing when to speak by the sounds of boots stopping behind his chair.

"You've got a mission," Fly said, sounding bored, as if talking to them was beneath him now.

"Where are we going this time?" Jenna asked, stopping herself from saying any more and outwardly showing her distaste for their last job, which could be construed as treason if the wrong ears heard it.

"Not you," Fly said with derision. "Just him."

"Okay," Jonah said trying not to show fear, shock, or anger at the news, "where am *I* going?"

"West," came the overly simple response. As if thinking about it, or perhaps saying more so he could judge their reactions, Fly explained more. "Seems that some of the terrorists took over another facility and want to force us to negotiate with them by threatening to hold up the food shipments."

"We heard," Jenna said, letting Fly know that they weren't totally ignorant as he assumed everyone was. "Why do you need him?"

"Technical support," Fly announced with a grandeur that made both twins roll their eyes. Fly let them enjoy their moment of fun before insulting them again. "We need someone to clean the drones when they're done destroying the enemy."

"Wait," Jonah said. "I thought the mission was to go and negotiate with these people?"

"And *I* thought," Fly said menacingly as he leaned his hands on the arms of Jonah's chair, "that last I checked, *you* weren't the Prime Minister or one of her senior advisors. Are you refusing your orders? Are you with us, or *against* us?"

"That's what you are then?" Jenna asked, instinctively taking the focus of Fly's attention off her brother, just as he would do for her unthinkingly. "One of the Prime Minister's senior advisors? Tell me, Fly, what do you advise her on? How to pick locks? How to get beaten up in a fight?"

Fly stood and flexed his chest as if that would intimidate her. To underline his emotions, he rested his right hand on the grip of the electrified baton he carried with the implied threat that he could or even *might* use it on them.

Jenna scoffed, her hatred of the young man she believed had been corrupted by power over others topped only by the fact that he now felt the need to rely on a gun and backup to make him feel bigger.

"That's what I thought," she said smugly. "Maybe you're better at just delivering messages that a simple phone call would achieve?" She leaned around him to look at the pair of armed men flanking their former friend. "And these two are your babysitters so you don't get lost?"

Fly turned his full attention on her now, gripping her chair as he had Jonah's and tensing his upper body for her to see how much bigger he'd grown since living well off the labours of the people.

"Careful," he warned her with a wicked smile playing across his face, "or I might find some orders for you too."

Jenna didn't back down, instead she leaned closer to his face and put her right hand behind her back as if leaning on the chair for support. Beside her, Jonah could see that she was actually folding the fingers of her right hand around the worn, wooden hilt of a knife sitting in a hidden sheath inside the waistband of her trousers.

"Fine," Jonah said, almost leaping out of his chair to

bring the attention back onto him before his sister did something that would get them both arrested for treason. "When and where? What do I need to bring?"

Fly stood straight and kept his cold eyes on Jenna, who still smiled to intentionally goad him. Speaking from one side of his mouth he kept his eyes on her, not out of a sensible caution but in a bid to remain intimidating.

"Vehicle bay," he said. "Six hours. And bring your own gear but no weapons because the real fighters will handle that stuff for you." He turned away and paused, looking back over his shoulder to add, "as always."

The twins watched him go, both of them remaining tense until the elevator doors closed again before Jenna let out a muffled grunt of anger and exasperation that sounded like she really wanted to scream in rage to let the pressure out. Instead, her emotions bubbling over unchar-acteristically, she drew the small knife from behind her back and twisted her entire body into a savage throw that sent the knife screaming through the air and embedding itself into a terminal monitor all the way to the hilt.

Jonah watched the knife handle for a moment, feeling oddly disappointed that there were no sparks as he'd have expected, then turned back to his sister, who was pacing a small stretch of floor in restless anger.

Jonah put himself in front of her, holding one finger to his lips to remind her she needed to be careful about what she wanted to say.

"I don't care," she snapped, stopping her pacing and stepping close to her brother to grab him by his upper arms before hugging him close so that she could whisper in his ear.

"You promise me," she hissed, unable to stop the anger she felt from coming out, "that if something doesn't look right, then you just go. Get out of there, go to ground, join the others, *anything*. Just get away from Fly and his new friends, because this all stinks to me."

"Me too," Jonah whispered, hugging her back. "And I promise you I will. I'll send you a message if I do, so you know to get out yourself, okay?"

───────

Six hours later, Jonah stood in a mostly deserted vehicle dock on the first level under the Citadel headquarters building. He carried a bag of his personal gear and despite what Fly had tried to order him to do, he carried his least favourite weapon on his belt, with three others he much preferred hidden in his bag.

An hour came and went, making Jonah check his memory of the instructions more than once, until finally others began to arrive and begin preparing both transport and technical support vehicles.

"You're early," a voice he recognised said from behind him. Turning, he saw Fly, still flanked by the same two men, smiling condescendingly at him.

"You told me six hours," Jonah answered, understanding that Fly had deliberately messed with him.

"I meant eight," Fly said with an annoying smirk on his face. "My mistake. Wow, you're *really* going to be exhausted later. You're in that one," he said, pointing at a support carrier. "I'm assuming you remember how to fly a Bat drone?"

Jonah said nothing, simply picked up his gear and walked to the vehicle where he took a seat, strapped himself in and closed his eyes.

"Joke's on you, dickhead," he murmured to himself as he focused on slowing his heartrate and breathing. "I can sleep anywhere."

CHAPTER THIRTY-THREE

INTUITION

Rebecca sat in the rear of the transport going along the smoother roads heading north, which were kept in better condition than the western routes. She said nothing for hours, which suited Mouse. He found conversation about nothing to be tedious and distracting to his task of mining the downloaded files he'd decrypted so that his brain didn't have time to wander down the multitude of rabbit holes he found himself in when he was awake and inactive.

The task wasn't a priority one, but he rarely found himself having the luxury of time when nothing else needed his attention. He was currently immersed in files, doing what he usually did and creating a kind of virtual reality world in his head where the symbols and characters on the screen before him came to life, allowing him to try different ways to unlock the doors designed to keep out anyone not given authorised access.

It wasn't always doors. Often he found walls that appeared odd, and only by retreating from the imagined rooms and looking at the layout from another perspective could he see that they were intentionally hidden, even from those who had originally had access to them.

"Got anything yet?" Rebecca asked, startling Mouse from his construct and back into the cramped vehicle's interior of his actual reality.

"What?" he asked, unsure what she'd said but knowing that it had been aimed at him.

"I asked if you'd found anything yet," she said. "About the people we're investigating?"

"Oh, no. Sorry. Did you want me to look into them?" Rebecca sighed, making him feel uncertain if he'd annoyed her or accidentally ignored a request.

"No," she said. "There's no rush, I just thought that was what you were doing." Mouse said nothing for a few seconds before returning to the keys.

"What were you doing?" she asked, accustomed to Mouse's social ineptitude and forgiving it easily for the gift of his inhuman abilities.

"I was looking through the encrypted files from the Party's archives," he explained. "I've got almost three hundred exabytes of the stuff and I'm not even ten percent through it."

Rebecca made a noise that attempted to sound interested. She spoke again, making Mouse fight the urge to sigh at the interruption, but he guessed that she needed to speak to cover her own feelings.

"Found anything useful in there yet?"

"Different versions of history," Mouse told her. "Nothing that changes things, really. There were some sealed personnel records I came across a few months ago which got me excited, but they were so old that only one of the people on the list was still alive and they're almost a hundred years old."

"What kind of records?" Rebecca asked, genuinely

intrigued.

"Some sub-division of a secret department doing experiments on people," he said. "No point in reporting it as a war crime because, like I said, the only one left is so old he doesn't know what's going on. I looked into his medical records and he's under care for dementia."

"So, there's no point in putting a senile old man against the wall for crimes he can't remember?"

"I don't think so, no," Mouse answered, wondering now for the first time if he was right not to report it.

"Me neither," Rebecca answered with a sigh. "Wait, what kind of experiments?"

"From what I can tell, it looks like some kind of prequel to Project Erebus."

"Psychological conditioning?" she asked, intrigued and preparing to be horrified.

"Along with genetic manipulation stuff," Mouse answered almost absently, as if the gravity of what they were discussing didn't matter to him. "Master race of perfect soldiers or something."

"Anything more recent?" Rebecca asked. "Anything we can use to, I don't know, get Black removed from office and tried for something?"

"No... I can look for that if you like?"

Before she could answer, the bulkhead separating crew from cab thumped twice and the muffled report of being ten minutes out came back to them.

"Some other time," Rebecca said. "Now listen, these places are... *different*. The people here aren't like they are in the Citadel. They're suspicious of us and in some places, they see us as another species. Think you can handle that?"

Mouse made a show of considering her words before answering.

"Like living underground for months with the Nocturnals?" Rebecca silently chided herself for forgetting that Mouse had been places even she hadn't.

"Not like that," she told him. "I hope not, anyway." She lifted her wrist to illuminate the face of the watch issued to her by the Party so long ago, one which she'd never had cause or opportunity to replace as so many other reminders of life before revolution had been replaced or reinvented.

"It'll be past the end of the working day now," she said, "so we won't be doing any work tonight. We should be able to get some food and settle in, ready to start first thing tomorrow."

"Fine by me," Mouse answered, shutting down his mobile terminal and rolling up the flexible keyboard he carried everywhere with him.

True to her driver's word, they rolled through the gates of the compound as the guards manning the position exchanged words with those of her detail riding up front. She heard one of her men ask where the charging stations were, and she assumed their battery-powered transport must have been running low on charge, given the distance they'd travelled in a day.

The transport set off again, jerking off the mark as the power was transferred to the wheels instantly, and Rebecca waited until it stopped to open the rear doors and step down onto the rough concrete outside a building that looked more like a bunker.

She climbed the steps towards the main doors, bag over her left shoulder and her right hand free, should she, for some reason, have need of the holstered sidearm. Rebecca's face broke into a smile of warmth and recognition at the woman walking towards them.

"Rebecca!" Samaira Nadeem said, holding out her arms for the younger woman to step into the embrace.

"Minister Nadeem," Rebecca said more formally, earning a *pfft* and a dismissive wave from her host. "It's Samaira," she chided, "or '*oi*'." Rebecca smiled, instantly falling under the beautiful woman's spell and finding herself unable to remain in the funk she'd felt trapped in only moments before.

"If you've come personally, then this must be serious," Nadeem said conspiratorially. "We only reported a few messages and secret meetings; we didn't expect the Citadel to send a departmental head to investigate."

"It's not what you think," Rebecca said. "I've bee—"

"Not here," Nadeem cut her off. "Let's get you two some food, shall we?" She forced the trademark warm smile back onto her face. It was the kind of smile that made a person feel as if they were the only person on the planet, and for those who saw it for the first time, it could be an enchanting thing to behold.

Rebecca had seen it many times before. Samaira Nadeem had been elevated from her dual positions in both the Party and the Resistance and given a position in government to represent the new Citadel in the northern outposts. Knowing that smile, Rebecca also saw how forced it was on this occasion.

The four of them followed the hypnotic sway of hips into the main building, where a young man with a tablet checked them in and informed them of their allocated quarters.

"I'm sure your young men will enjoy some rest," Samaira said sweetly, seeing Rebecca's escort turn into little boys with flushed cheeks.

"Stand down," Rebecca told them. "Report oh-seven-hundred." The two men walked away, lingering as though they both wanted to speak to Minister Nadeem for longer, but then following their stomachs instead.

Samaira ordered some food to be sent up to her rooms and led the way directly there, greeting people she passed along the way with their names in an impressive display of memory. As soon as the door to her suite of rooms closed, she dropped the public face and acknowledged Mouse with another embrace.

"So good to see you in one piece," she said to them both, sounding more concerned than ever before. "I was worried after you sent me the message, especially as I couldn't respond."

Mouse beamed at a spot on the floor beside her shoes and dug in his pack for a tablet that he held out for her. Usually an unsmiling person, Mouse was overtaken by the same boyish infatuation as Rebecca's detail had been struck with.

"You can now," he told her, unable to look her in the eye. "I've put a guidance note on there too, so you know how to work it."

"Thank you, Mouse," Samaira said warmly. "And how are Jenna and Jonah?"

"They're fine," Mouse answered past his grin. "Still arguing all the time about everything."

"Shared a womb but can't share a room," she said with a giggle which quickly faded away as she grew serious again and turned to Rebecca. "The fact that you've been sent here tells me there's something going on, either here that I don't know about – which worries me – or back at the Citadel, which worries me more."

Rebecca unzipped her jacket and sat heavily, telling the story from the beginning.

CHAPTER THIRTY-FOUR

NOT OUR WAR

Eve slept for an entire day, not waking until late in their second night with the Nocturnals. When she did, she was in so much renewed pain that she couldn't speak, but a herbal remedy carefully spooned into her mouth seemed to soothe her, along with the application of a fresh poultice of something that smelled a little like pine leaves to Mark.

Whatever they gave her, it worked, and her breathing settled down to a largely pain-free rhythm before she drifted back off again.

"Shouldn't she eat something?" he asked the small figures fussing around her. "She hasn't eaten for over a day now."

The response came to him rapidly, so that he barely made out a single syllable of it. He did understand the general feeling conveyed through the unintelligible words, however, and that told him to be quiet and mind his own business.

"He will see you now," Helghor said from the doorway. Mark stiffened, not having heard him approach, and stood to follow. Mark walked with him, stooping low through the old tunnels as he looked ahead for the newer areas excavated to a higher level.

"This man, the *gwithyas*, calls himself *Tarosvan*. He is a man of ambition who earned great honours in the battles on what your people named the Frontier."

"So he's a warrior?" Mark asked. Helghor canted his head to one side in thought before responding.

"He is, but I do not think this will help you as you want it to. He *is* a warrior, a capable one, but he is no friend to your people. He is one who thinks all outsiders are the same, and he is not alone in that." Mark paused, himself, thinking as Helghor had done before answering.

"So, you're telling me to be careful, because the man I'm about to ask for help has a loyal following and doesn't care for me and others like me?"

"I see all *kowr-den* are not stupid," Helghor responded with a smile Mark could barely make out in the low light.

They walked for minutes, taking the twisting turns along the unmarked tunnels and through larger chambers until the surroundings became more familiar to Mark from the time he had spent there with Adam and Mouse. He tried not to allow himself to be in the same mindset as the last time he was underground beyond the Frontier, because he knew that without the king there and without Dren, the King's only offspring bound to the fate of the pure born man Mark had trained from a young age, the attitude towards them would be colder, to say the least.

"Treat him the same as you would the *myghtern*," Helghor warned in a low voice as they waited to be called into the king's chamber. "*Tarosvan* has the same power in his place, but he is not the same man..."

Mark said nothing, letting the words sink in and reading between the lines to find words he did not like. *Tarosvan*, which to Mark's limited understanding of their language meant something along the lines of 'Ghost', had a following large enough to make him formidable, but his views weren't the same as the man he was standing in for. The king was magnanimous and open-minded, not to mention obviously sympathetic to their last cause, butt this man would need convincing to offer any kind of assistance.

Two guards, both armed with long, curved knives sheathed on their hips and both carrying short spears that seemed more ceremonial than functional, stepped into the antechamber they occupied

"*Hoyla my,*" one said, jerking his head in the direction he'd come from. Mark shot one last look at Helghor before he stepped under the archway and through another tunnel to enter the throne room.

"*Ow gwithyas,*" Mark said with the deep bow that he held to indicate supplication and respect to the small man sitting on the raised dais looking down on him. He raised his head when nothing was said to him, seeing a look that was unkind and predatory.

"I speak your tongue," *Tarosvan* said in a voice like a hiss. He leaned forwards, one elbow propped on the arm of the throne to sneer down at the outsider. "And I know why you are here."

Mark met his gaze, seeing nothing but malice reflected at him, and knew in an instant which way the conversation was going to go. This man had already made his mind up, regardless of anything Mark could say to him.

"Tell me, *Tarosvan,*" he challenged. "Why am I here?"

The interim leader of the Nocturnals stood and hopped down from the platform to land lightly on the smooth floor packed down under generations of feet paying tribute to the kings of old.

"You are here," he said, "because you have squandered the freedom bought by the lives of my people. *Your* kind are unable to put aside your petty squabbles and hunger for power, and so you come to us to beg for help in taking that power away from your friends."

Again, Mark said nothing, figuring that the man had the absolute measure of things, even if his prejudice was skewing his perception of it. He gave a small shrug and tried to educate the man to another point of view.

"What you said is true, in a way," he admitted, "only the ones in power are infected with the ideas of the men and women they replaced and they want to maintain the same ways." Mark paused just a fraction before continuing. "But do you know what is happening north of here?"

Tarosvan shifted his position, walking around Mark as if assessing a meal before he spoke.

"I know you have fought between yourselves over control of important resources, just as your kind has always done."

"Do you know that the fight was one-sided and unfair?" Mark asked. "Do you know that the victims of the attack simply wanted to live their lives under their own rule, just as you do here?" *Tarosvan* turned on him, stepping in fast to press his face close to Mark's before whispering harshly at him.

"It does not matter how you try to twist this. You have decided to fight among yourselves after we shed blood to set you free, so what you do now is your own decision."

"And when they've crushed us? When they've driven the will to live from everyone just as it happened before, what then?"

Tarosvan faltered as he stepped around Mark again. His words caused the man to stop, to pause as his brain took over every function of his body for a second.

"You are saying they will come for us?"

The words hung heavy in the chamber, heard and

absorbed by everyone as the tension grew. Mark knew that the way he answered the question would dictate how the rest of his time there went, so he thought carefully before opening his mouth.

"I think, if they won, then eventually they would, yes."

Hissing noises of anger and disbelief filled the edges of the chamber and sucked the sound from the room. At least two blades were drawn by guards close to their leader but as those men stepped up, *Tarosvan* held one hand out to his side and they froze.

The noise died down instantly in response to the small gesture, and that told Mark that the man was feared and obeyed. It remained to be seen if he was respected.

"Speak carefully, *dyowl*," *Tarosvan* warned.

"I'm no devil," Mark snapped at him, easily recognising the word he used. "And I'm not your *keth* or your *eskar*. I'm on the right side of this, and if your hatred of my kind blinds you to what's going on out there, then I don't want your help."

It was a gamble, he'd known that before he spoke and he knew it more when he turned to leave the chamber and heard the whispered sounds of more blades being drawn.

"Stop," *Tarosvan* barked, reminding Mark of how deep and resonant the true king's voice had sounded in that chamber.

"If what you say is true, we will not stand by and let them grow into an enemy we cannot defeat... for now, *kowr-den*, this is not yet our fight. You must seek *venjans* by yourself instead of coming to me..." he waved his hand in the air dismissively, "*krodvolhas*."

Mark looked at him for a moment before nodding and turning away to duck under the archway and leave.

Helghor waited in the tunnel and fell in step beside him as he walked.

"It went as you expected?" he asked Mark.

"Better, actually." Helghor stopped but Mark didn't. Running a few steps to catch up, he asked what he meant.

"I went in there expecting at the least to be sent away, but what I left with was a guarantee that help would come in the future if we didn't succeed."

"I do not understand. How is this a good thing? You will all die before that happens."

Mark stopped and turned on him. The smaller man was all but invisible to him in the gloom, but he was sure that his own features were clear enough to make out the earnest expression on his face.

"That's the difference between me and him," Mark answered. "I don't care about what happens to me, only what happens to the people in the long run."

CHAPTER THIRTY-FIVE

NEGOTIATING IN BAD FAITH

Fly woke Jonah up with a kick to his chair and a cruel look of satisfaction at the shocked expression he wore. Fly had been left in charge of the entire project for a while, that of Project Genesis, even if half of them had been missing or captured at the time and his resentment of his former brothers and sisters was palpable.

He still resented Mouse for disappearing, only to return with more knowledge and an affiliation with the Nocturnals that only made him more valuable. Adam and Eve, the arrogant killers raised in better standards than he had ever lived with, were never close to his heart as they were always distant and somehow *above* him. The twins, as far as he could see, were of little use to anyone as neither of them possessed the skills required to do what they all did.

If he'd been more aware of his own feelings, Fly would've known that he projected that anger at them because he was struggling to find a place for himself in the world. He was no killer – his only interactions with the enemy had left him injured and weak for days on end – and he was no awkward genius like Mouse. He couldn't climb buildings and wield a blade like the two killers, but the twins? He felt superior to them in every way and hated the fact that everyone saw him and the twins as the backup.

"We're here," he growled at Jonah, barely able to keep the hatred and jealousy from his voice. Jonah said nothing, just sat up and seemed instantly awake in an inhuman way. Fly wouldn't countenance the notion that he was jealous of them, of how people *wanted* to work with them, but his anger and arrogance wouldn't permit him to admit that even to himself.

The brakes of the transport squeaked before the rear doors opened to reveal armed officers forming up in ranks under the supervision of men and women who looked enthused instead of exhausted after a bumpy ride west.

"Detail!" barked Black's voice. "Form on me. The rest of you remain here under the command of Inspector Keenan." One squad of armed officers, looking every inch the part of the former Party soldiers Jonah guessed they were – only without the black visors – fell in behind Black, who was dressed for a fight himself.

He marched past, followed by his murderous minions, and Fly leaned out of the rear doors to speak.

"Good luck, Chief Inspector," he said, trying to sound firm and confident but coming across as a sycophantic boy. Jonah scoffed, and Black merely looked at both of them with disdain.

Fly spoke to cover his embarrassment, ordering their driver to move the transport up and telling Jonah to ready a surveillance drone. Jonah turned to his console, settling back into the seat which had been his bed until very recently, and hit the keys to bring it to life.

"Not that one," Fly snapped over his shoulder. "Take number four."

"But that's unarmed," Jonah argued, half turning to see the expression on Fly's face showing that he knew, and that it was entirely intentional. Jonah did as he was told, recalling his sister's instructions to keep his head down and not to do or say anything that would cause them to take a closer look at any of them. As he worked, he saw the options for the other drones nestled in the charging cradles on the roof of their transport turn grey as his ability to access them was withdrawn by Fly sitting behind him. He took a breath, steadied himself, and quelled the immediate urge to respond. All Fly wanted was to get a reaction from him, something he could run to a superior and cry treason over, but Jonah proved he was the more stable of the two and simply did the job given to him.

"Four up," he announced, banking the drone low and fast over the heads of the waiting officers and hiding the smirk when the images of them ducking away from it flashed over his display.

"Maintain safe follow," Fly ordered, as if Jonah had been sent there as his personal servant. Jonah didn't respond but he did do as he was told, watching the group of people marching over the bluff of higher ground as the walls of a facility came into view just ahead.

He saw it first as his proxy eyes were thirty feet higher up than the people on the ground studying the low walls and open gates with an eye for breaking into it. What he saw didn't fill him with any kind of confidence that a bunch of farmers, even augmented with a handful of real soldiers, could ward off an attack by Black and his robots.

He hovered his drone, scanning a quick three hundred and sixty degrees, seeing an icon flash up on his display to identify another drone. It was one from their transport, and the code told him nothing specific, but he knew it was an armed stealth drone following his own. That could only be Fly, watching what he was watching.

He said nothing, turning his remote-controlled attention back to the proceeding negotiation party, and lowered the drone to be able to eavesdrop more effectively.

He reached out with his left arm as if stretching, surreptitiously picking up an earpiece connected to his console, without betraying himself by turning to see if Fly was watching him. He stuck it in his ear and activated the audio feed to go along with the video.

———

"Here they come," a voice said beside Black, who had seen them coming out of the gate but said nothing as he didn't need anyone to point out the obvious.

"Stop on my word," he said to his small escort team. "Let these fuckers come to us."

They did. The others fanned out to the sides, making a show of leaving the talking to be done without an audience, but to anyone with a military basis in logic, it was clear that they were forming into ambush positions flanking the envoys.

"Inspector Black," a man in scruffy clothing and sporting an unkempt beard said in greeting.

"Former Minister," Black said in gruff response, setting out his stall early. Harvey smiled, conceding the first point to the visitor as if it didn't matter to him one bit.

"I'd assumed my position had been nullified," he told Black, still smiling, "but I see your standing has grown?" His eyebrows went up to match the small smile when he spoke, citing the new rank insignia on Black's uniform.

"I'm here to demand that you concede control of this facility to government forces," Black told Harvey. He spoke deadpan, as if he were simply conveying a message and didn't care much either way how it was received. His diffidence didn't confuse Harvey, who stuck to his guns.

"This facility is under the protection of an alliance we're forming. You've noticed that there are people moving back to the Citadel? Well, you see, we gave them a *democratic* choice of where to go and what to do."

"An alliance?" Black asked, smirking as if he'd just been threatened by a child with a toy gun.

"I'll happily share the details with an appropriate representative of government," Harvey said, heavily implying that an attack dog wasn't an appropriate envoy to send but playing along, nonetheless.

"You'll tell me," Black demanded, "or you'll answer in your trial." He shrugged again, conveying that it made no difference to him. "Or you won't."

Harvey's face dropped a little at the obvious death threat and he took a step closer, speaking in a serious tone.

"We aren't after a fight," he said, speaking more loudly as Black began to laugh. "But we *will* give you one if you insist. We're proposing peace."

"Peace?" Black retorted. "If I stole one of your towns, threatened to starve you out and choked off your supply routes, would you believe me if I told you I wanted peace?"

"That isn't what we're doing," Harvey began to say before reconsidering. "Okay, that's a little of what we're doing, but only to get your attention so that you took us seriously. We. Want. *Peace*. We want to trade you the food for other supplies we need out here – you have the manufacturing and we have the food. The north has the raw materials and we have the food. You understand this? We have the food!"

"So, this is just a shakedown? It's blackmail, you realise that?"

Harvey shook his head sadly. "It might be if we wanted something for nothing, but we want to trade, and the only cost is some reciprocal shipments and the ability to govern ourselves. Is that too much to ask?"

"What it looks like to me," Black said, "is that you wanted control of the Citadel for yourself and when the Prime Minister beat you in the election, you scurried off like a rat to find another way to be in charge."

"Is that what she thinks of me?" Harvey asked, anger flashing over his features as he took another step closer to Black. Guns were half raised and officers took defensive stances. Those stances were mirrored by Harvey's own people responding to the threat, but he was oblivious to how close they were to a bloodbath.

"You tell me now, Black, that Helen thinks this is me trying to get control."

"It's what *I* think," he snarled back. "And like it or not, I have orders to bring this to an end. The Citadel owns these facilities, the people inside them are subjects of the government, and I'm taking them back."

Harvey deflated in disappointment, which Black misread as him backing down.

"I'm sad you feel that way," he said. "Innocent people will be caught in the crossfire, but that's the way of revolution, isn't it? Weren't there martyrs throughout history?"

"Martyrs?" Black spat. "No, there are dead heroes and there is scum like you, profiting for personal gain off the back of other people dying for your personal vendetta." He raised his voice, speaking to the collection of civilians and former Party soldiers behind Harvey.

"You're all willing to die for his cause? You're willing to die to give him power over you?" He saw some of them shift their eyes uncomfortably, uncertain if they were on the right side of this just as he intended them to feel, but the majority were steadfast.

"It's not about who's in charge," one said vehemently. "It's about one slave master taking over from the last one." Black fixed the man with a cold gaze until he faltered.

"You're right. The Party treated you badly, and now this man—" he pointed at Harvey without looking at the man, "—wants to put you under his own heel so he can get one over on the woman who beat him in a fair election."

"I only ran to give options," Harvey argued. "And that was after Helen begged me to so that it appeared there was more than one choice of who to vote for. I never tried to become Prime Minister and he knows that. He's just trying to undermine your faith in what we're doing here."

"No," Black told him with a grin. "*This* is me undermining you…" he raised his voice so that all of them could hear his words. "Any person who reports to me in the next six hours will be pardoned for whatever part they played in this treason. Everyone else will be treated as a criminal and punished according to their crimes."

"You bastard," Harvey said. "You never came here to negotiate, you just came to threaten me and save face when you attack and kill innocent people like the last time."

"Innocent people? You mean the terrorists who fought us after we gave orders to lay down their weapons?"

"Twist it however you want," Harvey said. "We won't be threatened. We hold the cards, and if she's serious about negotiating with us, then tell her she needs to send someone with a vocabulary that includes something other than threats and violence. This isn't the old world anymore, Black. Just because they didn't find evidence to convict you for what you did for the Party, it doesn't mean they won't figure it out eventually."

Black smiled, seeming to enjoy the threats and the insults to his character.

"I think we have all we need here," he said, turning his back and walking away.

Harvey waited until he was out of sight before he relaxed.

"Tell everyone to get ready," he said. "They'll come in the night and try to take the facility back by force. You know what to do."

————

Jonah watched at distance from the drone he'd taken up to a higher altitude and zoomed in as much as was possible with the camera and directional microphone. He made out Harvey's last words, figuring that there was a nasty surprise waiting for Black's troops when they inevitably forced their way inside.

"What was that?" Fly asked, startling him.

"What was what?"

"What that traitor said?" Fly was leaning on the back of Jonah's chair and tipping it awkwardly as if trying to demonstrate his weight advantage.

"I didn't catch it," Jonah lied. "Too far away." Fly didn't press him, but demanded he create a short loop of video showing Harvey. He went back to his own console and manipulated the controls for his own drone. Jonah risked a look at the screen, seeing a zoomed view of Harvey and following him back to wherever he was going.

CHAPTER THIRTY-SIX

GHOST IN THE MACHINE

Like all good military commanders, Black knew that the most effective time to conduct covert military activities was during the darkest hours, but he was also highly aware of the risks they posed.

Detection at night was risky, and it went without saying that being caught skulking in the shadows behind enemy lines was a sure way of being shot at. It was also easy for a person to become confused, to get turned around and disorientated, and to open fire on their own side.

The choice of tools for the job was wide-ranging but abiding by the Prime Minister's wishes, he opted for the specialist, low-profile option. He took the tablet with the footage he'd requested from Fly, a man he considered a residual growth on his command, a sub-species who was raised in the underground tunnels like a wild rodent. Then he stepped inside another transport vehicle that was guarded by an entire squad of his people, all looking outwards.

"Briefing," he said to the sole occupant, who rose from her sitting position to stand in front of him. He tapped at the tablet and turned it around, showing it to the rigidly still form and speaking a single word.

"Target," he said, watching the flickering eyes dance over the footage she was being shown, memorising every facet of the target, down to the way he walked so she would be able to recognise him as a shadow moving in the darkness. Black replayed the footage twice more until he turned the tablet back around and opened another file.

"Target location," he said, showing aerial footage of the sprawling compound until that too played through and ended with a marked location. She watched that again and again, memorising the routes and alternatives to get her exactly to where she needed to be and accomplish exactly what she needed to achieve.

Black took the tablet away, telling her that she had five hours and needed to rest before deployment. She nodded, going back to rest and ignoring him entirely. Black smiled, liking that kind of brutal efficiency and the lack of attitude requiring him to second guess what people were thinking and what their own personal agendas were.

"If only I had a hundred of you," he said to himself as he stepped down from the transport.

———

"It's too soon," a woman told Harvey adamantly. "We can't fulfill that order yet, it's just not possible."

"Well, we have to send as much of it as possible," he said. "We need to show them that this is in their interest and that *we* are acting in good faith, even if they aren't."

"You want us to go without supplies instead?" the woman demanded.

"No, of course not, we just need to make this offering

to show we're more than good for our word. And they need to go via a route those soldiers aren't blocking."

"By pushing up a schedule by two weeks and working our people to the bone?" she asked. Harvey stopped and rubbed his face with his hands.

"You know what I'm trying to achieve here, don't you? You get that I'm trying to keep everyone free and stop those marauders from just bursting through the gates and killing everyone they see to send a message?" The woman deflated, flipping closed the cover on her rugged tablet and looking him in the eye before she answered.

"I understand all that," she said, "I just want to make sure that you understand we can't do this the next time. Or the time after that."

"I know," Harvey told her with a sad smile. "And hopefully we won't need to. The convoy going out should stop any attack on us now and buy us more time to actually negotiate and not have some rabid mongrel sent to intimidate us. This is the best way."

"If you say so," she told him. "If you're so close to the Prime Minister, why don't you just call her?"

"Believe me, I've tried," he answered tiredly. "Funnily enough, I can't seem to get through to her."

"Can't get through, or can't get her to believe you?"

"I can't even get to speak to her," he admitted.

"No harm in trying again…"

Harvey agreed, watching her rushing away to yell at someone for loading the wrong pallet of something or other onto the wrong transport truck. He was sure his plan would buy time at the very least, and at the best it would bring serious consideration to the negotiating table.

He expected something like what had happened, with Black turning up and stamping his foot like a spoilt child not getting his own way, and he knew that right now he'd be sending his recommendation to assault the complex immediately, so the idea to send the planned food shipment ahead of schedule was his best shot at sending a message to everyone.

If Helen was telling the people inside the Citadel anything, then receiving the food shipment would blow apart the reason for crushing what was being called treason.

He went to the small command office – not the former Party control centre but the transport hub where the planning of shipments was organised – and sequestered himself away in the communication room.

Keying in the correct authorisation codes, he tried to connect to the headquarters building and found himself cut off three attempts in a row. Sighing, he tried another way. When that met with a brick wall just as fast, he dropped his head onto the desk and groaned in exasperation.

The terminal beeped softly, making his head jerk upwards at the sight of a dialogue window popping open on the display and a word was typed out.

[Hello?]

"Who is this?" Harvey said aloud as he typed a response.

[Not important. You're trying to reach the PM]

Harvey frowned, wondering how whoever it was on the other end of the connection knew that.

"What if I am?" he asked, his fingers translating the spoken words into text.

[Record a video message. We can take it and send it.]

"How?" Harvey asked.

[Communication lines cut off. Accessing this terminal through remote data link. Record message now.]

Harvey hesitated, his eyes roaming over the display,

unable to find the icon he needed. He could almost feel the annoyance of the ghostly presence growing impatient at his delaying, as the cursor moved over the screen and activated the correct application to record video. His face filled half of the screen as the camera built into the terminal came to life.

He looked momentarily shocked at his own appearance, making a failed attempt to tame his unruly hair.

[Hair looks fine. Record message now.]

He tried not to feel anger towards the anonymous entity he felt was mocking him and instead, he took a steadying breath and tapped the trackpad to activate the recording software.

"This is a message for my friend, Helen, who I once saw as a brave leader of the Resistance. Helen, Prime Minister, I don't know if you're aware of what your people are planning to do but if you see this message and it isn't too late, *please* call them off."

He looked down, gathering his thoughts as he sighed and steadied himself to speak again.

"For everyone else who might not know, my name is Harvey. Until recently I was a member of the government, and before that a member of Command when we took back control from the Party and freed the people."

He sighed again, feeling his heart rate increase with the words coming to his lips next.

"I'm in an agricultural distribution centre in the west. We fled here after we were attacked and many of us were killed. And what was our crime? Treason. We're deemed traitors because we want to live our lives away from the Citadel, to be our own government, to be truly free."

He waited, letting those facts sink in for whoever might see the message.

"Right now, we're accused of holding the next scheduled shipment of food ransom to force the Citadel into meeting our demands. We are not. In fact, a few minutes ago the majority of that shipment left this facility headed for the Citadel as a show of good faith that we fully intend to uphold our end of the proposed agreement and not to stop the shipments of food. A senior military commander by the name of Black is orchestrating this to appear like we are the aggressors, when it was he who killed dozens of unarmed men, women and children. Their only crime was wanting to live free from his kind of oppression. We can't go back to how it was before, and unless we claim our freedom to choose, then we might as well never have tried to remove the Party from power."

He took a breath, getting the air back into his lungs as he'd realised he was in danger of getting carried away and angry.

"We want to live in peace, to govern ourselves far away from the Citadel but to remain allies and friends. We want to trade, to exchange food for goods manufactured inside the city walls... we are not your enemies, and your government has a responsibility to you. Helen, again, if you're seeing this, *you* have a responsibility to the people. Give them choice. Give them true democracy. Don't give them lies, and don't force their obedience through violence."

He hit the button to end the recording, barely able to remember most of what he'd just said.

[Nice] the dialogue box told him.

"What are you going to do with it?" he asked, not bothering to type the words as he now understood that he was being watched through the camera.

[Show everyone. Good luck.]

CHAPTER THIRTY-SEVEN

FEAR THE REAPER

Far away from where Harvey sat, Jenna unplugged the signal rerouting device from the port in the side of the terminal she was using, taking another small box with her that contained the message.

She picked a careful route out of the headquarters building after setting herself up in a quiet corner to test the software Mouse had left her with, trying to figure out what signals were being blocked and intercepted, when she happened across the third failed attempt from the same terminal address.

Satisfied with her subterfuge and certain that she had remained undetected, she slipped out of the building and turned a sharp left into the shadows just as the sound of tyres on damp concrete drifted her way. Whoever was driving was doing so hard, pushing the transport to its limits before braking hard outside the steps to the head-quarters building.

"Shit," she hissed to herself, drawing out the sound in annoyance at herself before she melted away, leaving the sight of a dozen armed soldiers responding to an incident that could only be the result of her network tampering. Her right hand clutched the small device holding the recording and she sped up, walking with her head down as any person caught out in poor weather would do after their work allocation had ended.

"You," yelled a voice in the obvious tone of someone in authority wanting their would-be victim to make it easy for them. "Stand still!"

Jenna didn't respond, didn't falter in her pace, but carried on aiming for the corner of the street just ten paces ahead. Boot steps rang out behind her, echoing between the buildings on either side of the road as the soldiers – *officers* – ran after her.

She stepped around the corner and pressed herself into the nearest recess so she could stuff the two pieces of hardware into the depths of her clothing and reached behind her back to grasp the hilt of the knife she habitually carried.

"Romeo two-three," came a voice from only feet away. "Suspect last seen on sixth heading east. Total loss."

Jenna heard no answer, not that she expected either of them not to be using an earpiece and held her breath as she imagined the search for her focusing on her location. She glanced around the street for a way out as the first of her pursuers stepped in front of her, weapon drawn, and turned the beam of light directly into her hiding spot.

She acted instinctively, spinning the sharp dagger in her hand to reverse her grip and bring the hilt up into the man's jaw with a loud crack. She ran before he fell, disappearing into the next alleyway to search desperately for a route underground where she felt safe from the prying eyes in the streets.

Lifting up a grate, she dropped recklessly into the sewer system to fall ten feet and land ankle deep in water before running hard ahead of her to put distance between her and the chase.

———

"You need to see this," Rebecca said as she woke Samaira from sleep.

"What is it?" she asked, sitting up and throwing on clothing as Rebecca tried not to marvel at the woman's figure.

"Message from Jenna in the Citadel," she answered, holding up a data stick and activating the terminal in the minister's quarters. Mouse arrived just then, fully clothed and red-eyed, likely from hours spent at another terminal, to take over and hit the keys with an inhuman speed to mask whatever Samaira was about to be shown from any potentially prying eyes.

"She sent it a few minutes ago, after she was chased by officers in the Citadel."

Samaira accepted that information quickly, saying nothing as she leaned over Mouse's shoulder to watch the video recording from Harvey in silence.

"Play it again," she asked, waiting as the footage was restarted.

"What do we do?" Rebecca asked, aware that she was supposed to know these things but feeling frightened and out of her depth.

"What can we do?" Samaira asked sadly. "If we get involved in any way, if we let on that we know that this message even exists, then we're traitors." She said nothing for a while, deep in thought before she turned to Mouse.

"I need to make a call," she said, wearing a look of resigned fear.

———

Reaper stepped down from the back of the transport to look around and get her bearings. She looked in the direction of the facility and glanced back at Black, who was designated to her as the handler for this mission. He gave her the permission to proceed and watched as the shadowy figure ran off into the darkness to do what she was designed and bred to do.

Getting into the compound was a simple task for her as the wall was low and mostly unguarded. Only one person patrolled near to where she infiltrated, and she remained so still that he didn't detect her even though he passed within feet of where she hid in the shadows.

Reaper didn't kill him, even though to do so would have been easier than breathing, because the mission was her sole objective and killing a guard before she'd achieved the desired outcome would jeopardise her chances of success.

She felt no emotion over it, no quickening of her heartbeat or breathing, only the cold logic of a killer intent on another victim.

When the coast was clear she moved, gliding silently between buildings and twice more adopting a hiding position when her senses alerted her to the movement of people. Eventually, not that the amount of time she'd been skulking behind enemy lines had an effect on her, she reached the building she had memorised by both appearance and location and perched on a low rooftop to watch.

She was shrouded by the shadow of a vertical stack protruding from the roof that hummed gently but gave off very little heat. She waited, checking for any routine movement of guards on patrol or any sign of other security measures, until the lights in the building went out to leave the inside as dark as it was out there for her.

She dropped lightly from the roof, stretching to her full height to ease the tension in her muscles, before walking softly across the track to the single storey building and stepping lightly around the walls to decide on the best way in. Opting for the single clasp on a large window, she slid a short blade under the lower ledge and levered it up and down slowly until she'd stressed the material enough to give the blade room to move. Resting the edge against the clasp, she gently tapped her free hand on the back of the blade to bump it millimetre by millimetre until the small clasp gave up and popped open.

Reaper withdrew, crouching low away from the window and holding the exposed knife ready to kill anyone responding to the small noises she'd made. When no investigation came, she stood, sheathed the knife and held open the window to slip inside like something from a nightmare.

CHAPTER THIRTY-EIGHT

THE TRUTH

"Yes, I'm well aware of the time," Samaira said with barely disguised anger at the obtusely annoying questions asked of her. "It's imperative that I speak to the Prime Minister immediately."

The silence on the other end of the line was only disturbed by footsteps fading away. There was a short conversation, the words of which couldn't be heard through her terminal, before the footsteps returned, sounding softer than before.

Samaira looked up at Rebecca and Mouse standing behind the terminal in her quarters so that nobody else could know they were there.

A light came on, bringing the screen before her to life and showing a room decorated in a grand if not gaudy fashion. Gold curtains hung fat over gilded ropes keeping them in a decorative position, and the furniture was all dark wood and rich green velvet or leather. It was hardly to her liking, she favoured the sharp, clean lines of straight edges and white wood, but she saw how it might appeal to Helen.

"Minister," Helen said tiredly, sitting down to reveal a face with bags under the eyes and hair uncommonly out of place. "It's late, so I can only assume there's a very good reason for this call."

Samaira played her part well, having dressed in the clothes she'd taken off earlier to give the impression she was still up from the previous day.

"It's urgent, Ma'am, I assure you. I'll cut right to the chase – do we have forces or operatives engaged in active missions involving a transport hub in the western outposts?"

Helen's face gave the resounding and obvious answer before her eyes narrowed and her expression grew suspicious.

"First, tell me how you know this."

"I'll take that as confirmation," Samaira said hurriedly. "Whatever is happening there, we need to call it off immediately. I've just received word from the counter-intelligence officers here that it's a trap. A traitor they were interrogating let some information slip that Citadel forces would be tricked into attacking a distribution facility. Prime Minister, I strongly urge you, if there is such a mission, we need to call it off immediately!"

"How reliable is this information?" she asked instead, not denying any hostile action against civilians.

"No way to be certain," she answered, remembering the rehearsed routine Rebecca had given her. "But I'm told the source corroborated certain events that he couldn't have known unless they were part of a pre-arranged plan. Whatever is going on, it's a deliberate ploy to destroy our forces."

Helen stared at the screen for a long time, making Samaira act as hard as she had when pretending to court the former Chairman's attentions.

"Is this traitor still under interrogation?"

"I'm afraid he succumbed to some kind of medical issue not long after giving this information," Samaira lied.

"I'll call you back," Helen said, killing the connection.

Samaira relaxed, leaning back in her chair and looking up at her two co-conspirators.

"That went well," Rebecca said. "They'll delay the attack at least, and that gives us time to find a way to show that video to everyone."

"And if it doesn't?" Samaira asked. "My cover story that you interrogated that out of someone only goes so far. We need to give them a plausible scapegoat and the body eventually."

"Not if this thing blows wide open," Mouse interjected, earning the full attention of both women. He looked down at the ground before speaking again. "I mean, if we can show the people that the government are abusing the basic rights of the people they claim to protect, people will want to subvert their authority, surely?"

"You're talking about another revolution not long after the last. People won't take well to that," Rebecca said.

"The issue here," Samaira cut in to prevent them from arguing, "is that we just bought Harvey and those people some time at best. At worst? Who knows?"

The terminal chimed to indicate an incoming call which ended their conversation. Samaira stood, walked away a few paces and rushed back so that when the connection was made, it appeared that she was returning to the terminal.

"Prime Minister," she greeted Helen's exhausted appearance.

"I'm bringing you in on this as it's highly likely similar incidents might occur elsewhere. You are, of course, aware that recently certain elements have been active in the west, resulting in the loss of a major agricultural facility falling into the hands of traitors. What you *won't* be aware of is that I sent another minister there to discuss their behaviour and demand that they return control to government forces. The man I sent to do that was Harvey, and to all intents and purposes, it appears that he has turned his back on legitimate government and decided to start his own cult following there."

Samaira tried desperately not to glance up and check the expressions of the others to see if it was as transparent to them how the information was being so effortlessly twisted in favour of what they all believed to be the aggressors.

"That facility was taken by force, but it has since come to light that many of those traitors had fled to another facility where they are currently holding food shipments ransom to their demands of effective cessation from the Citadel. I deployed a force to negotiate this and demand the return of that facility. However, I have just ordered a temporary stop on any direct action until this intelligence can be ratified."

Samaira made a convincing play of trying to fathom the information she'd just received, shaking her head before she spoke.

"Prime Minister, forgive me, that's an awful lot to take in…"

"I understand," Helen said without a trace of genuine understanding in her voice. "I need you to increase security levels at all northern outposts and advise on *any* hint of something similar happening there. Is that clear?"

"Absolutely, Ma'am, I'll get right on it."

"Good. I'll be in touch."

The screen went black again and Samaira let out a tense breath before looking up with a smile.

"She just confirmed everything, and there's no way she can't know what Black and his goon squad are up to. Mouse, can you send that video to every screen under Par — under government control?"

"Let me try," he said, unfurling his flexible keyboard and crowding Samaira on her chair until she stood to give him space to sit. He typed furiously, hissing and huffing as he worked until giving up with an exasperated noise.

"Not from here, no," he said angrily. "Data transfers have all been clamped down on, so the only way it can be done is through direct access. I can play it to this facility and any others that use it as their main access point to the Citadel mainframe, but as for showing the city? No."

"Jenna," Rebecca said. "She can do it, though?"

"She'll have to access the mainframe, but yes."

"Do it," Samaira said. "And let Jenna know to do the same."

———

"Chief Inspector?" a voice asked nervously.

"What is it?" Black snarled back into the darkness ahead of their stalled convoy.

"Urgent communication, Sir, it's the Prime Minister." Black growled and spun on his heel, eager for the time to attack and hoping that he wasn't about to be given orders to stand down. He climbed in the back of the command and control transport and snatched the receiver from a terrified operator.

"Black," he barked. "Send message."

"Chief Inspector, it's the Prime Minister," the voice on the other end told him, making him feel a smug satisfaction that *she* was on hold waiting for *him*. "I'm giving the order to delay any hostile action at that facility. Is that clear?"

"Sorry," Black said. "You broke up… it sounded as though you ordered me not to conduct the attack as planned."

"Yes. I've just received vital information from the interrogation of a suspected traitor regarding that facility. We have reason to believe that the entire thing is a trap designed to lure government forces into attacking, so we are pulling the plug on the mission until we've learned more."

"Negative," Black told her disrespectfully, "assets already committed and assault imminent."

"Chief Inspector, I'm not sure you heard me correctly," Helen said sweetly before turning on the snarl in her voice and dialling up the intensity, "I told you to *stand the fuck down, now!*"

Black hesitated, gripping the receiver in his gloved hand so tightly that he came close to cracking the plastic before abruptly bringing it back to his mouth and speaking in the clipped, professional tone of a man accustomed to radio use.

"All understood, thank you, Prime Minister. Out."

Instead of handing back the receiver, he threw it angrily against the radio set, making the young operator flinch away as if fearing he would be the man's next target.

"Keenan?" he yelled, waiting for his second in command to scurry from the darkness to report to him. "Stand the team down."

"Sir?" Keenan asked reflexively, wishing he'd kept his mouth shut a half second later as Black turned on him with a fury that terrified him.

"Stand the fucking team down, I said. Are you deaf? Do you need me to clean your ears out with my fucking sidearm?"

"N...no sir," Keenan stammered, backing away from the threat.

He turned to give orders as Black walked away, pulling out a radio not connected to the net any of his other officers were using and spoke into it.

"If you haven't done it already, kill the target right now."

CHAPTER THIRTY-NINE

FATE

"What do you mean you're going?" Eve asked, struggling to sit up in the bed that was actually the right size for her small frame. Mark sat on a stool beside the girl who was healing far faster than even he'd expected after witnessing more than one medical miracle performed by the Nocturnals using nothing but mud and herbs.

"I mean I'm not welcome here. The King is over the sea, Adam and Dren are nowhere to be found and the man in charge here has no love for our kind."

"So what? You're just going to walk back into a fight you can't win?"

Mark shrugged, admitting to himself that he didn't know what to do, only that he had to do something.

"What about me?" she asked. Her tone bore something bordering on an accusation and her eyes bored into him in the dim light of her chamber. Mark sighed, unsure how to say what he wanted to say.

"Just spit it out," she said, recognising his indecision.

"Go home," he told her. "Forget about the Citadel and just live your life like you wanted to before you got dragged back into it all. You've done more than almost anyone, sacrificed too much of your life already."

Eve slumped back a little, still staring through him.

"Why do you care?"

"Because... because I don't want you to get hurt. Or worse. I don't want to lose anyone else."

"You mean Adam?" Mark looked annoyed for a moment, his features flashing angry before he controlled himself.

"No, he went his own way and I... and I always knew he would. You should... you shouldn't have to make any hard decisions like that because you've done more than enough."

"Did you ever have children?" she asked, shocking him with the small leap in their conversation.

"No, I... I wanted to once, but she..."

"She died," Eve finished, assuming the worst, given the collectively depressing past they all shared.

"What? No! She... she chose someone else."

Eve's brow furrowed as she reorganised her thoughts and leapt to the next conclusion.

"So, you took on Adam to train him as the next best thing?" Mark nodded slowly.

"So, yes, I'm upset he isn't here anymore, and you can see why I don't want you involved either. I... I care about you, Eve. Cohen did too, in place of having her own children—"

"What?" Mark stopped talking, mouth hanging open as he tried to think of what to say next and how to say it.

"She chose not to have children," he told her. "She said you were her responsibility and that you – what you needed and what you'd become – were more important."

Eve's mind swirled. It spun with guilt and responsibility

and the pain of loss and tears threatened to come before she sniffed and rubbed her eyes dry.

"And she's dead because of me," she answered sullenly. "She died in front of me, *because* of me."

"You can think about it that way if you want to," Mark told her kindly. "Or you can believe that she gave her life willingly for you, just like any mother would."

Eve scoffed at the mention of her mother, conjuring visions of a selfish woman who didn't want her. She was angry, upset and she was in pain, both in her heart and her body. To know that she was being offered a chance to walk away from the fight and step down because she'd apparently already done enough stung her, and it did so because she felt responsible for starting this whole new episode in their tortured history.

"If you want to go and leave me, just go," she said, choosing to push him away rather than admit her feelings. She knew he'd already made up his mind anyway, and her imagination ran riot, thinking that he was hoping to throw his life away in the hope that when Adam eventually returned, that he'd learn of his mentor's fate and avenge his death, bringing down the full might of the Nocturnals with him, courtesy of his lethal partner.

Mark stood, leaning down to gently plant a light kiss on her forehead, and left the room.

He went to Helghor, who waited for him nearby, equipping himself with provisions for the journey and thanking the man who had helped him when the majority of his people saw Mark as an unwelcome guest with no place in their underground world.

"You are sure of this?" Helghor asked.

"I am," Mark told him as the shorter man led him above ground to where the spoils of war sat in storage. When the Nocturnals swarmed the Frontier, at the same time the Dearmad and the Nua stormed the defences in the west and the north, they had captured significant amounts of Party hardware which Mark now needed.

He took guns, which he knew intricately and was able to use courtesy of the chip still implanted in his neck, which Mouse had upgraded to allow him to access almost everything under government control. He started up a transport which was kept charged thanks to the ingenious way the Nocturnals harnessed the power of the coastal waters to generate electricity.

"You are sure I cannot convince you to stay here? To wait out this conflict until the *Myghtern* comes home?" Mark sighed with deep resignation.

"I don't even think he'd side with me on this," he told Helghor. "But if Adam does come back, please tell him what happened and where I went. He'll know what to do."

The two men shook hands solemnly, and Mark started the transport to head north and face all of his responsibilities at once.

———

Reaper slipped back through the shadows to the spot on the road where Black's entire team was loaded up ready to head east. She said nothing, as none of them there even knew she was capable of speech, but when Black demanded her report, she showed him the dried blood on the exposed fingertips of her hands and watched him smile and nod in satisfaction.

He gave the orders, stepping up into the front passenger seat of the second vehicle in line, and didn't lose that small smile of satisfaction for miles.

When the lead vehicle reported an obstruction ahead, the smile dropped. He snatched up the radio handset and demanded to know what it was, then the smile returned at the report.

"Overtake it and force a stop," he ordered. "All units prepare to deploy against the convoy. I want all enemy personnel taken out without hesitation."

"But… Sir…" the same hesitant sergeant who had spoken out of turn before their mission cut in. "We can't know if they're hostile or n—"

"Consider *all* personnel hostile," Black said angrily. "Deploy!"

The convoy of transports sped past the lumbering caterpillar of four heavily laden trucks, forcing them to brake and stop or hit the government transport vehicles. They were all volunteers, all of them fully committed to what Harvey was trying to achieve on their behalf, and all of them felt safe in the belief that they were non-combatants and hence would be spared the violence visited on the others who fought back in the other facility.

Armed men and women swarmed from the transports to point weapons at the drivers sitting high in their cabs. They raised their arms, each experiencing varied levels of fear but all of them certain that their payloads would be searched, and their journey to the Citadel would be resumed.

None of them expected the barrels of those guns to flash brightly, sparking off a chain reaction event of everyone pulling their triggers to riddle the glass of their windows and drill the projectiles through their bodies.

The entire one-sided, bloody ambush was over in seconds, leaving only one person shouting.

"Cease fire!" screamed the sergeant who had questioned Black's orders for the last time. "Cease fucking fire, you bastards!"

Black snatched his gun up into his shoulder, eager to

satisfy his bloodlust after being denied the chance to wipe out the facility and fired three fast rounds from the weapon into the sergeant. All three hit him hard in the chest and slammed him down to the ground on his back, where he lay looking as if he didn't understand what had happened, gasping for air as his hands fluttered feebly at the body armour that had saved his life.

"I told you to get onboard," he snarled, looming over the man before raising his voice so that every one of his people could hear him. "We all know the penalty for treason," he yelled, glancing around him to make sure he had the full attention of his audience before spinning back to the downed man and firing a single round into his face.

Jonah watched, mouth open and hands shaking with rage as the bastard executed the innocent drivers before killing his own man for trying to stop it. He slipped out of the transport, drifting through the standing soldiers like the shadow he had been raised to be, and angled his approach to Black from behind.

He knew it would be the end of him, but he was okay with that if it meant stopping this murderous piece of shit from taking even one more life to get the war he wanted.

The knife slid from under his jacket silently and he drew back his right hand to shoot a straight thrust of the blade through the small patch of exposed skin above the man's collar and below the line of his helmet. He tensed, summoning all of his strength to strike the fatal blow and make it count, when suddenly the power melted away from the hand as if the supply was cut.

It had been. And it had been done by Fly, who had stalked Jonah from the transport and waited for the perfect time to reach forwards and run his own blade across the wrist to cut blood vessels and tendons alike.

Jonah gasped, dropping the knife and clutching at his

bleeding wrist as Black turned and made direct eye contact with him.

Pain exploded low down on the right side of his back as Fly, ever the jealous, angry coward, drove his knife upwards between Jonah's ribs to pierce his heart.

As he fell, first dropping to his knees before slamming forwards to thump his lifeless body onto the roadway, Fly smiled at Black and tried to sound strong.

"I've got your back, Sir," he said, earning the first look of approval he'd ever received from the man.

CHAPTER FORTY

BACK UNDERGROUND

Jenna stopped running, feeling a tightening in her chest which she attributed to the desperate running as she bumped into pipes and fallen debris in the dark tunnels. She gasped, worried why she couldn't catch her breath, and felt tears sting her eyes without any reason she could understand.

She forced herself upright, pushing further through the underground maze until she could get her bearings and double back to their refuge. She couldn't understand why she was short of breath, why her chest felt as though someone were standing on it and grinding their boot into her body.

Eventually reaching their hidden haven, she collapsed into the chair Mouse habitually occupied and sucked in air. She gasped, fighting panic and tears like a distraught child unable to comprehend why they couldn't have their own way.

She told herself it was just her body's natural reaction to fear. She told herself it was an excess of adrenaline combining with her emotional state. She told herself it was okay, that she was safe for now, and she didn't believe anything she said.

She collapsed forwards onto the desk and let out a sob, still unable to control her breathing, and nudged the keyboard to wake up the terminal. Her attention was drawn away from her body by the dull flashing dialogue box similar to the one she'd used to communicate with Harvey. She gasped, knowing it could only be one of a few people on the other end of the connection because it was a method used by Mouse to bypass the communications network.

[System upgrade available] the text read. [Please sign in to proceed]

She entered details that would identify her to anyone watching on the other end and waited.

She waited for minutes with no response until the dialogue box disappeared and a text notepad function appeared. Mouse – it *had* to be Mouse – was remotely accessing the terminal at the same time.

"You got away safely?" he asked her.

"Just about," she told him. "Pretty sure I'm burned now though. Can we get word to him?"

Mouse didn't need to ask who 'he' was.

"Tried already," he answered. "Not connected. Diagnostic request sent. Waiting."

Jenna swore and banged the table, fearful that her actions had placed her brother in danger when she was trying to save people by doing it. She thought before typing again.

"What now?"

"You need to access the Citadel mainframe," came the response. "Upload that footage and stay hidden." She racked her brain for the best place to do that. Accessing the mainframe with a direct hardware connection would entail breaking into a primary server, and there were only a few of those not inside the Citadel. Mouse must have anticipated her logic.

"Head north," he told her. "Grid eight-three."

"Communications hub," she said aloud, not bothering to type her response as he knew precisely where he was sending her.

"Understood," she said as she tapped out the words in reply.

"Behind you," Mouse wrote back. "In the metal cabinet."

Jenna rose, glancing back at the small screen as if an explanation might appear there. Turning back, she opened the stiff door and forced the neglected hinges to open, revealing a tumble of sheer, black material hanging limply on a hook. She took it down, finding one of the few, precious suits reserved for the silent killers of their last campaign that she naively thought was over months ago.

She was a little taller and heavier than Eve, but the suit would fit her well enough. Behind the suit was a selection of weapons, each of them higher quality that the utilitarian dagger she carried daily, and she tried them out until she found the right combination for her desires.

Selecting a long, needle pointed blade, she fixed the sheath into the elasticated folds designed to allow the wearer to choose variable ways of carrying their tools. As a backup weapon, she chose one of the short, curved weapons that were part knuckleduster and part surgical steel. It wasn't that she anticipated engaging in hand to hand combat, more that she'd be happier knowing she was equipped for it, should that happen.

She stripped off her layers of clothing and slipped her feet into the suit, finding that it both fit her better than she'd expected and was far warmer, courtesy of whatever material was used to create it. She tied her hair back, having grown it longer in the days since they overthrew the Party, and tucked it into the hood, which she pulled up to cover her head.

"Thank you," she typed, sitting back in front of the terminal.

"Go now," Mouse told her. "Stay underground as much as possible."

She went, snaking her way through the underground labyrinth with only a fraction of the memory capacity Mouse possessed to guide her. She spent hours making her way slowly in the right direction only to find her route blocked by numerous, intentional, tunnel blockages where the wide grates above ground had been opened and rubble tipped inside and covered with tonnes of poured concrete to make any removal of the obstruction either too noisy or too difficult to achieve quickly or quietly.

It was almost as though the new government had learned from the way they had undermined the dominance of the Party and were eager to prevent anyone else using the same roadmap to their downfall.

Twice she risked peering through a grate at street level, willing to risk the open air for a chance to move faster, only to find herself even more frustrated as it seemed every person in a uniform had been turned out onto the streets to patrol.

Her fear and paranoia told her it was all for her, but as there was no other logical explanation for the increased activity, she had to believe it was for her. She went back underground, fearful that she was taking too long as the sun was already beginning to rise the last time she'd poked her head up to check.

———

Black returned at daybreak, riding in the lead vehicle of the convoy ahead of the laden trucks riddled with bullet holes and stained with the drying blood of the innocent drivers.

He sent his orders ahead by radio, demanding a small fleet of video surveillance drones to record their triumphant return to the Citadel and climbed out of the transport to bound up the steps and turn to address his small army.

"Brave, loyal citizens," he yelled. "We have been betrayed further by the traitors in the west. You won't know this, but last week we took back control of a facility where this *scum* was planning to overthrow the government and hold our food supply as ransom to meet their demands that we relinquish full control to them and their dictators."

He paused for effect, scanning the faces looking up at him and focusing on appearing like the strong leader they all needed.

"Indecision, capitulation, *weakness* allowed them to take a foothold which we shattered last night. They promised good faith, but instead they tried to betray us again and kill innocent people. These trucks…" he pointed, waiting for some of the drones to turn and swarm over the trucks to show the carnage which Black twisted into his success instead of his barbarism.

"…These trucks were sent to the Citadel, purportedly filled with food supplies, but instead we found that they'd filled the back of one with explosives intended to destroy the gates and open the way for them to invade."

He took two steps down, looking over his people before fixing the drone nearest him with a stern look.

"We want a peaceful existence without the constant threat of attack. We need to unite, to show strength against the terrorists, and we must show it now. That is why I will be calling for a general election, and I, Arthur Black, Chief Inspector of the Citadel Defence Force, will be running for Prime Minister."

He turned and walked away, heading directly into the headquarters building and through security to scan his eye against the reader on the elevator and hit the button for the command floor.

CHAPTER FORTY-ONE

POWER

"Prime Minister," Helen's senior aide said as he walked into her residence to find her dressed in a robe sipping from a teacup. She appeared startled but said nothing as the man's demeanour spoke clear volumes about the seriousness of his intrusion. "You need to see this," he said, picking up the remote and pressing buttons until the news was displayed on screen.

Helen's expression froze as she watched the man she had so recently promoted give an impassioned speech about strength and weakness, reading the clear subtext that her leadership was weak, whereas his was strong.

"How dare he?" she snarled, dropping the cup into the sink and marching to her bedroom to get dressed. She appeared minutes later wearing a black suit and blue blouse beneath, pausing only to snap at the aide to follow her.

She continued that power stride directly to her offices where her secretary rose from behind her desk in the outer office and tried to stop her before she opened the double doors and found a sight that enraged her further.

Black was sitting at her desk, his muddy boots resting on the polished wood and wearing a smug smile of arrogant victory.

"You bastard," she snapped at him, glaring from his face to his boots and back again. He didn't flinch from her anger, nor did he remove his feet from her desk.

"Madam Prime Minister," he said in a voice dripping with false deference.

"What the hell are you thinking? You know you can't call for an election, don't you?"

"Not technically," Black answered, "but think of how it will look when you refuse to allow one on such a technicality. The *people* want an election, who are we to deny them their democratic rights?"

"The people will only want an election because you *told* them there would be one!" Black shrugged nonchalantly.

"Maybe, but what's done is done, wouldn't you say? Aww, come on, afraid you won't win a rigged vote like you did the last time?"

"It wasn't rigged," she bit back reflexively. "And what you're doing is illegal."

"So, by all means address the public and tell them that," Black told her with a smile. "While you're at it, why don't you tell them about what happened in the west? Maybe explain that people are trying to attack their new way of life and all *you* did was nothing?"

"That's not true. I sent you there to—"

"Exactly," Black snarled, launching out of her seat so fast she recoiled two whole paces in fear. "You sent *me*. *I'm* the one who is fixing these problems, and you're doing nothing."

"You won't get away with this," she told him as he

walked towards the door. Black hesitated, one hand on the doorknob.

"Said every person on the losing side ever," he answered. "Do yourself a favour and call the election. I might keep you around afterwards if you make it easy." He smiled wolfishly, walking out and leaving the door open. Helen waited until the sound of his footsteps echoed into silence, only then did her aide and secretary poke their heads around the door.

"Prime Minister?" the aide asked, hopeful that she would know what to tell him to do.

"I need communications to Minister Nadeem in the north and Harvey." The aide paused, mouth hanging open and shooting a desperate glance at the secretary.

"Ma'am... the communications network has been compromised. You were informed of that last night?"

"I most certainly was *not* informed of that! When? How?"

"The duty officer said they'd contacted y—"

"Not how did I know, how is it compromised?"

"It seems that... that..." the aide stammered.

"Oh, for God's sake man, tell me!"

"Well, it appears there was unauthorised communication with the distribution facility just prior to you calling off the attack."

"I..." Helen was lost for words, so she shook her head to clear it. "I wouldn't have called anything off had I known that was going on. Let me guess, the person who said they'd informed me works for *him*?" she pointed a finger angrily in the direction of the corridor where Black had gone. The aide looked at the secretary again, as if she could save him.

Helen made a noise of exasperation and stomped behind her desk, sitting down heavily before brushing the dried mud off the polished wood, as if livid that the man left a trace of himself everywhere.

"Ma'am, I suggest w—"

"Leave me!" she barked, cutting him off and waiting until the doors closed behind the fleeing man before she dropped her head into her hands and cried.

———

Black went public again an hour later, as if the man didn't need to sleep. He told the public how the Prime Minister had agreed to call the election, forcing her hand in either capitulating or outright calling him a traitor.

He didn't think she would do that, not after she realised that every troop leader in the city was suddenly too busy to return her calls or was absent from the offices she walked into, desperately searching for anyone brave enough to arrest him.

He spoke grandly, explaining his vision of a strong and stable government which would protect the people and refuse to allow any terrorist threat to endanger their peaceful way of life after crawling out from under the cruel boot heel of the Party.

Those who knew, those of his officers and troops who, like him, were guilty of many crimes that couldn't be attributed to them, knew that he'd been on the verge of breaking through the upper ceiling of middle rank and gaining a foothold in the Party leadership through military competence. He was lucky that none of his deeds were attributed to him by name, instead his actions which the now dead Chairman considered to be his successes were chalked up against the city's quick reaction force.

He played his hand well, spending months making himself invaluable to the new government, which he considered to be nothing but unqualified peasants elevated to positions of power by other desperate, witless peasants, and one of his finest coups was the removal of two women who had the uncanny ability to see directly through his façade.

Secretly, without any authorisation other than his own, he dispatched a convoy of trusted troops north to deal with that future threat once and for all.

CHAPTER FORTY-TWO

THE SET PATH

Mark made it to the junction where the northern road from what used to be the Frontier offered him options left and right. Right, to the east, led him directly to the Citadel, where the best reaction he could expect was imprisonment and interrogation for desertion, and the worst case would be a bullet to the skull on sight.

To the left, heading west, lay the distribution facility where the equipment loaded into the back of his troop transport could be put to good use against the government forces who were, in his eyes at least, far worse than the Party he had once been a member of and had turned on to fight against.

Before he reached the facility, something on the roadway ahead of him caught his eye. He stopped, climbing out and shouldering the rifle to scan all around him, before approaching the unexpected source of light reflection to find evidence littered all over the ground that told an obvious story to anyone with an eye for such details.

Pebbles of safety glass lay strewn in patches on the

road's surface, and all around him were scatterings of dull brass which he took as the unmistakable signs of a fight so one-sided that it might as well have been an execution.

Looking all around him again, he took in the scale of the scene, counting up what seemed to be four distinct ambush sites all in close proximity.

At the last one, much to his horror but offering little in the way of surprise, he found the four bodies of men, civilians, who were so riddled with bullets that his imagined analogy of the firing squad might have been a reality.

"Bastards," he grumbled to himself, lowering the rifle and walking fast back to his transport to get to the facility, hoping he wouldn't find it a smoking ruin littered with the bodies of more men and women, the victims of ambition and a desire for freedom.

"Who are they kidding?" Mark asked himself as he drove hard, recklessly almost, towards the gates ahead.

He was met by armed guards, all but a few of them holding their weapons uncertainly as though they'd been shown the bare basics of how to handle one but lacked the years of muscle memory that made holding such a destructive thing seem natural. Their fear of the weapons, of themselves, was obvious to him.

The few who possessed that natural look eyed him cautiously; too disciplined to open fire but trained well enough to be ready to if he gave them the slightest provocation.

He got out, hands away from his body and opting to leave the rifle inside the cab where it couldn't be misconstrued as a ready threat to them.

"I'm Mark," he said. "I was with Harvey at the last facility, and the one before, for that matter…"

"Driving that?" a woman asked, hatred in her words and showing on her face. Mark turned, not for the first time seeing the Party emblem stencilled on the front doors of the transport, as though he'd resurrected some old enemy to haunt them.

"I picked it up on the old Frontier," he explained, realising that the truth sounded implausible. "I've been with the Nocturnals asking for their help."

"And are they coming?" a voice asked from behind the armed guards. They parted to allow a woman through, one that Mark recognised as being an aide to Harvey from before. She'd come from the Citadel with him, and like half of his people – Mark included – had decided to stay and fight the good fight.

"No," he admitted. "I need to speak to Harve—"

"Where's the girl?" she demanded. Mark saw that her eyes were puffy and bloodshot then, knowing that what he saw on the roadside was just the beginning.

"She's hurt. She's still with the N—"

"Bullshit," the woman spat, chin quivering now with either anger or upset. "I'll ask you again, where is the girl?"

"You mean Eve, right? I told you, she's with th—"

"Take him into custody," she barked, standing tall as half a dozen of the militia rushed him. He let the first one come, slapping aside the barrel of the rifle as it came too close inside his reach and hitting it onto the bridge of another's nose. He dropped, turned his body sideways and launched all of his weight into an elbow driven into the gut of the one whose rifle he'd knocked aside before standing and stamping a kick out into the chest of another.

A woman – he could tell buy the grunt of effort and anger – jumped on his back to try and claw at his eyes, so he took two long paces backwards to slam what he guessed was her lower back into the front of the transport to make her fall away, screaming in pain.

Another went for him, swinging the rifle like a club as

though a hand tool was more natural in his hands than a gun, and Mark ducked the wild swing easily to rise up and deliver a brutal punch which he unleashed into the soft part of the body where the liver sat.

That man fell like he'd been shot in the head, leaving only two others to face him.

These two were the ones who held their rifles in a manner that made him believe they knew how to use them. They stood out of reach, both of them staggering their approach so even if he did manage to draw a weapon and shoot one of them before they could shoot him, then the other would have all the time in the world to take him out.

He stopped, standing tall and holding his hands up again.

"I'm not your fucking enemy," he huffed, short of breath after the explosive burst of power needed to free himself from the ragged attack. "Back there, on the road, *they're* your enemy. The bastards who killed four civilians in an ambush sometime last night."

The woman calling the shots looked shocked, even lifting a hand to her mouth as she looked from left to right, as if expecting there to be someone beside her to reassure her that what Mark said wasn't true.

"Go and check if you don't believe me," he said, hoping to capitalise on her stalled momentum. "If not, I need to see Harvey right now."

"Harvey's dead," she told him. Mark blinked, taking his turn to be shocked into being speechless.

"He's what? How? When?"

"Last night. He went to bed, and when he didn't get up this morning, I went to check on him and... and found him..." she faltered, her chin quivering again only more forcefully than before.

"I need to see him," Mark said.

"Why?" one of the men holding a rifle trained on his chest demanded. "To see if your little pet did her job again? Just like she did on Horrocks?"

"Listen, Eve didn't do anything. She's in a hospital bed after nearly dying becau—"

"Save it," the guard snapped, tightening the grip on his gun as if wanting to shoot him just so that he stopped talking and disagreeing with them.

Mark turned his attention back to the woman and tried again. "I *need* to see him. If you think it was Eve then you're dead wrong, but if it *looks* like it was Eve, then it can only have been a few others…"

"Bring him," she said, turning on her heel as the sidearm was pulled from his holster and inspected before being tucked into the back of a man's belt; a man who eyed him acidly past the blood running from the split skin of his nose.

———

The scene was undisturbed, not for any need to preserve evidence, but for the fact that nobody knew what to do about it and so they'd locked the door and posted a guard.

"It was still locked from the inside," the woman told him. "We had to break the door down to get in when he didn't answer."

"Old mechanical lock?" he asked. "Key still on the inside?" She nodded an affirmative to each question and Mark stepped inside, following his nose towards the acrid tang of dried blood which, if his senses weren't fooling him, came from a *lot* of blood.

He wasn't wrong. Harvey lay on his back on the bed, spread-eagled as though he'd fallen there from a great height, and his throat was cut through so cleanly that the ice-white skin barely contrasted with the exposed tubes and bones of his neck which were laid partially bare by the savagery of the cut.

"I can tell you for certain that Eve didn't do this," he said again, quieter this time. "Because she's still in the south west. But I can see why you suspected it might be her."

"Because that's her style, right? Sneak in when it's dark and slice people open?"

Mark shook his head sadly to disagree with her.

"What Eve did at the last place was… she thought she was doing the right thing. Just like when she killed the Chairman." The reminder of what they all owed Eve went a tiny way towards helping his case, but he knew he still had some convincing to do.

"So, who did this then?"

Mark surveyed the room, noting the raised window latch and inspecting it, finding small blade impressions.

"This window was jemmied open from the outside. Whoever did it climbed in and…" he gestured at the body on the bed, still with its eyes open wide to stare lifelessly at the ceiling.

"Other than Eve, there are only a few people I know with these kinds of skills – to get in and out undetected after doing something like this."

"And you can vouch for all of them, I suppose?"

"All but one," Mark said. "And that one isn't like any of my people."

"You need to see this!" a voice yelled from out in the other room. They ran in after exchanging a look to find the screen on and playing a video of the man lying dead in the bedroom behind them.

CHAPTER FORTY-THREE

THE TRUTH WILL SET YOU FREE

Jenna waited for hours, watching through a storm drain with only millimetres of space either side of her head between the concrete and steel, until the activity surrounding the communications relay lessened and the nearby klaxon sounded to indicate a shift change in a nearby factory unit.

She retreated three streets before climbing up to street level and pulling on a hooded coat to cover her appearance, then began walking with the resigned shuffle of a worker in between shifts, using the cover of human traffic to mask her approach on the last leg that couldn't be achieved underground.

She walked with the flow, blending into invisibility easily but feeling exposed and terrified inside, before ducking out of the path of people and into an alleyway.

She shrugged out of the coat, standing tall and breaking into a run to hop up and grab the vertical waste pipe running down the side of the building to shimmy up it as easily as the workers in the street below were putting one foot in front of the other.

She was no Eve, and she was no Mouse, but that didn't stop her being a formidable weapon of espionage and secret lethality in her own right.

For years she had been on the sidelines, standing guard for others or carrying their bags, when she felt just as capable as they were to conduct most missions. She reached the roof, rolling up and over the edge, only to find herself looking at two approaching drones flying on a preset search pattern, and she panicked, recalling in time to tuck herself into a ball with her face turned down in the shadow of an industrial vent until they completed their pass.

She waited until the sound had faded into the distance before uncoiling and running low over the rooftop to a skylight she began to silently pry open after checking for any wires or other indication that it was alarmed.

Lifting it slowly, trying to avoid the seized hinges making any sound, she lowered herself down and found footing on the pipes bolted to the structure to slip inside.

———

"We've received orders," Mouse announced. "From Black, demanding our return to the Citadel immediately."

Rebecca looked up, catching Samaira's eye as Mouse didn't look up. The two women exchanged fearful looks, both understanding that the orders, and more specifically, the origin of those orders didn't bode well.

"Does it say anything about the current tasking?" Rebecca asked.

"No, which tells me plenty about why we were sent here in the first place," he told her.

"Like it was a bullshit reason to get you out of the Citadel while he did something," Samaira said.

"There's more," Mouse told them, eyes flickering over the screen and widening in horror. He made a choking noise and turned away from the screen, suddenly panting for breath.

"What?" Rebecca asked. "What is it?"

Mouse couldn't speak. He turned away from the screen and stood, staggering a few paces away and stopping before his knees gave way and he sank to the ground.

Rebecca moved around to read the communication, gasping aloud as Samaira joined her.

It read briefly, demanding their return to the Citadel immediately, going on to explain that Jenna was now a wanted terrorism suspect following unlawful communications activity, and that Jonah had been killed by the terrorists occupying the western distribution facility. It added that an escort detail was already inbound to bring them back safely.

They read it again, still in shock, with tears in their eyes. Behind them Mouse wept quietly, having lost one of the closest people to him he had ever known.

"*He* did this," Rebecca snarled through tears and gritted teeth. "And there's no way he's going to let us live. This is him taking control, and what are the chances of us getting back to the Citadel alive?"

Samaira had picked up her own tablet after reading the message a third time, tapping on the screen and confirming her suspicions.

"You're right," she told her. "I've got a ministerial bulleting calling a general election with Black as a candidate."

The room was silent for long seconds as they all tried to take it in.

"He's going to take it back to how it was," Rebecca

said. "And we're all in the way, just like everyone else in the Resistance... *shit!*"

"What?" Samaira asked.

"The Resistance. My covert operatives. He'll have access to all of them now."

"So what do we do?" Mouse asked, looking up at them in turn.

Rebecca stared hard at Samaira, the idea forming into words in her head.

"We join the others," she said firmly. "We play that video, we join them, and we deal with Black."

Samaira nodded, accepting her plan before adding her own advice.

"We need to make it look as though we're complying. Send an acknowledgment, and when that escort arrives, we take them prisoner." She moved to her wardrobe and began changing her clothes, as unashamed of her body as she always was.

"What are you doing? Rebecca asked.

"I'm going to address the facilities in the north and tell them that the Citadel is under the control of the Party and ask for their help."

"You think they'd do that?" Mouse asked, earning a smile from the woman as he sat back at the terminal and began rattling at the keys to send the video out as a prerequisite to Samaira's call to arms.

"Mouse, it's taken me months to get them to accept that there was a new government in the first place. Given the chance to rebel, they'll be queueing up to fight."

———

Jenna slid between the server stacks like a shadow, searching for what she needed until she discovered the specific panel required to complete her task. Folding up the rugged screen on the terminal built into the system, she used generic access codes courtesy of Mouse and memorised through repetition, and then pulled out the two devices required to make it work how she wanted.

First, connecting the box of tricks that allowed her to broadcast through the data lines instead of via communications, she tapped at the keys far more slowly than her northern counterpart, and when she'd established a link ready to transmit, she plugged in the data stick containing the video and readied it to play.

Wish a steadying sigh, she hit the return key and watched as Pandora's box was opened.

CHAPTER FORTY-FOUR

RESPONSIBILITY

Eve rose and stretched, feeling better than she had done in as many days as she could recall. It was odd, she thought, that despite her issues with being contained after her detention as a prisoner and spending almost her entire life underground through necessity, that she'd feel comfortable being denied sunlight.

Living alone in quiet peace had entailed at least a few hours each day outside, exposed to the elements in whatever weather, but somehow being with the Nocturnals was peaceful and cosy instead of cold and dark.

She was healing, far better than with the drugs she'd been given after she was injured, and she felt her strength returning with each minute. She ate, tearing a thick chunk of dark bread with her teeth and chewing it before adding a slice of sharp cheese to enjoy every bite of the food that felt so rich and natural to her inexperienced taste buds.

She swallowed, washing down the lump of food with a gulp of cold water, before picking up the bowl of salty stew and spooning the contents into her mouth.

She was juggling the food and drink with stew running down her chin when there was a knock at the door and she managed to call out through a mouthful for whoever it was to enter.

Helghor, the man she recognised from before her consciousness had fled her, and who had visited her three times since Mark had left, stepped inside and bowed a greeting to her.

"Hi," she said, feeling inadequate in the presence of his respectful manners.

"I apologise for intruding on you again," he said, "but I feel that this matter cannot wait."

"What is it?" Eve said, putting aside the food as his tone made her forget it instantly.

"A few things," Helghor told her. "All of them concerning."

Eve sat up and watched him, waiting for the list of bad news to begin.

"We know that a force from your city is readying to come here, and as they are not invited, we are preparing to fight them. We know that your own people fight amongst yourselves, and that there is to be a change of leadership…"

"And?" she asked, expecting there to be more.

"And I want to ask what you are planning to do. There is a man, our spies say, who is taking control over all of your fighters, and he is from the people before who tried to kill all of us."

"Black," Eve said with a dark sneer of hatred.

"Yes. This is the name we have been told."

"I need to go," she said, standing stiffly and gauging her own abilities at under three quarters of normal.

"You are not yet fully healed," he told her, concern in

his words as he stepped into the room, fearful that she would fall. Eve fixed him with a look that rooted him where he stood as she reached for her sheathed sword and picked it up.

"You're right," she said. "I'm not, but I have a responsibility to deal with him once and for all. I knew there was something wrong, but I didn't listen to my instincts, and now people are dying. I have to go, Helghor. I have to get back to the Citadel and end this."

―――――

Mark's status as a potential traitor to the people of the distribution facility was rescinded after he explained everything he knew. He still received sullen looks from the four people he'd easily bested when they'd rushed him, but they were the least of his concerns.

The video played on constant loop, projected from somewhere inside the Citadel, which told him that Black and his minions would probably be tearing chunks out of the place to find the source of their lies being exposed to everyone.

"We should make a move now," he argued, cursing the sudden lack of leadership among the would-be separatists. They were peaceful on the whole, believing the propaganda that their actions were just and that the government would allow them to live separately if they did nothing to anger them.

"With what?" a woman asked. "Trucks and tractors? We have enough guns for one in three people, and not even half of those know how to fight properly."

"Then we don't fight conventionally," Mark explained with as much patience as he could muster. "We undermine them, ambush small patrols, we lure them to us on *our* terms instead of being drawn into engaging on theirs. You think this will be over in a day? It'll take weeks, *months* even to wear them down."

"And all the while we're doing that, they're punishing the people for our crimes against them," a man said, his voice wavering as he seemed to regret every life choice he'd made recently.

"You think they'll do that?" a woman almost shrieked. "My sister's still there… she has kids!"

"Settle down," Mark said with both hands raised. "Just because the Party did that, it doesn't mean they will. They're telling the people they're legitimate, that *we're* the enemy, so public executions to punish them for our actions would go against them."

"So *you* say," someone grumbled from beside him, making him turn and fix the wrong person with a glare.

"Enough," Mark said. "As far as I see it, we have two choices: we can stay here and prepare for an assault, but it's fairly obvious they can get people inside without being detected, we can go and fight them or we can argue and do nothing."

"That's three choices," someone helpfully pointed out.

"The last choice isn't a choice," Mark said loudly, covering up his inability to count as he spoke. "It's giving up."

They argued for another hour before he finally convinced enough of them to join him, leaving behind a large portion of fighters to offer the civilians at least some protection. As the group he led stocked provisions and weapons, he ran through the list of priority targets he needed to hit first in order to have a hope of succeeding.

With much of the Party's military infrastructure left

intact, he decided on drone control systems, along with communications, to be attacked as a priority, and as they set off towards the Citadel, he racked his brain for just how in the hell he was going to achieve any of it.

CHAPTER FORTY-FIVE

STRIKING THE FIRST BLOW

The escort detail nominally sent to bring back the counter-intelligence officer and her team arrived only hours after they were informed one was coming for them. The convoy of four transports – three more than were strictly required – was permitted to roll through the gates of the mining facility where the majority of Party soldiers were once billeted to cover the region.

They dismounted, all of them armed and alert, to find a mostly deserted compound. The man in charge, an inspector who appeared to be cut from the same cloth as Black, looked around for anyone of rank to report to and pass on his orders but found nobody.

At the back of the convoy, out of sight of their leader, men and women appeared from inside buildings, from behind vehicles and stacked containers, to advance on the convoy and raise weapons to face them. By the time the inspector realised something was wrong, he found himself staring down three weapon barrels and knew he'd been a fool to expect the lambs to march to their own slaughter.

"Radio," Rebecca demanded, holding her sidearm in

her right hand and gesturing with her left for the man's communications. He reached for it slowly, eyes not leaving hers, and when he handed it over, he intentionally dropped it to bring his weapon up at her.

His back arched to the sound of the crackling pulse of electricity coursing through his body. Making a noise like a mating animal, he went rigid before toppling over like a felled tree to reveal Mouse standing behind him holding the modified baton in his hand. He smiled, gave a shrug, and turned to see the others being disarmed with less violence required, now that the show of force had made its impression.

"Now what?" one of Rebecca's escort officers asked.

"Now we escort ourselves back to the Citadel," she told him, adding silently to herself that she didn't have the first clue what to do after that.

———

Black raged, throwing things across his office as the third person he'd tasked to remove the video from every screen in the Citadel came back to him empty handed. He roared about their incompetence, demanded that the feed be cut and ordered someone to get the right people to his office to record another video refuting the footage as fake, as an attempt to subvert the rightful leadership, and branded anyone repeating the words they saw as a terrorist sympathiser.

No matter how many people summoned the courage to tell him that he was making a mistake, that he was acting too strongly and that detaining citizens for such minor crimes would go against him when there was an election, he raged further.

"There won't *be* an election at this rate," he yelled.

"These damned fools will believe anything they see on television, which is why I want it shut down now!"

"Sir," a man said, "the only way to do that is to kill the power to the entire city."

"Do that then," Black demanded.

"Sir, that comes with certain risks involved…"

"I don't give a shit," he snarled. "Take that video down any way you can. If you can't trace the transmission source, then pull the plug."

"That's the thing," another man offered from the safety he enjoyed behind two other people who would be hit by anything thrown his way. "There *is* no signal to trace. It's like it's coming from inside the communications mainframe."

Black stopped, turning half over one shoulder to glare at the frightened officers hovering by the doorway ready to flee.

"Did it occur to any of you that it might just be the case?" Black asked quietly, seeing them exchange looks and scurry away to give the orders to search the communications hardware for any sign of infiltration.

It took them hours to find the oddity there, to discover the small boxes plugged in where they should be none, so that by the time the video feed was cut, the city was already under lockdown, and the wind began to blow hard with the setting sun.

Black was furious, still pacing in his office and fielding reports of incidents all over the city as the people already began rebelling against authority. What made that worse was the fact that entire swathes of uniformed forces were joining them, with each small pocket of people deciding that the time for revolution was then and it was all in their hands.

"I want this damned place locked down," he yelled.

"Nobody on the streets, and if any of the filth who called themselves the Resistance shows their faces, I want them brought to me."

He stormed to the corridor, angrily waving off his armed escort as he accessed the elevator to go down and bring back his last line of defence against whatever the night was going to bring.

CHAPTER FORTY-SIX

AN END TO EVERYTHING

Eve had accepted the offer of transport back to the Citadel, and with only a mile to go on foot, she said farewell to her driver and began walking stiffly towards the lights of the Citadel.

The night was dark but there was still enough ambient light to make out her path, just as the lights of the city lit her way well enough when she drew closer.

The gate was open, the position seemingly abandoned as the sounds of very distant gunfire rang out sporadically.

It was already beginning, she hoped, but if she were honest with herself, she knew it was more like Black had seized control of the Citadel and was dealing with anyone who defied his orders.

She knew this place, had heard this song sung before, only by a bigger choir and with much better harmony. From the little she knew of Black, he was no Nathaniel. Sure enough, the man had been cruel and ruthless, but at least he was efficient, she mused. Black had no subtlety. No guile. No... *finesse*.

Nathaniel had, and he never pretended to be anything

other than what he was, apart from when he'd almost fooled her into believing that she had been fighting on the wrong side her entire life.

She hadn't, she knew that now, but she had been convinced into fighting on the wrong side this time, and her actions had allowed everything to fall apart so rapidly that she hadn't even begun to properly recover from her injuries before a second coup was taking place.

She'd believed at the time that they had been right to show leniency, to show mercy to those who swore their allegiance to the winning side, but she now realised that they'd mostly been biding their time until a new leader emerged with the strength to make them believe they were the dominant power again.

She didn't want that, not for her and not for anyone else. She was alone. Adam was gone, Cohen was dead, she didn't know if Rebecca and the others were her enemies or not. Everything she had been bred for, raised for, was for nothing if she couldn't do this one last thing.

She stepped through the streets of the Citadel, winding her way inexorably towards the tall building at the centre where she guessed she'd find the man who was bringing death back to their country, all the while avoiding patrols of uniformed men and women on foot and in roving vehicles who would likely all jump at the chance to take her out, or take her in alive and earn even more reward, like loyal dogs returning a prize stick.

One patrol caught her out, not that she was being overly cautious at not allowing anyone to detect her, and when the first man threatened her, she knew what would happen even if they had no idea.

She took all three out, leaving two jerking on the ground in shock as their muscles spasmed from their own tasers and the other unconscious. She shrugged out of the heavy coat she wore and revealed her frame to the night, sheathed in shimmering black material just like the first time she'd walked these same streets so long ago. No armour, no fancy technology or bullet resistant plates, just her and her sword the way she intended it to be.

That was when the voice she recognised called her name.

She saw Fly, resplendent and somehow repulsive in his uniform and carrying a gun as though he'd abandoned their religion and sided with non-believers.

Her side hurt from the walking and the exertion of the brief encounter with the guards, and she knew she was in no state to outrun a bullet, so she ran.

———

Only minutes after Samaira, Rebecca and Mouse arrived in the dark city from the northern gate, Mark approached the western opening to find it closed.

He made a play of not seeming concerned, as though he knew the guards there were automatically on his side because doubt, no matter how small, had a compound effect on how fast a person pulled a trigger.

"Open the bloody gate!" he called up, seeing the helmeted skull he'd singled out with his gaze look left and right, as if someone else could tell him what to do.

"Who the fuck are you?" another voice came down from the other side of the portal.

"Captain Evans," Mark lied smoothly. "Formerly of the Party QRF and bringing troops back home to support the new Chairman. What's *your* name?"

The threat of punishment from on high was subtly delivered and quickly obeyed as the gates opened and he climbed back inside the lead vehicle packed with irregular fighters, just as the ones behind him were. Only his transport bore the Party emblem, and the sight of that symbol of power was enough to confuse the guards into not noticing that the three vehicles behind bore no such insignia.

"Straight to the main drone relay," he said, twisting around to pass the word to the men and women in the rear section. "And we stop for nothing."

———

"Done," Mouse said as he slammed down the cover on his laptop terminal, not elaborating on what he had just achieved. He jumped out of the transport and looked around before setting off in a specific direction.

"This way," he said, leading Samaira, Rebecca and her two loyal officers away from the underground vehicle bay and into a service elevator that led directly to their workshop and offices.

"Don't access that," Samaira warned as Mouse bent to scan his eye to the reader. "They'll know you're here!"

"No," he answered, mumbling to his boots as he fiddled with the end cap on his baton. "They won't. I've programmed our scans to rotate and randomly use any file with the same level of security access."

"You can do that?" Rebecca asked, unsure why she hadn't utilised his full skills before.

"Of course I can," he answered, unsure why they wouldn't believe him.

"Can you cut the access of other people too?" Samaira asked.

"Like Black?" Mouse shot back, still looking down but smiling at his boots as the elevator rushed upwards.

"You already have, haven't you?" Rebecca asked,

mirroring the smirk. Mouse didn't answer, just issued an odd laugh through his nose.

They reached the workshop, opening up a secure storage locker to add more weapons and magazines to their equipment, and set off for the command floor.

———

Jenna, after a night and a day spent awake in the cramped tunnels under the city, found her way back above ground near to where she'd first run from the soldiers sent after her.

She stuck to the shadows, avoiding the patrols easily in the dark but spending more time hiding than moving, thanks to every single drone the city possessed being in the air searching for any target.

She could tell from the pitch of the buzzing rotor blades that these were the slightly heavier but more compact version, not like the usual surveillance drones, and she recalled the specifications of the Wasp units with unnerving clarity to know exactly what the heavy ammunition they carried would do to her body if she was spotted.

She watched as a transport drove hard around a corner, tyres squealing as the body leaned, to disappear down the ramp into the vehicle bay ahead of her. She ran, trying to reach the opening before the shutters dropped down and sealed her out, but was forced to dive into the cover of a statue depicting some former Chairman in all of his military glory as four drones buzzed low past the corner of headquarters.

By the time she thought it was safe to move, the shutters were down and she was left out in the cold.

She had to find another way in, and she couldn't count on anyone to take out Black but herself.

CHAPTER FORTY-SEVEN

INEVITABILITY

Fly joined Black and his small team of loyal followers and aides on the command floor. He saw Helen and two others, both senior members of the ruling council and ministers of the now dead government cowering in a side room which was guarded by two armed men sporting the reflective black face masks that had so recently been banned.

He suppressed a shudder at the sight, not from fear but through an ingrained learnt behaviour that formed an automatic response to the anonymity of the Party soldiers.

Black was wearing his old captain's uniform, having discarded what he thought was a sign of weakness in his enforced *peacekeeping* role.

These people didn't need peace, Fly knew, they needed strength. They needed to be told what to do because when they weren't, well, shit like *this* happened. The people needed smacking back in line, and Fly was eager to volunteer himself for the role.

"What the hell are you doing here?" Black snapped at him, earning a hurt and pitiful look before Fly found his words.

"It's Eve," he said. "She's in the Citadel."

"You *saw* her?" Black asked, accusation heavy in his words. Fly nodded, opening his mouth to answer before he was cut off.

"So she's dead then, right? You obviously killed her, which is what you're here to tell me. *Qtherwise*," his voice doubled in volume and intensity, "why would you be here?"

"I... I came to protect you," he answered, only now realising how pathetic he sounded as the men carrying guns and wearing heavy armoured vests laughed at him. He felt like a child with a toy gun in front of these brutal people, but he refused to let them see his self-doubt.

"Trust me," Fly said, trying to sound tough, "if she gets in, you'll want me around."

Black scoffed at him, looking him up and down like he was unsure what he was even looking at. "I have that covered, thanks," he said sarcastically, raising his voice in summons to say, "Reaper!"

The tall, muscular and almost androgynous woman stepped into the room behind Fly and stood so close that he felt his blood cool and thicken in his veins.

"Now," Black told him with a sneer, "if you want to be helpful, then get your ugly face out of mine, get back outside and bring me someone's head on a fucking spike."

Fly nodded weakly and went to step backwards, managing only to bump into the human robot behind him and gasp at how hard and cold her body felt.

He fled, taking the elevator back down to do as he was told without the first clue how to achieve it.

———

Eve tried the eye scanner on the main doors of the head-quarters building, expecting it to flash red and set off a klaxon to bring a squad of soldiers down on her so she could buy her entry with their deaths.

To her surprise, the panel turned green and the door hissed aside to allow her entry.

"Too easy," she said, aiming for the elevator where she tried again, receiving the same simple obedience from the system that, by rights, should be screaming at the top of its voice that she was there.

She went up, aiming to search the first place she'd ever laid eyes on Black so she could kill him and let others figure out the rest. That was what she was good for: killing. She wasn't a diplomat or a leader. She couldn't get people to work with her or vote for her. She was barely capable of growing her own crops or cooking her own food. She couldn't use computers, couldn't build things, but what she could do was kill, and that was precisely what she intended to do.

As the elevator doors opened, she readied herself to fight, which was what she needed to do as two men were aiming rifles at the door when it opened.

Eve whirled aside, using the reinforced metal of the structure to protect her from the lethal projectiles. The firing paused and she heard grunts of conversation as the two men who had her pinned down worked out the fastest way to kill her.

The faint, distant *snick* of metal pulling on metal sounded, followed by the dull thump of something that bounced twice and rolled into the elevator to rest in the middle among the scraps of debris thrown down by the gunfire.

She stared at the cylindrical grenade for a half second, contemplating it closely before she used the sheathed sword to smack it back out into the lobby where it detonated with a blinding flash and a percussive *whump* that left her ears singing high notes.

She'd closed her eyes so only her hearing was affected by the flashbang, but the two soldiers hadn't been so lucky.

Both had dropped their aim away from her position as they tried desperately to fight the disorientation. She felled them both with small daggers which she whipped through the air to hit one in the left eye socket and the other in the back of his neck. Both men fell down dead and opened up the way for her to proceed.

"Reaper!" she heard, freezing to the spot in the long corridor. "Kill her!"

Ahead, twenty paces further into the floor, an armoured apparition appeared brandishing more weapons than one person could ever need. The two locked eyes, sharing none of the bond they had once teetered on the edge of, before Reaper launched herself at Eve with no regard for her own mortality.

Eve turned and ran back to the lobby, needing more space to be able to use her sword and gain whatever advantage she could over the soulless young woman. She turned, starting to draw the long blade before Reaper was on her, flying through the air to extend a foot and slam Eve backwards off her feet to slide across the polished floor and into the wall nearest the elevator.

Reaper landed on her feet, spinning and turning to draw two guns from her thighs as though using a gun on a girl with just a sword held no shame. As if only the outcome mattered, and how it was reached bore no relevance to the world.

Eve, gasping for breath and hurting, was no lamb volunteering for slaughter. She rolled over, kicking her feet into the wall to add speed and momentum and rise up with the sword singing from the sheath and cutting a sweeping, upwards arc designed to take both hands off at the wrist and end their dance as quickly as her opponent intended to.

Eve was fast, even injured, but Reaper was faster.

She leapt back, saving her hands but losing both weapons as the blade bit into the metal and plastic of one and knocked the other from her grip. She took three fast paces away to give herself room to draw another weapon but Eve was not in the mood to fight fair and spun her body to whip the sword out and send the gun wedged on its edge flying into Reaper's face to hit her hard and disorientate her long enough for Eve to advance and spear a thrust at her opponent's neck.

Reaper reeled away again, succeeding in whipping two batons out to extend one in each hand as the blood from a cut to her forehead ran into her right eye.

"You don't have to do this," Eve said, speaking in laboured gasps and only talking to slow the fight so she didn't collapse from the pain. "We were on the same side once, remember? We can be again."

"No," Reaper growled, uncertain of the sensation of speaking as if it went against her code. She twirled the batons in each hand once and advanced on Eve.

"Don't you understand?" Eve yelled. "I don't want to have to kill you!"

"But I must kill you," Reaper answered.

———

In the street hundreds of feet below them, Fly stomped out of a side exit and into the street. He was unsure what to do, having found himself on the ground floor heading for the outside before he'd even thought to question his orders.

Will Black even win? What will I do if he doesn't? Where will I go? Could I say I had nothing to do with the takeover?

His tumbling thoughts froze as a shadowy figure emerged from the darkness ahead. At first, he feared it was Eve, but recognition took over and he knew who it was a second later.

"Jenna," he breathed. "I'm so glad you're okay." As he said it, he knew it sounded false, sounded weak, but it was too late by then.

"Are you?" she snapped back.

Something inside Fly snapped then. He hated his old life, hated being not even second best but third or fourth, and in his former freeborn comrade, he saw a way to earn renown and earn a place back in the inner sanctum.

He lifted the baton out of its holster and knew exactly how he would beat her.

"No," he said, smiling. "Just as I wasn't glad to see your brother on my mission, but at least I didn't have to suffer him coming back."

"What did you say?"

He could tell she was close to tears, close to losing control from just the implication of what he was about to tell her.

"You didn't know?" Fly teased mockingly. "Oh, little Jonah got it into his head that he didn't like Black... so I had to..." he shrugged, giving her a wink to imply that he'd enjoyed doing what he did. Still he didn't say it, waiting to force her over the edge into a desperate attack so that he could kill her more easily.

"You didn't," she snarled, close to sobbing as a long knife appeared in her right hand. "You couldn't have."

"I did," Fly said. "Straight into his heart with this." He produced the blade he had indeed used to kill Jonah, turning it so the light glinted off the edge.

Jenna screamed and lunged, just as he knew she would. She stabbed straight out, aiming at his throat with the point of her blade, but he turned and seized her arm, curling his own hand underneath to bring the tip of the baton towards her face so he could watch her expression as the lighting hit her.

The tip didn't glow, didn't crackle to life, and instead of the sensation of cold metal in his hand, he felt only a hot wetness. Glancing away from her angry expression, he saw a curved blade complete its circuit of his wrist before the baton fell to the ground, because he had lost all strength to keep it in his grip.

He staggered backwards a pace, disbelief fighting with pain and weakness for control over his body. Reaching awkwardly across himself to draw the gun with the wrong hand, he watched in rage as Jenna ducked low and drew back her arm holding the long knife to skewer his hand into his thigh and pin it there.

Agony tore through him. It forced him to his knees and prevented him from being able to utter a word, only make strangled sounds as she rose over him and twirled the hooked blade on the ring around her index finger.

"He was too good to die by your filthy hands," she said, spinning the blade once more as if pondering her next move. "But you're not worth dying by anyone else's but mine."

She slashed once. The pain only came at the end, such was the razor edge of the weapon, but the same hot flood washed down the right side of his neck as the blood fountained out and left him fading in an unconsciousness he'd never wake from.

CHAPTER FORTY-EIGHT

TO THE DEATH

Eve and Reaper battled through the abandoned offices, and each second that they fought meant that Eve was getting further and further away from Black, who had fled upwards into the nearest stairwell. It also meant that every dodge, every parry of the batons, sapped her strength further and left her in a weakened state that she knew she couldn't maintain.

Gunfire from the corridor behind Reaper made Eve's adversary duck down, but as it wasn't aimed at her, Eve was forced to apply her strength to kick in the nearest office door and seek cover, even if that meant trapping herself inside.

More shots erupted in the corridor, with shouted commands and a cry to retreat. She risked a look out, glancing back in the direction she'd come from to see Rebecca of all people aiming a rifle down the corridor.

Looking back to where she'd last seen Reaper, she caught only the black rubber of her bootheel disappearing into the same stairwell Black had run through.

"Hold your fire," she shouted breathlessly to the people

she knew for certain were on her own side now, because she could see two of Black's men lying dead on the deck. She waited for the shooting to stop before tearing recklessly after the people she needed to kill. In the stairwell she looked up, seeing running people go through a door two floors up and forced her exhausted body upwards, gasping for breath, before Reaper swung over the railing to her right and slammed her hard into the wall with both feet.

She couldn't breathe. The pain exploding in her side was worse than it had been since she'd been shot the first time and her vision was blurry with the compounded effects. Her sword was behind her, trapped half under her body but the wooden sheath was still in her left hand and she jabbed it hard into the point where Reaper's muscular thigh met her groin in a weak attempt to debilitate and distract her.

It worked, as the first thrust of the baton fell away in flinch response to allow Eve to roll backwards and raise her blade to smack the weapon in Reaper's other hand out of her grip. She sliced at her ankles, aiming to drive her back up the steps and maintain her upwards momentum before she ran out of steam. Reaper jumped, dodging and retreating upwards as Eve hoped she would, and she kept pressing the attack at her vulnerable lower legs with thrusts, intending to open up her flesh somewhere and release the blood from her body to slow her down.

Even in her best condition, Eve wouldn't consider any conflict between the two to be a certainty at all. In the state she was in – out of breath, exhausted, and in so much pain that she feared her internal wounds were bleeding freely again – she knew that if she let up even one little bit, if she backed off to catch her breath or showed any sign of weakness, then she was dead.

The stairwell hindered her use of the sword more than

the corridor did as she lacked the space to swing the long blade to its full effect. With enough space, as she had shown before, the sword could cut through steel and bone or decapitate a person with an alarming ease, only she couldn't get that full swing now, so she was forced to use it like an ungainly spear to herd the woman who wanted to kill her back up the steps one at a time.

Gunshots behind her made her flinch but given that she heard them and didn't *feel* them, she guessed it was those on her side coming to her aid.

Reaper wheeled away, almost casually throwing an elongated diamond of bright steel in Eve's direction which sailed past her ear and ended the gunfire with a gasping, choking, bubbling noise. Looking back, she saw a young man in uniform, eyes wide in shock and pain, with the fingers of his left hand fluttering desperately at the dagger buried in the very base of his throat where it protruded grotesquely from his ruined windpipe. She recognised him as one of Rebecca's men, but didn't have the time to think or feel anything about his death.

Their bullets had driven Reaper to flee, and that opening allowed Eve to advance up the stairs with difficulty.

"You're alive," Rebecca panted from behind her. "How are you alive?"

"I… didn't die…" Eve answered, not realising how inanely simple her response sounded until after she'd said it. She could barely get enough oxygen into her body and her heart banged loudly in her ears as if she were still suffering the effects of the flashbang thrown into the elevator. Rebecca didn't ask any more questions, and their small group managed to reach the next floor up unimpeded, until a hail of bullets forced them back into the cover of the concrete steps.

"Cover your ears," Samaira said as she lowered her gun and stepped up to the front of their stack, holding a device and showing a grimace of determination as she yanked the stiff pin from the grenade.

Eve ducked back, expecting the same effect as before, until the flames and screaming shrapnel told her that Samaira wasn't fucking about with a non-lethal device but had tossed up the real deal to blow the door and the doorway to pieces, along with anyone stupid enough to be there.

They moved, with Rebecca firing twice into the scorched torso of a soldier trying in vain to reach for his weapon. Piling through the smoking ruins of the door, they came under fire again, this time with Samaira taking a ricochet in the back of her vest and pitching forwards as Rebecca opened up with a long burst of gunfire to clear away any of their enemy still in the open.

Eve again saw Reaper fleeing the bullets and went after her, needing to put this soulless creature down for good and trapping her in a large room with a huge picture window overlooking the city below.

Reaper turned, recognising that she was trapped, and drew two long knives from behind her back as she faced Eve, readying her sword for their final dance.

Instead of adopting a fighting stance and stepping for her cautiously, Reaper drew back and hurled one of the knives savagely, forcing Eve to duck and pop up as the blade buried itself deep into the plaster of the wall behind. The second knife followed, making her twist desperately to narrowly avoid it before Reaper was on her, closing the distance fast to use her hands and feet inside the lethal reach of Eve's sword.

As much as she hated to, she dropped the long weapon and snatched up the last remaining dagger from her thigh, holding it in a downward grip while she blocked and traded blows with Reaper.

She felt as if she were made of stone, and each hit that connected with her body seemed twice as devastating as anything she could deliver. She knew she couldn't win on strength, maybe not even on technique with how slow and damaged she was, but what Eve knew and – she suspected – what Reaper *didn't* know, was how to fight dirty like an underdog.

She clawed at Reaper's eyes when she aimed a blow at her face. She kicked her hard between the legs, knowing what debilitating damage she could do and with each block, she jabbed the point of the dagger into her flesh in the hope of getting through to a nerve cluster to kill the sensation in an arm or a leg.

Reaper broke off, recoiling backwards and trying to take stock of the dozen minor injuries she'd just received tussling in close quarters with the smaller woman.

Their eyes went to Eve's sword at the same time, then back to one another, and as Reaper made the dive to grab it first, Eve let her, twirling the throwing dagger in her hand and pulling back to send it just where she needed it to go.

The fingers of Reaper's right hand hit the warm wood of the sword's hilt and closed around it, just as a hollow crunching sound seemed to move throughout her entire body. She froze, knowing something was very, *very* wrong but didn't yet have the information feeding back to her brain to understand it.

She stood up, trying to lower her right arm to her side and finding that she was unable to. Lifting her arm and looking down, she found the very edge of the dagger's blunt end sticking out of her armpit.

As the visual confirmation of her grievous injury made

it real, she dropped the sword from her numb fingers and staggered backwards towards the big window to stare open mouthed at Eve, who advanced on her. She was bent double, clutching her left side in serious pain, as the two women seemed to come to a silent agreement that, deep down, they both knew that they couldn't both occupy the same world. They were counterparts, opposites, they were destined to go from two to one, but the outcome was never certain.

Reaper, her face contorting as though she understood that fact and refused to accept it, lunged with both hands for Eve's throat, forcing her to twist and roll her head under and around Reaper's grab where her left hand found the protruding knife. She yanked it out hard before reversing it and avoiding a second, wild swing of sluggish arms, to rise up and bury the point upwards under Reaper's chin.

They stood, face to face as blood gurgled from Reaper's lips, when the glass behind Eve's worthy adversary and most recent victim exploded to fall away and let the howling wind snatch Reaper's body outwards into the blackness.

A second shot, this one not missing, slammed into Eve's left shoulder blade to spin her around and leave her face down by the edge. As her eyes tried to stay open, she saw boots walking slowly towards her and heard Black's gloating voice.

———

Rebecca searched frantically for Eve, for Black, for anyone else but the pair of shots seemed to call out to her and promise an ominous ending for someone.

She ran towards the sound, stopping in the doorway as

she heard Black's voice ring out over the screaming of the wind outside.

"I wish you hadn't done that," he crowed. "She was very valuable to me. It helped when dealing with scum like *you*."

He grunted, sending out the sound of a kick meeting a body with great force as she stepped inside and saw him aiming another boot at Eve's prone form to send her out over the precipice of the shattered window.

"No!" she screamed, raising her weapon just as Black turned, abandoning his kick, to smile at her.

"Inspector Howard," he said, as if what was happening wasn't really happening. "I didn't expect to see y—"

He didn't get to finish his words. She didn't think he deserved the opportunity to speak, so she fired twice into his chest to rock his body and send him staggering backwards to trip over Eve and teeter on the edge of the window.

He looked at her, disbelief and hatred fighting for supremacy on his expression before he was gone.

EPILOGUE

Eve woke, keeping her body still and her breathing steady in case anyone was monitoring her. She kept her eyes still and reached out through her other senses, drinking in the smell of the air first and relaxing.

She opened her eyes, sitting up and stretching with only a slight wince at how tight her left side felt and how her right shoulder didn't reach up as far as it used to because of the shattered bone and the tendons and ligaments that had all had to be fixed back into place only a few months before.

She swung her feet out of her bed and walked across the floor, her bare feet appreciating the new carpet that had come with her from the city. She poured herself a glass of water and drank it down in a series of large gulps before she dressed and slipped her feet into thick boots to brave the cold weather outside.

A cat, multi-coloured and loyal only when she offered it food, was waiting for her outside and made clear its displeasure at being kept out in the cold for longer than it wanted to.

Eve ignored the yowling remonstration and stepped out to suck in a full chest of the chill air high above the sea. She walked around her small property, letting the chickens out of their small hut to scratch and peck at the ground where she scattered the inedible leftovers of her last meal. Speaking softly to them, thanking them for playing their part in the symbiotic relationship they enjoyed, she reached inside to gather the four eggs the night had yielded and slipped out of their domain to leave them to their scratching.

She went back inside, shutting the door to ward off the cold, and began heating a pan to cook the eggs.

At her feet, still explaining how unhappy it was with the facilities and services, the cat ran short, slinky laps around her ankles as it yelled upwards, demanding something.

She broke three eggs into the pan before cracking the fourth into a shallow dish that was eagerly anticipated by her feline companion and stood to carefully lift the edges of the clear substance going white to make sure it didn't stick and burn.

Her ears, still as sensitive as ever and not dulled by the injuries she'd suffered, forced her head to turn and look out of the window which gave onto the only track leading to her small home, to see a transport bumping along it, not an entirely unexpected sight.

She took the pan off the stove, replacing it with a kettle to begin heating the water. If that transport contained who she thought it did, she expected a comment about the occupant dying of thirst if she didn't make it clear she was making him the drink any decent hostess would offer.

If it didn't contain that person, if it was someone else, then... then she was still Eve. She carried no fewer than three blades on her, not that they were obvious, and the sword still hung on its sheath on the wall by the fire.

Mark climbed out from behind the wheel and knocked out of courtesy as he opened the door and stamped his feet to rid the boots of any substance unwanted inside her home.

"Brrr! Get that kettle on," he said with a shudder intended to explain that it was cold outside, as if she didn't know. The water, kept warm by the stove that heated her home, began to bubble inside the metal container, so she prepared a pot with a scoop of dried leaves in, ready to pour it.

"It's already on," she said.

Mark said nothing, just took a seat and leaned back ready for the cat to jump up on his lap and turn to offer him a close-up sight he hadn't asked for. Pushing the animal gently aside, he watched as Eve poured the water into the pot and stirred it with a long spoon.

"What brings you out here?' she asked. Mark shrugged.

"Thinking of setting up down here myself," he answered as if gauging her reaction to the prospect.

"Not going back to the Citadel?" she asked with a raised eyebrow. "Or the west?"

"They don't need me," Mark said self-deprecatingly. "I'll leave all that stuff to people who have the energy for it." Eve replaced the lid of the pot and let the infusion sit for a minute as they spoke. "They're all just working out trade for raw materials, processed goods, food, manufacturing… I don't have the head for what they're calling *economy*, so I think I'll stay retired this time."

"How's Rebecca?" Eve asked dutifully. "And Mouse?"

"They're doing fine," Mark said. "They asked me to ask you to come back. Obviously, I said you wouldn't, but

I'd ask you all the same." Eve smiled and gave him a look which he understood.

"I said I'd ask for them," he said. "And that's done now, so there."

"And Samaira?"

Mark smiled at just the thought of the woman and gave some airy, dreamy retort about her being just as magnificent as always.

Eve poured the tea into two cups, using a tiny strainer to catch the leaves, which she found to be good fertiliser when she mixed it with the soil under her vegetables. She gave him a cup and sat down opposite him, wearing a look that he recognised.

"Uh oh," he said. "You've been thinking, and that never bodes well."

"I have," she told him. "And I've been wondering if it's all worth it, or whether it's just going to be a repeating cycle forever."

"It wasn't done properly the first time," Mark admitted. "They accepted defeat too easily and people were too quick to take them at their word. It's different now, I'm sure of it."

"How can you be sure?" she pressed him. "How can you know it won't be the same again in a year, five years, fifty years?"

"I can't," he admitted. "Not for sure, but I can hope and I can believe."

He could see she wasn't convinced, so he put down his cup and sat forwards to speak.

"Last time, all they did was remove the leader. That left too many people hiding in plain sight, telling lies to our faces just to save themselves, and when the opportunity arose to seize back control, they tried to take it. Could they have succeeded? Maybe. Probably yes, at least to begin with. But this time we've disabled the whole thing. Military, the drones, the surveillance, it's all been torn down so the tools of oppression can't be used again."

"So, you burned the old way to the ground to start from scratch?" Mark leaned back and picked up his cup again.

"Did Cohen ever tell you about the Egyptians?"

"The what?"

"Ancient Egypt – it's kind of a place and a time I suppose – well, it was thousands and thousands of years ago, and they had a legend about a bird that lived for a long time, only when it died, it burst into flames."

"Sounds awful," Eve cut in.

"And out of those flames," Mark said, continuing as if she hadn't interrupted, "came a young bird – some say the same bird – starting its life cycle all over again."

"So, you're saying we can burn down the city and start over again and it'll be fine?"

"That's exactly what I'm saying," Mark told her. "Only it isn't our responsibility any longer."

"Not our problem," she agreed. "Not our problem."

FROM THE PUBLISHER

Thank you for reading *Phoenix,* the final book in Defiance.

We hope you enjoyed it as much as we enjoyed bringing it to you. We just wanted to take a moment to encourage you to review the book on Amazon and Goodreads. Every review helps further the author's reach and, ultimately, helps them continue writing fantastic books for us all to enjoy.

If you liked this book, check out the rest of our catalogue at www.aethonbooks.com. To sign up to receive a FREE collection from some of our best authors as well as updates regarding all new releases, visit www.aethonbooks.com/sign-up.

JOIN THE STREET TEAM! Get advanced copies of all our books, plus other free stuff and help us put out hit after hit.

SEARCH ON FACEBOOK:
AETHON STREET TEAM

Printed in Great Britain
by Amazon